RISEN FROM THE DEAD

by

Rod Hacking

To Sue Tilley and John Wilson

Wonderful friends I am proud to have married

"Resurrection has nothing to do with what follows our death
But the hope and possibilities we have here and now"

Some of the characters in this book have previously appeared
in
The Auld Alliance
and return because I like them

Chapter 1

The marquee was, as she had expected, packed and noisy. There were Scottish farmers everywhere tucking into their cooked lunches as if they had never eaten before. The Border Union Show was the highlight of the year for many, most of whom would be hoping the local police would not be too keen as each one returned for afternoon milking. There were lots of faces Rhona knew and ever since her boss, Anne-Marie, had blotted her copybook by getting pregnant, she was now the favourite female farmer in the area and enjoyed all attention this brought her in the way of free lunches at the cattle market and many cups of tea. Some younger ones, and even one or two of the older, had tried to chat her up, but the last thing she wanted was to leave the farm at Galashiels, the day-to-day running of which was hers, and which she loved. She was so happy and fulfilled and felt she had been made for this life.

She took her tray and looked around for somewhere to eat its contents. She could see only one table where there was a young woman, perhaps slightly older than herself, eating and reading a book. She must be a tourist, thought Rhona, as there were few signs that she came from a farm, especially reading a book

'Excuse me', said Rhona, 'but may I join you? Otherwise it's out with the pigs for me.'

'I'd love you to,' said the woman. Rhona sat down.

'Are you a farmer?'

'Oh dear, is it the smell?' said Rhona.

The woman laughed.

'It's the clothes. They're a bit of a giveaway. You look like a farmer and I can see you attract a lot of attention from the male farmers around here.'

'Oh, don't be taken in by that. All they see is a free potential farmhand, cook and breeder of children. Besides which, running a farm leaves no time for a man in my life, even if I'd met one worth having. Anyway, I'm Rhona.'

'And I'm Charlotte, though usually I'm known as Charlie.'

'It's great meet to you, Charlie. Your accent suggests you're from Wales so what on earth are you doing at the Border Union Show, especially given that even this wondrous event cannot compete with the Royal Welsh Show in Builth Wells?'

'Have you been?'

'Twice, when I was a student at the Royal Agricultural University in Cheltenham. It was brilliant and although it's too far to travel to now, I would like one day to take livestock to show there.'

'Have you got a lot?'

'They're not mine. I'm sorry to say, but yes we do. About a thousand yows and sixty ladies to be milked each day and calved each year, and my boss has recently invested in small Chinese pigs, because she's crackers and taking maternity leave at the moment so I have to look after them.'

'When is she due back?'

'It's her farm so when she decides, though I miss working with her. We're great friends and she's an outstanding farmer from whom I'm always learning.'

'So do you have to do it all by yourself now?'

'I have two part-time men. One was a University Professor of French in Edinburgh and is married to a delightful French woman and they have a new baby, and the other was the Senior Civil Servant to the Scottish government and is married to Anne-Marie. He's training to be a counsellor and possibly a psychotherapist, and milks the cows every Sunday. Neither are all that hot with the yows however.'

'You used that word before. What's a yow?'

'Posh people in England and Wales call them ewes, ladies that we hope will bring forth lambs in March and April. But what are you doing here in such an out of the way place?'

'Well, I work for a writer as one of his researchers. He's called Edward Challen and mostly writes what I would call large biographies. My colleague Henry, mostly works with him at home in a place called The Gate House, near Hereford. He's at work now on a new biography of Archie McHugh, the poet, and my job is to go sniffing around the places and people who knew him and dig up whatever there is to be found.'

'Gosh, however did you train for that? You must have had to study espionage at uni.'

'Not at all. I've not been to university, but Edward said when he met me that I seemed to be nosey enough for his needs, which I think was a compliment.'

'Did you apply for the job out of curiosity?'

'No. It fell in my lap. I was living in a village not too far from Cardiff when my accommodation came to an end and I had to find somewhere urgently to live and some employment. I asked around and a nice lady telephoned Edward and he invited me to see him, and that's how it happened.'

'I can't say I've heard of Edward Challen nor the poetry of Archie McHugh.'

'That's alright, I hadn't heard of yows!'

They laughed.

'Did Archie McHugh ever visit the Border Union Show?'

'I would imagine he did as he lived not too far away, in a place called Jedburgh. But you might well not have heard of him as he was something of a recluse.'

'Have you a purpose in being here today?'

'Yes. To enjoy myself and meet you.'

'Where are you staying?'

'I'll drive on to Jedburgh and find somewhere.'

'No. Come back to the farm with me. I've got a spare room and I especially enjoy showing someone round the farm.'

'That would be great. Thank you, Rhona.'

Those with milking schedules to keep were already leaving Springwood Park creating a traffic hold-up, but once they were on the main road it took no time at all with Charlie doing her best to keep up with Rhona. As they drew near to Galashiels, they left the main road and approached the farm up the long lane. Rhona parked the Land Rover and indicated to Charlie where she should park. It was a very hot afternoon and Rhona would need to dress down for milking which, this afternoon, when she would be sharing with Adam who no doubt welcomed the opportunity to have a break from Jerome, the new baby which he and Anaïs had produced. The parents mostly spoke French when together and so the son would no doubt grow up bilingual. Talking about anything was almost impossible during milking even though the numbers involved at the moment were smaller than usual, a number of cows being dry. Adam thought the best thing about that was that they need not begin so early in the morning, or at least he thought that the case until Jerome arrived since when he had been more than happy to arrive early!

There was no one around when Rhona and Charlie arrived. Ed and Anne-Marie and their son Gregor were out to afternoon tea with a very important political person, for whom Ed used to work, but she expected them back before too long. The Boss (as Anne-Marie was universally known), having decided to take a proper maternity leave had held to it and was not in any way interfering in the farm's work which had surprised and impressed Rhona. Rhona was wholly in charge as her two distinguished helpers knew. She liked them both very much and respected them but that did not inhibit her when she needed to correct them, something on the whole a daily occurrence. Ed on a tractor was a total liability and when it had come to sheep shearing time, Adam managed to find no end of new ways to find himself in the wrong place time and again. The shearers, who came from New Zealand, thought this amusing on the first morning, but less so as the days of shearing went by, however Adam redeemed himself a little when it came to putting the newly shorn sheep through the dip and became the master of pushing them under the water and managed to drown not one though most seemed to give him the evil eye as they resurfaced. Rhona led Charlie into her home, originally an annexe to the farmhouse, and showed her the room she could use and then told her to feel at home.

'I need to look at the yows and the pigs, and by the time I've done that it will be time to start milking, and Adam will be here. Anne-Marie and Ed will be back soon. If it's ok with you I'll suggest he pops in and you can see if he knows anything worthwhile about Archie McHugh. Even if he doesn't you'll enjoy his company. It wouldn't surprise me to know he's read some or even all of Edward Challen's books. Is that ok with you? I can prepare food when I get back.'

'You're so very kind, Rhona, and yes I'd love to meet Ed, but before you go can you let me have your wifi password so I can communicate back to base?'

'It's on that piece of paper on the sideboard. Ok, that's enough of humans, now to the real top of the evolutionary tree: sheep.'

Charlie laughed in response as Rhona disappeared through the back door. She looked around. It was simply furnished but with love and attention. There were books, but mostly concerned with animal husbandry, no novels and no biographies. It had been a long day with a long drive and in no time at all she was fast asleep in her comfortable chair.

She awoke with a start as the door opened and in came a good-looking man.

'Hi there, you must be Charlie Holly. I'm Edgar, the farmer's husband and father of Gregor. She ruled my life at one time, now he does.'

He stretched out his hand and took hers.

'Hello, Edgar.'

'Ed, please. I'm still trying to shed the formalities of my previous occupation as a civil servant. Anyway, welcome to the farm. As you will have no doubt heard from Rhona, she is the manager whilst Anne-Marie, my wife, is on maternity leave. She works mainly with Adam who is proving to be a quick learner but nevertheless commits the occasional faux-pas, about which we know because we can hear Rhoda's voice cursing him 800 yards away.'

Charlie laughed.

'I gather you are a researcher for Edward Challen. That's quite a job. What sort of background do you have to have won a prestigious role like that?'

'Education-wise, nothing. I was in care for some years and then left to free-float, and mostly made a mess of everything. Then one evening I was badly beaten-up in Swansea by a sadistic sexually perverted detective sergeant. I had to have surgery and told that what he had done would make my chances of having children very small indeed. Thanks to two women police officers I found the way out of the maze. A friend of Edward's lived in the village where I was enjoying protection and we got to know each other, and she could recognise someone who was inquisitive, or "nosey" as she so-charmingly put it, with terrier-like tenacity, and despite the absence of formal educational qualifications, Edward thought my other skills were what he needed in his second researcher, whom he would send to do some "sniffing".'

'Ye Gods, Charlie, what a story. You should write it up. What happened to the policeman?'

'A few days after what he did to me, he raped his own 14-year-old daughter and was arrested. He was held on remand in Cardiff Prison where one morning he was found dead in his cell. The inquest heard that he had been poisoned but could not say whether it was by his own hand or that of another.'

'What do you feel about that?'

'I rather suspect there might have been several of us forming a queue outside his cell door. And yet, ironically, what happened to me has enabled the first steps in my rescue operation, so somewhere inside there is a tiny bit of ambivalence. Oh, hang on a minute, Ed. Didn't Rhona tell me that you were in training to be a psychotherapist? No wonder you've managed to get my life story out of me so easily! I'm trying to decide whether it was crafty or impressive.'

They both laughed.

'Whichever it was I can promise you I wasn't using any technique. I was however profoundly moved and shocked by your story, and although it's biologically impossible, I wonder how many men could have withstood what you have been through and emerged remarkably unscathed. I have long believed that women are emotionally much stronger than men. In government I worked with one such, and I'm married to another, as is Adam, and then there's Rhona. Men can be so pathetic. After the death of a wife, men either marry again quickly or die, which is why there are so many more widows than widowers about the place and especially in churches. But you're not here for psychoanalysis which I couldn't do if I wanted to, you're here to learn anything I might know about or suggest to you regarding Archie McHugh.'

'Rhona thought you might know something that could give me a clue where to begin tomorrow when I get to Jedburgh.'

'She flatters me. We, that is those of us who see her at work regularly, believe that Rhona should go to train as a vet, and I might add our vet thinks so too. When he has to come, he always works closely with her and asks her advice and often often defers to her because she has a formidable capacity for working closely with animals, far exceeding anything even Anne-Marie has, and believe me, that is saying something.'

'So why doesn't she?'

'Because she says she loves farming too much and couldn't bear the thought of lectures and students younger and considerably less experienced and knowledgeable than herself. Neither does she want to have to spend most of her working life castrating dogs and testings cows for TB.'

'I can see her point. What about income? I can't think farming can set you up for the good life.'

'I think Rhona and Anne-Marie would tell you that *this* is the good life. It's true that you'll never be rich but when I see their faces even during lambing when they get utterly exhausted, I know they think without a moment's hesitation that it's all worthwhile.'

'And do they do it all, except, I mean, when not having babies?'

'There's no question of that, though I've always done the milking at the weekend, and Adam has really taken to it, though I suspect that he talks to the cows in French which is pretty confusing for them. But to the matter in hand, our great Scottish poet, Archie McHugh. I'm interested to know why Edward Challen is interested in him as it's not obviously his normal field of interest. If it's just his poetry then the person you and he need to speak to is my wife. Anne-Marie worked for *The Poetry House,* the leading publisher of poetry, and I'm sure she would have some suggestions with regard to his published and unpublished works.'

'It's a biography he's writing not a commentary on his poems and I'm not here to find out anything about his poetry as lots of people have done that already, and besides which I'm not equipped to deal with it any more than I would know how to milk a cow.'

'Poetry's cleaner than milking.'

Charlie laughed.

'Look, I need to go next door as I'm cooking, but what about a conversation in the morning, or do you have to get off early to Jedburgh?'

'I'm in charge of my own time so if you are able to spare me some, that would be great, thank you.'

'Come and join us at breastfeeding time, though you and I will have to make do with the stuff that comes from the cows Will 8 o'clock be ok?'

'I am already looking forward to it, and especially to meeting Gregor and Anne-Marie.'

Ed stood and made his way next door. At this time of year it would barely get dark, which he loved, and not least walking around Edinburgh with its beautiful buildings until quite late. Opening the door, Anne-Marie and Gregor in her arms were almost asleep as they sat together on a kitchen chair. He paused and smiled, pulled out his mobile and took a photo. Anne-Marie surfaced.

'How did you get on with Charlie?'

'She's really nice with a lovely Welsh accent. I've invited her to join us for breakfast at 8-00 in the morning so you and the wee boy can both meet her. I don't know if you have anything intelligent to offer her on the theme of Archie McHugh, but I have one or two snippets of information which might come in handy.'

What's her background?'

'Not in biographical studies, that's for certain. She says her boss hired her because she's nosey, which is an important requirement in a researcher. Challen's biographies are always worth reading and he certainly is not scared of dealing with the scurrilous. Did you ever read the one he wrote about Angela Hargreaves, the tv newsreader who entered parliament and died in her 60s from cancer?'

'No.'

'Members of her family sought legal redress for printing appalling lies about her which, when their respective solicitors met and evidence was produced, brought about a sudden reversal by the family who largely withdrew in amazement. It's all there in the book. But he doesn't just write salacious works. He also produced a very fine work on Alexander Selkirk, of Robinson Crusoe fame.'

'What will he make of Archie McHugh I wonder?'

'A good question, but the prior question is why he is interested in writing the biography of a Scottish poet who did nothing of note other than write poems, or at least as far as I know?'

'Are you suggesting that Challen might know something of greater interest than poetry?'

'I just don't know, but I'll make a couple of calls and see if there are those who do.'

'Of course my darling, but there is first the little question of something to eat. Gregor's had his, but I am starving.'

When Rhona arrived back from milking, Charlie was surprised to find her all dressed in white in the sort of kit worn by police forensic investigators she had seen on television.

'How come you went out in one set of clothes and arrived back in another?'

'We have strict rules regarding hygiene after the milk leaves the cows. It is transferred to the dairy where we begin treating it and preparing it to be taken away tomorrow morning. We have to take off our milking clothes and put on these paper clothes to work in the dairy. I suppose it makes sense but a previous generation of farmers never had to do this and even now when I meet with them they continue to complain about it.'

'And were you doing the dairy work by yourself?'

'Oh no. Adam was doing it with me.'

'Where does he live?'

'About a mile on the edge of Melrose, with Anaïs and Jerome, who are often here in the daytime, as the two new mothers love chatting together and comparing notes. Anaïs is French but her English is superb and she works as a psychotherapist in Edinburgh, which gave Ed the nudge in the same direction. She's Adam's second wife, the first, Alice, was also French and died of breast cancer in her late twenties. I met her twin sister Simone once when she came here. I don't know the full story as it took place in France, but whatever it was has shaken Adam a great deal. I know they do not allow therapists to treat members of their own family but I gather from Adam himself that whatever it was that took place, it has been vital to his recovery that Anaïs is there to help and support him. What I also know, and he confirms it regularly, is that although he was a university professor of French, he has never enjoyed himself more than when working on the farm. What will happen when Anne-Marie returns I don't know. Financially there is no way that we can afford three of us, but I guess we'll just have to wait and see.'

'You never know, do you, what people's lives have held. Perhaps all of us have fantasies that everyone else is having a good time and we are the ones who are not, but when you scratch the surface it is amazing just how much some people have to live with and endure,' said Charlie.

'You are right. There aren't many of us who get through this life unscathed. The farming community is a classic example. Most of us love what we do, but increasingly more and more find that it has become a massive struggle to manage financially. The unpredictability of the market in the light of political changes has meant that many farmers have to cut back dramatically and as that has happened so I regret to say, suicides have risen, shotguns in the mouth being the favoured means.'

'Good heavens, that's terrible. Do you have one?'

'Certainly. You see that metal box on the wall over there, that is where my gun and ammunition are stored. And every year a policeman comes to check that it is secure. To be honest I've hardly ever had to use it but I wouldn't hesitate to do so if our lambs were at risk from a fox, or a badger, and especially crows which are partial to the eyes of newborn lambs .'

'Surely you're kidding me.'

'I'm afraid not. It's called living in the country and making a living in the country. Farming is one job where you literally cannot afford to be sentimental. I love the lambs but I don't cry when I take a load to the market because that's what pays my wage.'

'Do you think enough is known about farming?'

'I know there is a very strong anti-farming lobby operating, the vegans and othersMost farmers have ambivalent feelings about _Countryfile_, the TV programme. Yes, it has done a great deal to open people's eyes to what we are dealing with on a daily basis, but it is difficult to escape the sentimentalisation which underlies a great deal of what they do, for example their pretty animal picture competition for their calendar. What the public needs to do is listen to Radio Four on weekday mornings at 5-45

Whilst drinking the tea she picked up a farming magazine from the table and began to look through it. Most of it was in farmer speak and therefore inaccessible to her but she could recognise the appeal and very much hoped that before she left later in the day to begin her work in Jedburgh, there just might be sufficient time before haymaking began for Rhona to show her some of the animals. Looking through the magazine she could see that some farmers were only in the business of growing things and didn't have animals, which struck her as most odd. As she sat back and thought about it all, she realised that what she most admired here was the fact that the farm was being run by women. They were in charge and the men, both of whom had astonishing qualifications, were hired hands, the labourers.

Charlie went upstairs, had a shower and washed her hair. What, she wondered, did the day ahead hold for her? Her boss had said he thought she would only need a week or so to pick up such snippets of information that could be of use to him. She had seen the video of Archie McHugh and decided she didn't like him, or at least she wouldn't have liked him had she been around when he was. There was an entry for him in the Oxford National Dictionary of Biography, though its author had now died, and she had gone over it with a fine-tooth comb hoping to find possible starting points. Although she had looked at it, his poetry felt inaccessible. She'd always found poetry and plays quite impossible at school, though if she was being truthful, she would admit that she found everything impossible at school, though her teachers had found her even more so. Whether this job was really for her she doubted, but she had little in the way of an alternative and, at the least, was determined to give it a go. Seeing Rhona gave her an example of what a happy and fulfilled woman could be, and doing that with no need for a man.

'It's going to be a big breakfast,' said Rhona as she came in through the door, not attired in white but in her normal clothes.

'What I mean by a big breakfast is that everyone will be there. Besides you and me there will be Adam, Anaïs and Jerome, plus Ed, Anne-Marie and Gregor.'

'Gosh, should I offer to help get everything ready?'

'Don't worry, Anne-Marie's speciality act is doing the impossible. You'll like her, in fact you'll like us all.'

'I certainly envy you all, living here and being happily fulfilled in your lives and work.'

'Are you not?'

'I haven't the first idea to be honest. I've no idea why I'm doing this job and I feel out of my depth already, before I've even started, and I shall be making it up as I go along.'

'Have you got a family?'

'No. I was given up for adoption but the couple weren't able to cope with what they had taken on, so I went into care when I was 4. I had several foster parents all of whom found me impossible to deal with, but not as difficult as I found the last pair, who seemed to have pulled the wool over the eyes of Social Services who had told me they were thoughtful and kind. Let's just say they were not. So I have no one.'

'Have you traced your birth parents?'

'No. I could never see much point. I reckoned that if they didn't want me when I was born, they were unlikely to do so when I was on the streets taking drugs and waiting to die. I'm afraid I joined the girls who turn to immoral earnings to finance the drugs I craved. We were under the control of a disgusting creep called Ollie to whom we had to hand over most of our earnings, and then I received a visit from Detective Sergeant Hughes though at least that has enabled me to break free from the life I'd lived in my teens. I've been perfectly clean of drugs for some months now, I no longer smoke, and I've got a job. That has to be an advance.'

'Edinburgh has a big drug problem, which is why

Trainspotting was set here.'

'I've never seen it.'

'You have missed little though perhaps that's as well. I should think you've had more than enough of that existence.'

Breakfast was a noisy affair. Being mid-summer and already warm there was no porridge, but Anne-Marie had provided cereal and a wonderful cooked breakfast which Gregor seemed to eye enviously before attaching himself to her breast, gently murmuring his satisfaction and allowing bacon to be kept for another day. Jerome was still asleep from the car journey allowing Adam and Anaïs to tuck in undisturbed. To Charlie they all came over as strong and happy people, though she also knew that how things looked was not always how things were. From what little she had learned from Rhona, she knew full well that Adam had been through a very difficult time, though other than telling her about the death of his first wife, Rhona had said little more. Anaïs had a slight French accent but had no difficulty understanding anything anyone said, though only the two men had a Scottish accent besides Rhona.

They were discussing the day ahead, and thoughtfully not plying Charlie with questions. Anaïs worked in a psychotherapy centre in Edinburgh (where Ed was hoping to be placed for his closely supervised practice) and was due to hand over Jerome to Adam after he had done a morning's baling with Rhona. Ed would take over from Adam, who would be back later to milk. Anne-Marie had a lot of paperwork to do, she said, and it was clear that she was feeling frustrated not to be out there working on the farm, though she intended taking Gregor out later to meet the Chinese pigs.

'What about you?' asked Anaïs, 'are you going straight off to Jedburgh?'

'No. Ed and I are going to have a chat so he can fill me in on local knowledge of Archie McHugh. After that I shall make my way.'

'I very much hope you will return to see us. These others are so very boring that a new face is so welcome!'

They laughed.

'I am including neither Gregor nor Jerome in that. They are always interesting and to be honest I have some very good conversations with my son when there is no one around, though always in French.'

'So do I', said Anne-Marie, 'and unlike my husband the only answers I get are in the form of burps.'

At that moment, almost in response to his name being spoken, Gregor detached himself from his mum and basked in the limelight of attention.

Rhona had promised Charlie a quick tour of the pigs and cows after breakfast, the sheep being far too scattered on the hills behind the farm.

'It's been great having you here, Charlie,' began Rhona, as they walked back the farm.

'Oh, but you've been wonderful and welcoming from when we met in that hot and crowded tent in Kelso. I'll keep in touch and if I get the chance I'll come back and see you.'

'Mind you do.'

They gave each other a quick hug and then Rhona set off with Adam who had been waiting, to get the two tractors going and to get on with haymaking. Charlie could hear them chattering and laughing as they made references to the big kit, as they called their workhorses. It had been a warm night without dew and so, unusually, they could get to work at once.

Charlie turned and then made her way back inside the kitchen where Anaïs was engaged in the feeding task and listening to Anne-Marie talking about something or other, beyond the ken of Charlie's mind. Anne-Marie broke off.

'Ed will be here in a minute or two so pull out a chair and come and join us until he does.'

'Thanks, I will.'

'Have you got children, Charlie?' asked Anaïs.

'No, and sadly I'm unable to do so. I was the victim of a horribly violent sexual assault in Swansea of which the perpetrator was a corrupt detective sergeant. He did so much internal damage with an implement that I had to have extensive surgery and the surgeon told me afterwards that I could forget children.'

'God, that's awful,' said Anne-Marie. 'What's happened to him?'

'He's dead. A couple of days after dealing with me he raped his own 14 year old daughter and was arrested and remanded in custody in Cardiff Prison. Somehow or other, and no one knows how, he died suddenly on the day he was due to be moved to a different prison. When it came to the Inquest, I gather even the coroner didn't extend herself in returning a verdict of suicide by means unknown.'

'You can't have lost much sleep about him.'

'None, but what he did to me and the support I received from two women police officers has been the occasioning of a major change of life, but sometimes life's like that.'

'As I know only too well,' added Anne-Marie, 'but we won't go into that now.' She had a glint in her eye.

'It sounds like I ought to come back sometime and hear the story.'

'Not my finest hour.'

'It certainly wasn't,' said a voice at the door.

The three women turned to find Ed there, smiling.

'Ed was so used to listening in to conversations without being noticed all the time in his previous job that I have to watch everything I say even to Gregor here just in case his daddy is listening,' said Anne-Marie jokingly.

'Quite right too,' continued Ed, ' and the wee lad tells me all sorts of things.'

Charlie stood.

'Are you ready for me?'

'Aye. Rhona wants us to walk up to Brona End, to see if there are any strays over there.'

'Darling, are you sure that's wise? You know we think you may have a summer flu coming on.'

'I'll take it easy – I promise.'

They headed across the farmyard, over two fences and began making their way upwards, passing the Chinese pigs on their left. Charlie pointed towards them.

'They're tiny as pigs go. They will hardly make sausage meat, so why are they here?'

'Anne-Marie's always fancied them, so here they are. But you'd be wrong about meat. They will get larger but we keep them for the Chinese food market in this country. They want only Chinese pig meat, so that's what we're providing and my wife is a wizard with farming finance so she had a good idea how much we would make from them.'

'Doesn't she mind when they have to go off to be slaughtered? I'm sure I would.'

Ed laughed.

'No. Farmers have to be as hard as nails in that regard and she is. The great secret is not to give any of them names, I gather. Rhona's exactly the same. On the other hand we don't go in much for Chinese Take-aways.'

'I should hope not. I think I would feel like a cannibal. Anyway Ed, you said you'd see if you could find out anything which might indicate a possible starting point for sniffing around Jedburgh.'

'H'm. I'd be interested to know what your employer knows and why he has sent (if you don't mind me calling you this) a novice researcher. I assume he's been here himself.'

'Not as far as I know. He said only that he was interested in McHugh and thought how good a subject he was for his next biography.'

'Well, I'm intrigued why he should think that, because as far as I have been able to work out there was nothing in his life at all which could be of interest to others, apart that is, from his poetry and there have been a number of books published concerned with that. I have been told that he wasn't particularly well-liked in his community, and at the end of his life alienated from his son Malcom, who still lives in Jedburgh. And I'm intrigued that he has sent you to do this and for only a short while, which any researcher would agree is worse than useless? I asked Anne-Marie if she knew anything from her time in *The Poetry House*, but she said McHugh had died some time before she worked there, but she knew that her uncle Oliver who was the Founder and Editor refused to accept his works for publication saying that he was uneasy about the voice of the poems.'

'I don't know what that means.'

'It means he had doubts about how genuinely Scots the poems were. He apparently always had doubts, though other publishers did not, but Oliver was no fool where poetry or beautiful Italian women are concerned, but if it would help, Anne-Marie is happy to call him in Sicily and let you speak to him.'

'Thank you for that and Perhaps I should try to speak to Anne-Marie's uncle but I'm quite perplexed what to do next. You rightly call me a novice, but even that may be to flatter me, and sets me sharing your question as to why he took me on. The thing is, Ed, and I feel can tell you, before someone suggested me to Edward, I was living in a police safe house. The man who had attacked me was in prison and awaiting trial, but my two protection officers who I really enjoyed being with when they called in to check up on me, wanted me protected from someone else, an unpleasant guy called Ollie. He ran a string of prostitutes in Swansea, of whom I'm sorry to say I was one. I was meant to be giving evidence at the trial of the policeman in prison and Ollie feared I might jeopardise his operation. Hence the protection. It's been a liberation. I'm drug clean, don't smoke and wanting a new life having totally messed up my first one.'

'How much of this does Edward Challen know?'

'Some, but not all.'

They were walking on level ground again and both were keeping an eager eye out for misbehaving sheep though as there were none to be seen. It was another warm day and they were both sweating.

'Have you got any family?'

'No, I was brought up in care. I went round quite a few families, but I was never at ease nor them. I did nothing at school to speak of, and I never trusted the looks I received from my last foster father.'

'A familiar tale I'm afraid. Charlie. I want you to make sure you stay in touch with me while you're in Jedburgh but keep to the schedule you've got. Sniffing around is unlikely to bring about unwanted attention, but there's something very fishy about all this and I think you and I should try to get to the root of it, and there's someone else I would like you to talk to and see what she thinks.'

'There they are,' said Charlie pointing over to their left, 'or at least some are.'

There were twelve yows and lambs enjoying that which they had always maintained among themselves would be greener grass on the other side of the hill. Ed's phone was already in his hand. Rhona's tractor would have been too noisy for her phone, but the cab was equipped with bluetooth, and she turned the engine off.

'Ed. Hi.'

'Charlie and I have found 12 of what you've been missing, all with our mark. What do you want me to do, if anything?'

'There's nothing much you can do. I've got your position on my GPS, so I'll let Adam have a coffee break and I'll come up with Gyp as he's best with small numbers. Thanks.'

'D'ye know, Anne-Marie has an amazing eye for stock, but the day she found Rhona when she was paying a visit to her college in Gloucestershire, she was at her very best.'

'They're both pretty astonishing. And is it one or the other of them that you want to include in my little adventure?'

'Neither. This is not a farming matter, and we need someone with experience of strange worlds and complex motives, a former police officer and undercover agent.'

'And who on earth is that?'

'Anaïs Clément, with whom you had breakfast earlier.'

Chapter 3

Anaïs was quietly delighted to be asked to offer her thoughts on the mystery Charlie was already part of. Jerome was asleep in his buggy and was alongside Gregor in the small garden at the back of the farmhouse, being watched over by Anne-Marie. She was loving being a mum and was already greatly in love with Scotland and its extraordinary beauty, and her practice as a psychotherapist was already growing, but she acknowledged within herself that the one thing she was missing was a mystery to solve, though, to a degree, therapy presented her with these on every working day.

'I agree with you Ed,' she said after he and Charlie had brought her up to speed. 'Choosing to use you, Charlie, someone without experience or qualification, immediately suggests something fishy (which is a good English colloquialism I have recently learned from you, Ed). It makes little sense. I have a hunch that you should take great care and I would recommend cancelling your hotel booking before you set off. Book another at the same time in Hawick. Especially when you don't know what you might be dealing with, and it might be nothing, but you need to be in control and not predictable.

'I'm not working tomorrow afternoon, and I was thinking of

visiting Jedburgh and the McHugh Museum. Perhaps I'll see you there at three o'clock.'

'That would be a splendid coincidence.'

Charlie made her phone calls and prepared to leave. Collecting her bag from Rhona's she bumped into the great farmer herself.

'Did you get the yows back?'

'No, but Gyp did. She looked at me as if to ask why I thought I needed to be there, and I didn't. Anyway, I needed a break for a wee as it's the only thing the tractor doesn't provide.'

'Don't you get hot in the cab on a day like today?'

'No. It's got air conditioning, a computer with mobile broadband and stereo, but nowhere to wee, but one day it'll come, or at least I hope so.'

'I have to get going, Rhona, and I'm not sure what awaits me when I get there.'

'Do come again though. You haven't met the ladies yet or seen them being milked apart that is from Anne-Marie and Anaïs in the kitchen though it's a bit different with my ladies. You've got my mobile number so let me know how you're getting on, and as I say, if you get the chance to come back, we'd love to see you again.'

The journey was straightforward, mostly down the A68, passing close by Melrose where she was due to be staying overnight in the Station Hotel. Yesterday she had gone through Jedburgh on her way to the Show at Kelso and she had noticed where the car parks were. One of her hopes was to find time to visit Jedburgh Abbey, which dated from the 12th century. She headed up Canongate and followed the signs for the Abbey which from the outside looked well worth a visit, but not now. Once on Abbey Bridge Road she could not resist following signs for the Abbeybridge Coffee House by the river. Her breakfast had been more than satisfying but she felt she needed something extra now.

On a lovely summer's day it was full of visitors. The man serving pointed to the only spare table in the corner.

'You can say hello to the Jedburgh freakshow.'

It struck Charlie as a very odd thing to say and as she looked over all she could see was a woman minding her own business as she ate what appeared to be a toastie. She ordered the same with a coffee and went over.

'Hello. May I join you?'

I'd be delighted,' came the reply as she moved her bag to give Charlie more space.

'I'm Charlotte, though everyone calls me Charlie.'

'I'm Paula. You must be a visitor with an accent like yours.'

Charlie laughed.

'South Wales, but I'm not really a visitor as I'm here on business.'

'Gosh, that's a long way from home. Are you staying in Jedburgh?

'No. I have friends who farm just outside Galashiels. What about you?'

'Well, I live in Melrose but I work here as the manager of the Co-op Supermarket. Today's my day-off but I had to pop in to check on a new girl due to start today.'

'And did she?'

'Yes, as I thought she would, but I wanted to be there so she would at least recognise one face before handing her over to the tender arms of my assistant, Molly, who looks as if she once tossed the caber at the Highland Games, but is really as soft as they come.'

'Do you have a good team?'

'As they've all been appointed by me, I will have to say yes, but even so they are a good lot and I have had ever such a lot of support from them.'

'Am I allowed to ask what for?'

'About four years ago I began the long process of gender transition. I was Paul until then and now I'm Paula.'

'In which case they and you have done a fantastic job on the outward you. I would defy anyone not knowing to have the slightest idea that you were not 100% woman. The waiter said to me that you are the Jedburgh freakshow. I feel offended on your behalf.'

'Take no notice of Andrew. He and I have been friends a long time, and believe me, I can give as good as I get. But perhaps I am something of a freakshow. If I were to lift my skirt, which I won't in here, you would see that nine months ago I completed the surgical removal of my former male genitals, followed later by a bowel vaginoplasty, which is complicated to describe so I'll just have to ask you to use your imagination.'

'Paula, I am so full of admiration for you.'

Don't be, Charlie. I'm pretty certain that if I hadn't had it done the depths of despair in which I was living would have led to my suicide sooner or later, so it was a kind of life-saving procedure.'

'Really? They didn't teach us that when we were learning how to life-save during swimming at school.'

They both giggled.

'But that's the outward you, what about the inner you? How have people responded?'

'Habits die hard, and twice I've walked in to a gents lav in a motorway service station though I can't recall who got the greater shock, them or me? Otherwise I'm aware that people are trying, some of them anyway, to make their own mental adjustments, but others just can't manage it.'

'You don't have to answer this but given all you've told me, I what about relationships and sex now?'

'Before the change I was gay and I'm still attracted to men which as a woman makes me straight, and I have a boyfriend who's totally at ease with this and we have a pretty good physical relationship. I have no complaints, but I've been talking too much. Tell me about you and the business that has brought you here.'

'I work for a writer in Wales as a research assistant. His speciality is biographies and some of his works have won a lot of praise. Now he's beginning work on a biography of the poet Archie McHugh of Jedburgh and I'm here to root about and see if there are important things he's missing, but I'm only here for a short time so I don't think he's expecting much.'

'You know there's a Museum in what was once his house in Dean's Close, just past the Town Hall on the right?'

'Yes, thanks and I should be heading off there now. Did you know him by any chance?'

'Archie was a sort of recluse though I think he enjoyed being "the grand old man of poetry". Something of a joke really. But Charlie, you take care and I mean it.'

They both stood and walked towards the door, and then crossed the bridge and walked towards the Abbey ruins. Paula stopped and pointed.

'Here's Dean's Close,' said Paula, 'and the Museum's on the right, but I've had a thought. Charlie, why don't you come and stay with me. I've got a spare room and perhaps your farming friends can spare you for a night? It might also help your research in ways I can't explain now as we stand in the street.'

Charlie made her mind up at once.

'Of course they'll understand. I'd love to spend the evening with you. But what about your boyfriend? Won't I be in the way?'

'Erm, well, no. He'll be at home with his wife and kids!'

'Ah. Well, give me your address and phone number and I'll give you mine.'

They exchanged the necessary information.

'I'll let you know at what time to expect me.'

'Make it after five if possible. I shan't be alone until after then.'

The Archie McHugh Museum had once been his home and, a notice outside proclaimed, almost all of his poetry had been written here. There was no entry fee and a lady by the door welcomed Charlie as she entered. There were about six others already inside.

'We've kept the house more or less exactly as it when Archie passed away,' said the lady.

'Don't you mean "died"?' replied Charlie, who received an old-fashioned look in return.

'How much do you know about Archie?'

'Quite a lot. Yes, I'm visiting, but doing so in the course of my work as a literary researcher on behalf of my boss, Edward Challen, a well-known biographer, who has turned his attention to Archie McHugh.'

'Oh,' said the lady taken aback. When she had recovered her composure she said, 'I can't think he'll have much to work on. Archie rarely strayed from Jedburgh, and to be honest, not a great deal happens here. I imagine your employer will be familiar with Archie's poetry and if so he will know that Archie's journeyings were mostly inner journeys.'

'I think Mr Challen is well aware of that, but if you've read any of his other books, you'll be aware that he uses material such as poetry and other writings to weave together a story, and does so effectively.'

'Well, I'm sure we shall be delighted to see the finished work, and what about you, have got a copy of the *Complete Poems?*'

'It wouldn't have been wise to come without.'

'No, of course not. Anyway, do feel free to wander. Here is a leaflet which explains what is what and where it is.'

'Thank you.'

Charlie wandered around the museum looking at the detritus of the life of a Scottish poet who had either died or passed way some time ago. Her real difficulty was that she had no idea what she was looking for, but she was determined not to rush, so every so often she would pick up an artefact and loudly murmur 'H'm' or 'That's most interesting.' The fact was that she was bored and totally at a loss to know what she should do next.

'Have you found anything that catches your attention?' said the lady as Charlie drew nearer to the door.

'I think it's all fascinating and I feel I shall from now on be engaging with his poetry in a different, much deeper way.'

'I assume you have a background in the study of literature which you would need to do your job, so how would you rate his work?'

'I long since gave up trying to do that because it's never a case of comparing like with like, but I think Archie needs no words of praise from me. He must have known their quality and as I'm sure you do too.'

'Definitely, and you're right, such poetry cannot be ranked, not least because it's all so subjective.'

'Tell me, are there people still living who knew him well?'

'Yes. There's his son, Malcolm, and two former amanuenses who worked closely with him. If you'll wait here a moment, I'll write their names, addresses and phone numbers on a piece of paper for you.'

She crossed the room, opened a door and Charlie heard her going up some stairs. Meanwhile, she was wondering what on earth amanuenses were. She would have to ask Ed when she called him later. The lady returned and handed her a piece of paper.

'I'm sure they'll be pleased to hear from you though it's worth bearing in mind that Archie and Malcolm didn't always see eye to eye.'

'Thank you so much. What's your name by the way?'

'Sylvia Sirling.'

' I may pop back tomorrow just to get another sense of the place, so I may see you then.'

'That would be nice. And your name?'

Charlotte, though most people call me Charlie.'

'Are you staying in Jedburgh?'

'No, I have farming friends near Galashiels.'

'Enjoy the day light. The sun hardly sets at this time of the year.'

'So I've noticed. Bye.'

Charlie walked back past the Town hall and feeling she needed a break from conversation decided this was a very good time to visit the Abbey. She had no idea what "Augustinian" in its title meant and was genuinely sorry it was in ruins as once upon a time it must have been full of life. There were some visitors doing the rounds of its ruined walls but not so as to spoil it for her. She had grown up with no contact with religion but here in this place felt there was something very special and she wondered what sort of life the original residents might have led and whether there were any who still did live that life. Perhaps Paula could provide an answer later.

She spent a long time there, just wandering and wondering, and for the first time in many years, perhaps in her life, she felt happy and at peace. A lady she had seen as she entered the Abbey grounds came towards her.

'Hello there. You look as if you're enjoying yourself.'

'Hello. You're quite right, I am. I really like it here but thinking what a pity it is that it's a ruin and no longer used as it was intended to be used.'

'Well, not for the first or the last time that was the work of politicians operating in the name of religion. Are you religious?'

'I have no idea.'

'Ooh, that's an interesting answer.'

'Is it? I know little about religion.'

The lady smiled and took Charlie's hand for a moment.

'Some would think you very lucky in that case.'

'Is that what you think?'

'No. Not at all, but that's another story. How long are you here in Jedburgh?'

'I don't really know. I know that sounds bizarre but I'm researching into the Jedburgh poet Archie McHugh for my boss in Wales who's writing a biography of him. I was only intending to stay a week or so but I'm greatly enjoying myself and making new friends.'

'H'm. What an undertaking.'

'Is it? I thought it would be straightforward.'

'It depends on how deep you want to dig.'

'Oh?'

'I would advise you to stay with the official McHugh myth as expressed in the Museum.'

'As opposed to?'

'Who knows? But if you are coming back tomorrow we could have a spot of lunch together. Is that possible?'

'Yes. That would be good. Here at 1.00?

'Ok.'

'I haven't told you my name. It's Charlotte, Charlotte Holly, though I'm normally called Charlie.'

'I would prefer Charlotte. It's such a beautiful name and if you don't mind me saying so you don't look even slightly like a man and quite the opposite. I'm Eilidh Hart, and I'm so pleased to meet you. I hope to see you tomorrow, Charlotte.'

'I'll be here.'

She was being given hints, most of them almost warnings, which heightened her curiosity but also raised her anxiety levels. It was vital she should speak to Ed and already she was keenly anticipating the visit of Anaïs on the following afternoon. She had an enquiring mind, but as had been pointed out this morning both Ed and Anaïs, she was almost immediately out of her depth once she spoke to anyone, so why did Edward Challen send her? She didn't think it was mischief on his part and he was far too intelligent not to have done it for a reason, but what that could be she did not understand.

Chapter 4

Charlie returned to her car and looked at her watch. Although Paula had said it would be ok to arrive after 5 o'clock, Charlie thought it might be wise to leave it a little later. That being the case she decided to call Ed in the hope he had finished his afternoon of counselling in Edinburgh. He replied at once on his carphone.

'Hello Charlie.'

'Hello Ed. Is this a good time to call?'

'Ideal. I'm in a traffic jam which is not moving but in any case I'm on my hands-free. So how it is going?'

She recounted the encounters of the day including that slight sense of menace she had picked up in the Museum.

'Do you want to return to us tonight or visit your trans friend?'

'I think I might learn more from her somehow or other, but thanks for the offer.'

'Don't forget that Anaïs will be with you tomorrow. Tell her everything you have discovered, and I mean everything, and above all do what she tells you.'

'Ok. Ed, do you think I have grounds for feeling unsafe?'

'If you do, either get out immediately and come back to the farm or call me or Anaïs at once.'

'Ok. I'm setting off for Melrose now, but one more thing,

what's an amanuenses. It seems Archie had two of them, but I've no idea what they are.'

'They're people who write down what the master dictates. A kind of walking tape recorder.'

Something a poet might have.'

'No, I wouldn't have thought so. Odd then that he should have two of them.'

It was afternoon milking time, and both Rhona and Adam were hard at work and finding the parlour a very hot place. Both wore only their underwear under their milking kit and thought nothing of it as very often they saw one another dressed in nothing more as they prepared to go into the dairy.

Ed was making the food this evening and Anne-Marie feeding Gregor, but he found the time for a quick undisturbed call to Anaïs to report on his contact with Charlie.

'I shall be pleased to see her for myself tomorrow, and you and I must then consider whether we should encourage her to abandon what she's doing. Something feels most odd, but especially why Challen sent such a ludicrously under-equipped person on a mission like this. You said she was staying with a trans woman she met earlier today.'

'That's what she said.'

'It almost sounds like a mystery that would have intrigued Maigret.'

'I recommend you don't take up pipe smoking though.'

'I will try, not least because I don't think Jerome would appreciate it.

'Nor Adam. Pipes smell.'

'Hey, how do you think I feel when he comes in from work smelling as he does after a day on the farm?'

Ed laughed.

'Well, I have to say Anne-Marie now has a constant smell of

baby which I prefer to some of the aromas she has carried home in the past, such as when she has just delivered a calf or a lamb.'

'Did you know that that wicked woman Rhona encouraged Adam to have a go at delivering a calf?'

'How did he do?'

'Ok, I think, but the bit I most enjoyed but he maybe did not, was when he reported they were both down to their undies and covered in afterbirth and shit.'

'Wow, Even Rhona might not have been so glamorous attired like that.'

'Well, I hope not!'

They laughed.

The Eildon Hills standout for many miles around. They are not towering mountains as can be found further north, nor even are they Monroes to be bagged by keen mountaineers and countrymen and women. But to the locals they indicate the presence of home and most especially the small town of Melrose. Other than an Abbey which Charlie intended visiting before she left in the morning there wasn't a great deal to see though not too far off was the former home of Sir Walter Scott. Charlie knew nothing of him and had read none of his books but her guidebook told her that his house, Abbotsford, was well worth a visit. Whether she would make that was a matter of conjecture.

Paula lived in a typical Melrose terraced house which Charlie found quite easily using the satnav in the car. She collected her possessions from the boot and went towards the front door which opened as she approached.

'Hi there Charlie,' said Paula with a broad smile.

'Hi.'

'Did you find it easily enough? I was a bit concerned when you were late.'

'Oh yes. This is a hire car and comes with a very good satnav. I shall be really sorry when I have to take it back and I shall have to start giving thought to getting a car of my own.'

Paula led Charlie into her front room and immediately said she would make a cup of tea for them.

Charlie looked around and immediately noticed that there were no photographs. There was a huge television but not a lot of other furniture apart from the sofa on which she was now sitting and another armchair beside it, both of which had seen better days.

'I noticed at dinner time that you didn't take any sugar so I haven't brought any through.'

'You're quite right, I don't. My reason for being a little late was that I didn't want to take the risk of bumping into your friend who came to see you this afternoon.'

'He is gay and my own former regular partner when I was a gay man. I'm not really sure what he makes of it all now, especially my breasts and artificial vagina but little has otherwise changed for him and he still uses the same entrance, so perhaps he's happy.'

'And you?'

'Shall we say it's taking some getting used to and what I really want is a man who will relate to me as a woman in and out of bed, but that's unlikely here in these small communities where everyone knows me and has seen me change. I can fully understand how some might think.'

'Well I think you're courageous and I can well understand why you no longer wanted to be a man. Although I have suffered at their hands more than I like to remember, I've often wondered what it feels like to be so driven to want sex at any cost. It must be pretty difficult living with that.'

'I was a man for a long time. I suppose that in my teens I used to feel like that but of course it was never directed towards girls but towards other boys which was even more confusing because

I was growing up in heterosexual society and this was at a time when although the law had changed, societies still seemed to frown upon gay men. But by my early twenties something inside me had changed in a big way, and the result is here for you to see.'

'I haven't come across many trans women, but those I have always seen to make a point of being more feminine than the feminine. What I mean by that is you are wearing lovely clothes and not cheap I imagine, and look at me who has been a woman for considerably longer and I almost look butch in comparison.'

'Charlie, I don't think anyone would mistake you for a man, but I take your point about trans women emphasising our newly experienced femininity and I don't know whether something has actually changed in my brain but I simply adore going into clothes shops and buying lovely lingerie.'

'I think that's really cool.'

"Now, I hope it's okay with you, but I ordered us both a takeaway pizza and in my freezer I have some lovely ice cream. Is that okay?'

'Great. Thank you.'

'And after we've had our tea, there are one or two things I would like to talk to you about, important things about what you are doing here, but let's leave it until after we've eaten, and as neither of us will be driving this evening I also have a nice bottle we might share, one of the benefits of working in a supermarket being that I do the ordering.'

'I can imagine that the people you work with will have seen you through every stage of your transition. How have they been?'

'Frankly, they have been brilliant. And I'm not so stupid as to imagine they might not have said things between themselves, probably humorous at my expense, but in their dealings with me I can't speak highly enough of them. You see, I was close to them as a man, because I enjoyed the company of women considerably more than the company of men. They had always known that they could talk about anything including intimate matters in my presence without feeling the slightest bit of embarrassment either in them or in me. I think they've always known that I would support them in any way I could in whatever circumstances they found themselves, and when push came to shove, they did the same for me, and still do. In fact I would say they treat me exactly as the woman I want to be, if that makes sense.'

'So has there been no hostility?'

'Oh God yes, and not least from God's earthly representatives, meaning the Minister and members of the Kirk, who, because they have direct access to God's will, know exactly what is to be demanded even of those who have not the slightest belief and never attend their services.'

'So how did you deal with them?'

'The Minister and one of the Elders came to see me and I told them to fuck off. It was very effective.'

There was a knock on the door.

'I'm very much hoping that's our tea and not the Minister trying again,' said Paula as she rose and went to the door. While Paula was putting the pizza on plates and adding coleslaw, Charlie went upstairs to the room Paula had shown her and changed her top. It had been very hot today but was a little cooler here in the valley. The pizzas were very good and Charlie had felt ready for something substantial to eat. After the ice cream they quickly washed up together mostly chatting about the sort of nothings humans most enjoy. Eventually they came back to the front room and sat down.

'Before you tell me what it is you think I need to know and which, after all, has brought me here, I would welcome knowing a little more of your journey. To be perfectly honest I know nothing about it and although I'm not anticipating doing it myself, hearing from you an account of what you have been through would be really helpful, though it goes with saying that if this is all too personal then you must not feel under any obligation at all.'

'No, I'm perfectly happy to tell you about it and the first thing to say is that in no way is it a quick fix. It took a long time. The first stage was summoning up the courage, though it may have been the desperation, to visit my GP. That has to be the starting point for everyone. Dr Fernyhough's interrogation technique she learned from the Gestapo, so I can assure you that from the very beginning there was no way I was going to be allowed to do this without a lot of testing. In a way, the next test was the worst. She said she was perfectly happy to refer me to the gender clinic in Edinburgh which is what I wanted. Within a couple of days I received a letter from then acknowledging my referral but informing me that there would be at least a year's waiting list before I could go and be assessed. As you might imagine, having summoned up my courage, this was a great disappointment. I now know that waiting times in many other clinics are even longer, and although it's not done for this reason it is a good testing ground. You have to want to do it to wait all that time and I gather that quite a lot of people can't wait and give up the idea.

'The day I received an appointment was a great day. It was an initial assessment by a specially trained nurse, male as it happened, but who could not have been better though I have to say that he too was a graduate of the same interrogation school as my GP. I was recommended to go further in the process, though I was told again and again that if at any time the clinic staff thought this was not right, it would be stopped. The next stage was to see a psychiatrist, and I went to see him twice. I don't know what I was expecting but he wasn't anything like it. He didn't interrogate but had a wonderful way of encouraging me to speak. At the end of our second meeting he told me he was happy for me to go forward to the next stage and would make the appropriate recommendation.

'That meant that I began to take oestrogen every day. At first nothing happened, but gradually I noticed my body beginning to change. The muscles on my arms and legs seemed to get less bulky. I was never very hairy but such as I had begun to disappear. My breasts began to swell, not enormously but noticeably almost in proportion to my willy doing the exact opposite which was a bit disconcerting at first. I was given help with my hair and my eyebrows needed to be reshaped. Most amusing of all however, was going to a make-up class and receiving help with choosing clothes. That was the point when I had to face up to what I was doing by doing it publicly – going to work and being in public dressed as a woman. God, did I shit myself as I went out the front door on the first morning and most of all because of the sort of shoes I now had to wear.'

Charlie started laughing.

'That was brave.'

'I don't know about that. When I got home I immediately wanted to take everything off and put my male clothes back on but the point was made, and I see now that it was a good one, that we were not cross-dressing or playacting but we were becoming women and it had to be 100%. I did this for a further six months, still taking hormones and rather disappointed that my breasts were not as prominent as I hoped they might be even with the help of an uplift bra, when I had to go and see another psychiatrist who tried to assess how it had been and whether the process should be completed by surgery. This of course was the point of no return, not that I wanted to return. I was happier than I had ever been and for some people that is enough, but I wanted to do it properly. This doctor gave the clinic the green light and so I had surgery to remove my genitals, to enlarge my breasts and then to provide for me an artificial vagina. Surgery of course is never fun but I was so very well looked after by the clinic that I will never be able to stop singing their praises. And so, here I am.'

'Did you have special training on your voice? Looking like a woman, as you do, would be odd if you had a deep masculine voice.'

'Yes, I forgot to mention that I used to see a speech therapist. The clinic thinks of everything.'

'Thank you so very much for telling me that. I knew nothing about it.'

'Well, let's have another class of wine, because I have some other things to tell you and it will involve quite a lot of speaking on my part.'

She took a healthy drink and put the glass down.

'Charlie, are you going to meet with those who knew Archie, such as his son Malcolm or any other?'

'I've already met Eilidh Hart at the Abbey and Sylvia Stirling at the museum and in fact it was Sylvia who provided me with the address and telephone number of Malcolm though as yet I've done nothing about it.'

'I knew Archie McHugh or more strictly that should be that he knew me. I was about 10 years old at the time, still at the primary school, and being distinguished he was invited to the school to hand out prizes and make a speech at the end of the year. He gave the impression that he liked to be thought of as the Grand Old Man of Jedburgh. I think however, or at least I got the impression from my parents and some of their friends that not everyone liked him. I guess that poetry has always been a minority pursuit and it was only a small number here in the town that took an interest. He did however, seem to have the Editor of the *Southern Reporter* at his beck and call because it was rare indeed not to see his face in every edition.

'My dad often said to me that I should keep well away from

McHugh. What basis he had for saying that so often I didn't at the time know and in a way I was really disappointed because I'd heard from some of those with whom I was at school that he ran an unofficial after-school club to which they would go, but my dad had spoken and there is no way I would have gone against him. But then I did so. I was curious about what people were going on about at school with regard to being in his home once school was out. It did sound fun and so I decided I was missing out on the fun and just wanted it to satisfy my curiosity.

'It was fun indeed, like being at a birthday party. There was food and drink and pop music and I thoroughly enjoyed it and made my mind up that I would come again. As we were leaving, McHugh stopped me by the door and said that because I was new he would welcome a short chat. There seemed little harm in that so I agreed. There is no easy way to tell you what happened next so I will be as direct as I can. He led me upstairs where he pulled down my trousers and buggered me.'

Charlie said nothing but continued to look steadily at Paula's face.

'I did not return but neither did I report it to my parents when I got home. In the first place I was very sore and I was also profoundly shocked. I mentioned this to the first psychiatrist that I saw before I began to take oestrogen. Both of us knew that there was nothing that could be done because McHugh by this time was dead, but I think that what he had done to me lived on. Is it what has made me seek transition? Neither the psychiatrist nor I can answer that question but I would say that I wouldn't be surprised if it was. For understandable reasons I would never enter the museum and I've even sometimes given thought to the desirability of burning it down because for me it is an absolute outrage that it should honour the far from honourable.'

'Do you know of any others who had a similar experience?'

'I was very young and I would have had no idea how to go

about asking my friends what experiences they had had. Plus, if my questioning had became aware to my teachers then it's quite possible that I would have been held responsible for giving the local hero a bad name, and my parents would have come to know that I had disobeyed them. Back then it was assumed that children made up this sort of thing. So I said nothing, but your coming makes it possible that the truth can come out in the biography that Edward Challen is writing.'

Although her knowledge of how publishing worked was almost non-existent, as Charlie lay in bed and thought about what she had heard from Paula, she thought it likely that she would need to gather corroborating evidence from others and she wasn't at all sure how she might do that. She decided that acquiring a clip board and wandering the streets asking men of a certain age had they been sodomised by Archie McHugh probably was not the best way forward. Sadly, she had no access to a police computer, or any other sort of computer, which she might just contain records of complaints made against McHugh but then disregarded. In his previous job Ed might have had that sort of access, but not any more, and of what she had seen of the computer in the farmhouse, it only dealt with cows and sheep and farming accounts, which would not be of much use to her. She liked Paula and greatly admired her. She would be leaving very early in the morning to open up the supermarket, so if she wished to see her again, she would need to do some shopping, and once again remembered that soon she was meant to be returning to Wales with the hire car and her report. After all she was not working freelance but had a boss who was paying her to do what he asked but she would have to tell him she needed more time.

Chapter 5

It was going to be heavy day for Rhona and Adam as it had been three days earlier for after milking they would need to move all the cattle, including those which were dry, for the return visit of their vet Sam – Judgement Day. 72 hours earlier Sam had shaved a small area on the neck of each cow and injected them twice, once with avian and once with bovine tuberculin, measured the thickness of the skin and sent each one on its way. Today Sam would have either good news or catastrophic news to impart.

'Adam, can you make sure the crush is working properly, and if necessary liberally oil the moving parts. I'll go to collect the copies of what Sam left us and have a word with the boss and see if she wants to join us though I'm pretty sure she won't, and as it happens neither do I.'

'I'm more than happy to do it myself, if you want.'

'Thanks Adam, and I'm sure you mean it, but of course I have to be there and so do you. Moving the girls will require both of us especially if, and God forbid, we need to isolate any.'

'What would happen then?'

'Compulsory slaughter I'm afraid.'

'Oh.'

'Yes, but we live in a low risk area, so let's hope we are clear but until Sam gets going we won't know.'

'Ok, I'll go and attend to the crush.'

Rhona walked into the farmhouse kitchen but there was no sign of Anne-Marie, which suggested she would be out with Gregor on the lane trying to get him to sleep. Rhona sat down. She loved this place and she loved farming but this was the one day no farmer loved – TB results day. If it went bad she would lose some of her friends, taken off to what she thought was a wholly unnecessary slaughter and that included those in calf, plus restrictions on movement for 60 days, and milk from the others could only be sold with notification that TB has been found in the herd, which could ruin their business completely. Rhona shared the view of most farmers that the cause of a great deal of TB was the presence of badgers and had no compunction about shooting any she saw on the land. She prided herself on the quality of care with which she engaged in animal husbandry but had no time at all for those who had no idea what they were talking about, who mostly lived in cities and presumed to lecture farmers on what they did.

The sound of a motor vehicle which she recognised as belong to Sam (whom she rather fancied – it was such a pity about his wife!) brought her from her reveries and she left the kitchen and went out to greet him, though it turned out that she was greeting two of them, the other being what most men would think to be a rather dishy blond of her own age.

'Good morning Rhona, good morning Adam (who had appeared from nowhere), it's another lovely morning, and let me introduce to you Francine, who's just joined the practice from her home somewhere outside Geneva.'

Immediately Rhona knew that this was not good news. Adam had been Professor of French at Edinburgh University, and both his first and second wife were French. He could see that his eyes had lit up as soon as he saw Francine. It did occur to Rhona that a tactful phone call to Anaïs might be a good idea but, then again, why spoil Adam's day? And in any case most people meeting Anaïs thought her stunningly attractive.

Adam and Francine chatted away in French whilst Sam and Rhona prepared everything at the business end. It turned out that Francine was to do the tests with Sam recording and very quickly Rhona realised that she was very good indeed at her job. Adam kept the girls coming and Rhona returned those done back to their temporary paddock. So far, so good – no reactors.

There was no need for rush to get back to Jedburgh so Charlie delayed long enough for Melrose Abbey to open. The sign said it was Cistercian but she had no idea what that might possibly mean. It was smaller than that in Jedburgh or, perhaps, more compact might be a better way of describing it but she liked it no less and tried desperately to hear the sound of monks. She decided it must be wonderful to be able to feel so committed to something you could give yourself heart and soul to it, and for a few moments she wished she could live like that. Unfortunately, a lot of her life had taken place in the sordid and unpleasant places of the world which like tattoos stained her very being permanently. Even in the beautiful Scottish Borders and close to these monastic houses, she had uncovered things which she recognised from her former life. Her temptation was to abandon it all and return to Wales and tell Edward Challen she had found nothing, which might work but for one thing: somewhere inside herself there was an inkling that he already knew something of what had been going on, and so sent a halfwit to see if she could find out more by being clumsy in what she said to people, being too stupid to know better. She couldn't think of any other reason why she should have been sent by him.

Her first port of call she had arranged earlier when, to her surprise she had been invited for coffee. It was with Malcolm

McHugh, the son of the poet. She had explained on the phone exactly why she had been sent by Edward, and the mere mention of his name brought about the coffee invite. Malcolm lived a little way outside Jedburgh but Charlie had little difficulty finding the place and he made her warmly welcome. He lived in a bungalow which revealed no signs of any other form of life, whether wife, partner or children.

Malcolm brought coffee through to the sitting room where there was a lovely view of moorland from the picture window.

'So how can I be of assistance?' he began.

'I have no idea,' replied Charlie truthfully.

Malcolm laughed.

'You should get a job on television interviewing politicians.'

This time they both laughed.

'Edward told me was working on a biography about your father and was sending me to Jedburgh to see if I could find anything other than the normal hagiography or at least I think that was the word he used. Quite why he sent me I have no idea. I've read only a little of his poetry, most of which I don't understand, and seen him on one or two YouTube videos, and I have no background at all in literature or being a researcher.'

'And how are you doing in your quest?'

'About as well as you might expect in someone like me - so far, nothing.'

'Edward never mentioned being at school here?'

'Primary School?'

'No. Jedburgh Grammar. It's not a real Grammar School now of course, the politically correct educationalists determined to dumb everyone down to the same level have seen to that but in our day it was as good as any other Grammar in a Scotland which used to pride itself on its education. No more.'

'What was he doing there? He's not a Scot as far as I know and there's not the trace of an accent.'

'It was his father's work that brought him. We never knew what it was, and I was not entirely sure Edward knew either, but we became friends not least because we both played for the first XI Soccer Team in the year we won the Border Cup. He was a tough and uncompromising centre half and had mastered the sliding tackle to perfection. Opponents used to hesitate when face to face with him and he had a fierce reputation. How true it is, I don't know, but it was said that scouts came to see him from both Hearts and Hibs. He was a clever lad and did really well in his Highers and went on to St Andrews, when I lost contact with him. But Edward was always shrewd, so I can't imagine that your presence here is some kind of accident.'

'It would have been nice to know all that before I came.'

'Yes, but that may have been his intention, that you might in your supposed innocence be able to discover things otherwise inaccessible to a professional researcher.'

'Such as?'

'I've no idea. That's why you're here.'

'People, literary scholars don't usually bother with the life and circumstances of your father but with his poetry. Does it surprise you that Edward is concerned with more than that?'

'Yes, as he's not in the premier league of poetry commentators though that I would regard as a compliment. I regret to say that most of what is now being set forth in poetry journals, whether in print or online, my father would dismiss as trivial nonsense just as I feel about what is described as modern classical music and played as new commissions at the Proms in London. I've sat on the lav and farted better tunes!'

Charlie almost upset her coffee cup laughing.

'Are they likely to win you a recording contract?'

'O God, Charlie, it wouldn't totally surprise if they did.'

'I get the impression Malcolm, that you are not totally enamoured with how the country is developing.'

'Aye well, things are not so good, and the idiots in Edinburgh are now wanting another go having lost the first vote on independence. I voted Remain in the Brexit Referendum and we lost. It's called democracy and as Leave won, that is what we should do. Edinburgh didn't like the result of the first vote so they want another, and then another until they get what they want. I didn't like the result of the Scottish Cup Final a few weeks again but I'm not demanding it be played again, though it was a travesty that Hearts lost 2-1.'

Charlie was enjoying her time with Malcolm. He was a funny and warm man, and she also knew he was concealing things and knew she would have to come back to unearth. She also thought that a conversation with Edward was becoming more and more essential, though her afternoon meeting with Anaïs was becoming increasingly important in her mind.

Malcolm accompanied Charlie to her car.

'You have a nice car.'

'Alas it's a hire car but it drives ever so well and the satnav seems on the ball, so I'll be sad to part with it. Thank you for your time and coffee, Malcolm.'

'I've enjoyed it. If you get chance please come again. Where are you off to now?'

'The Abbey, which I really like, and then some lunch. I do hope to see you again too.'

She parked in more or less the same place but noticed there were more spare spaces available and was in time not just to meet Eilidh, but also to wander round the ruined Abbey again.

'Hello there,' said the familiar voice of Eilidh recalling her to the present at a time when she was envisaging the monks about their daily chores. Charlie turned.

'Hello Eilidh, it's good see you again.'

'Are you ready for some dinner?'

'Will they have horse on the menu, because I could certainly eat one?'

As they placed their order at the counter, seats were easier to find today.

'It's quieter today.'

'It's Farmer's Market Day in Kelso but the place will get busier during the afternoon. So how is your quest progressing?'

'I get the feeling that there's a great deal more that could be said than is being said. I can understand that if there are dark secrets the community here won't welcome them being brought where everyone can see them though I may be getting hold of the wrong end of the stick. And the secrets seem to go far back. I have just learned that my boss, the man who sent me here, was in fact at the Grammar School. That wasn't a surprise, it was more of a total shock, and at some stage today I'm going to ask him why he had not told me.'

'Perhaps if there are dark secrets the community would possibly thank you for bringing them into the light. Have you considered that possibility?'

'Do you know whether or not there are such secrets hidden away?'

'I do know that Archie McHugh was a secretive person. Those of us who lived here never felt we knew anything about him whatsoever. I think we would be particularly interested in the new biography, if it ever sees the light of day, to enhance our knowledge of the man.'

'Did you like him?'

'I had next to no contact with him though I knew his wife, Marjorie, slightly through a women's organisation we both belonged to, but she had clearly been instructed to say nothing about their life.'

'And what about Malcolm? Did you know him?'

'Yes. He was quite cheery lad though I think we all felt sorry for him living with his strange father.'

'When did he do his writing? He's written a great deal and the Complete Poems is very heavy. Not being a writer I haven't the first idea what it is that I'm asking, but it's something that did occur to me.'

'To find an answer to that you will need to consult either Peter McDonald or Jonty Dickinson. One or the other worked with him for a long period and I think they might be able to answer that particular question. They were his scribes, you might call them.'

'His amanuenses.'

'Yes.'

'Fortunately I have managed to discover their lairs and I shall later try to beard them there.'

'I am bound to say, Charlie, that for an out and out amateur in the business of finding things, you are doing remarkably well, but that makes me say that you must take great care. Don't they say that the tiniest of stones can begin an avalanche? Please remember that I'm on your side and that I will do all I can to help and support you, if you need it.'

Charlie was struck by the words "on your side". What did they imply? Was there some sort of conflict ahead?

All was going well with the TB testing, Francine worked well and fast, until, that is, one of Rhona's girls shot out of the crush and in unsisterly fashion landed one of her feet on one of Rhona's, who went down with a thud. Adam immediately attended to the cow and it was Sam who came to the rescue of his client, still on the floor and uttering the sort of oaths that Francine might not yet be familiar with. Sam helped her to her good foot and helped to a nearby barrel. Adam took over the identifying and recording as Francine worked on. The last few girls were soon conducted by Adam to the paddock and and he returned Francine and Sam were discussing with Rhona what they should do with her.

'Sod that,' said Rhona. 'Much more important is to know whether there are any reactors.'

'None at all,' said Francine.

'Well that's already helped the pain in my foot. Why the fuck didn't I put my boots on this morning rather than these useless wellies? You'd think I was a total novice.'

'Francine,' said Sam, 'can you please bring the portable scanner from the van? It's not the same as an x-ray but it might give us some idea what you've done though, as one who has experienced it myself more times that I can say, I anticipate only heavy bruising.'

With some difficulty Rhona removed her wellie, exhibiting thereby 'girlie' socks with lots of colours and patterns. Everyone laughed except Rhona.

'I don't think you should laugh – they're lovely.'

'Indeed,' said Sam, 'it's what every well-dressed farmer is wearing this season.'

Rhona aimed a gentle hit across his head.

'Gosh', said Francine, 'I did not know that Scottish farmers hit their vets.'

'Twice,' replied Rhona, 'once today and once again when I get the bill!'

Sam was already at work, Adam had found a convenient mains socket not too far away.

'Well it's good news on two fronts, Rhona. First of all you'll be pleased to know you're not in lamb, and the second is the sight of bruised tissue but no indication of a fracture.'

'Obviously I'm disappointed about not being in lamb, but heavy bruising is normally what you get when stood on by a cow.'

'Let's get you into Anne-Marie's', said Adam, 'as she's made some lunch for us.'

'And I'll complete the paperwork,' added Francine.

'Didn't you tell me on the phone you were intending to worm your yows and lambs tomorrow?' asked Sam.

'That had been the plan.'

'I would give it a day or two, but no longer as we're getting reports of liver fluke. What will you use?'

'Triclabendazole.'

'What do you think, Francine?'

'I assume you mix it with ivermectin in the drench?'

'Yes.'

'You have nice hilly land and not a lot of standing water I imagine, so you should do quite well here, and that is a good combination of drugs. It's my day off tomorrow and I would be happy in this lovely summer weather to come and take your place for drenching. I have done it many times before. The only thing is that your yows and lambs will have to be brought down.'

'That's a very kind offer, Francine, and Adam has done it before too, but the real problem is that only a few of them speak French, mostly naughty words taught them by Adam. The real problem is gathering .'

'Not at all,' said a voice behind them. 'If Rhona will babysit, I'll do that, and in fact I'd like to do so, just to keep my hand in. It was Anne-Marie with Gregor fast asleep in his sling.

With time to fill before the arrival of Anaïs, Charlie made her way to Queen St and the Mary Queen of Scots Visitor Centre. Charlie had not heard of this queen and was amazed by her life story as she wandered round, and horrified by the account of her death in England, a death ordered by Queen Elizabeth I. The locals clearly wanted to make the most of this to draw in visitors even though Mary was here for only a month. There were more people here than in the nearby Archie McHugh Museum but that was hardly surprising, but after leaving Queen Mary to her fate,

Charlie began to make her way to the Museum and her meeting with Anaïs.

She had heard a weather forecast on her way here which said the good weather was due to break tomorrow, but today was like its predecessors, warm and cloud free. She arrived at the Museum and looked about her to see if Anaïs was around, but then heard a French accent from inside and looking closely she saw Anaïs talking to the curator Sylvia Stirling. Anaïs was an extremely beautiful woman and her clothes enhanced that beauty, but her face was immediately striking as being highly intelligent, and although Charlie knew very little about her, she did know that she had worked undercover for the French Police and Intelligence and now was blissfully happy as a farmer's wife in the Scottish Borders.

'Hello Charlie,' said Sylvia as she entered the building. 'We have a visitor from France who has actually heard of Archie.'

Anaïs turned and held out her hand to Charlie.

'I was expecting a man when I heard your name but you don't look much like one.'

'You cannot always know these days,' said Sylvia. 'The manager of our supermarket used to be called Paul, but insists we now call him Paula. He says he's had all the necessary operations to make him a woman, but he's not a woman no matter what he claims even though he does a nice line in women's clothes.'

Charlie and Anaïs wandered round together pointing and commenting on various artefacts.

'Now then, would you welcome the opportunity of a cup of tea?' said Anaïs.

'Ooh yes, that would be lovely,' replied Charlie, and turning to Sylvia, 'Can you recommend anywhere?'

'The Abbey View Cafe and Bookshop is best.'

'Yes, I've seen that. Thank you Sylvia. I hope to see you again. I like coming into the Museum and being in touch with Archie in this way.'

'I will look forward to that.'

Anaïs waved as she left and they began their walk to the cafe first of all passing the Town Hall and then turning right towards the Abbey.

'I'm afraid my poor Adam is going to have to do the milking this evening by himself. One of the cows stood on the foot of Rhona leaving her badly bruised. However it is good news that the whole herd is free of TB but it is very bad news that a sexy Swiss vet is coming to treat all the sheep, what they call drenching, and will be working with Adam all morning tomorrow.'

'Anaïs, that's not bad news. You must be one of the most beautiful women in the world, and by the time they have finished, no matter how sexy you think she may be, I bet she won't look it then.'

They laughed together as they walked up the hill. The cafe was quiet and they found a table enabling them to talk relatively freely. At once, without any prompting, Charlie began to tell the whole story as she had received it. She was not interrupted once. Only when she finished the story did Anaïs speak.

'Who, if anyone, has told you the truth and who is either not telling you everything they know or simply lying, because you are being fed a mixture of them all. It's almost as if you have been spending your time with politicians. It's all to do with what they want you to think for whatever purposes of their own. The exception and most trustworthy person is Andrew.'

'Andrew?'

'You need to talk to him as I think he can be relied upon. Your friend from across the road at the Abbey . . .'

'Eilidh.'

'Yes. She knows a great deal more about things than she is saying just now, but obtaining this information requires that you maintain a position of total innocence and ignorance.'

'That won't be hard as it is exactly how I am anyway,'

'Really? I'm not so sure. You may be ignorant about what's going on here, but you're the ideal person to find it out. I don't know why your employer did not tell you he was at school here, though he must have known you would discover that, but sending you here was a shrewd move on his part, though quite how remains to be seen. There is one person I need to see today and that is Paula. Will she still be at work now?'

'Yes, she finishes at 5 o'clock.'

'Is it close by or do we need to travel by car?'

'It's nearby so we can finish our tea and cakes.'

Anaïs laughed.

'Of course we must finish our tea and cakes. Ah, the British make me laugh so much.'

Chapter 6

Anaïs and Charlie set off up the hill towards what was perhaps over-optimistically called a "Superstore" which seemed more an example of wishful thinking than anything else.

As they approached the door, Anaïs stopped.

'It's a lovely day, Charlie. I think you should go for a walk. Fifteen minutes at the most and then I will meet you by that red postbox down there.'

She pointed and then went into the supermarket in pursuit of a meeting with Paula. Charlie suddenly felt protective towards her new friend who had fed and housed her on the previous evening. She hadn't known Anaïs long but suspected she could run rings around anyone she chose. A fifteen minute walk was what she had been told to take and that is what she set off to do.

She was back more or less on time but there was no sign of Anaïs, nor in the next ten minutes. Eventually she appeared, waving to Charlie as she made her way towards her.

'I'm sorry to be late as it took me a little longer than I had expected.'

'And?'

'It took me a little while to find Paula but when I did was impressed. She has made herself attractive not least in terms of her selection of clothes. For the rest you need not trouble yourself but Paul is not quite as he told you.'

'Paul? Oh.'

'He certainly has not undergone the surgery he told you he had – you can trust me on that. I always thought that the person who had told you the truth was Andrew at the cafe who described him to you as the Jedburgh freakshow. As for the others there seems be a whole culture of either reserve or lies. The most obvious reason for this lies in the Archie McHugh cult. Charlie, you must speak to your boss this evening and find out what he really wants from you here, and I have to advise you to return to Rhona's farmhouse to sleep this evening. She's in a lot of pain and from the feeling of my breasts, I must get back to my son and that is the only milking I will get done today and it was not helped in the supermarket by someone trying to touch them.'

'You're joking.'

'No. Andrew said Paul was a freakshow and perhaps you did well to survive any advances from you last night.'

'But his boyfriend is a man.'

'Go and find Andrew and talk with him, and perhaps things will become clearer.'

'Anaïs, how did you discover the truth about his surgery? Did he tell you?'

'I put my hands up his skirt – sometimes the direct route is best!'

With Anaïs on her way back home, Charlie called Rhona.'

'Oh Rhona, I've just heard about your foot. How are you?'

'I'm sitting here watching a DVD as if I were a lady of leisure, apart from the fact that my right foot is in a bucket full of ice and throbbing.'

Charlie laughed.

'I'm sorry, I don't mean to laugh as I'm sure it's extremely painful. Shouldn't you have gone to hospital in case something's broken?'

'No need. My vet Sam was here and he checked it out for me and even scanned it with the portable machine he uses to see if a yow's in lamb. To be perfectly honest I'd always prefer to be treated by a vet than a doctor. I'm thinking of marrying Sam if only I could think of a suitable way of disposing of his wife, Betty. I've been looking on the Internet for pages called "How to murder your vet's wife and get away with it" but Google has let me down.'

'Is she really called Betty?'

'Alas no, she's actually called Iona and is as lovely as the island itself, but it makes me feel better if I call her Betty.'

'Oh poor Rhona. You live a tortured life.'

'Actually, Charlie, foot and Sam not withstanding, I think you would have to travel far to find someone happier and more fulfilled than me, and today all the girls passed the TB test, so I'm in ecstasy. But what about you?'

'Anaïs spent the afternoon with me and has left my head spinning. I can well believe she worked for French Intelligence, but she told me – not suggested – that I was to come back to you for the night, if that's ok with you.'

'Ok? It's brilliant. Chinese or Indian?'

'Oh, Indian. I can call in at a place I saw in Melrose, if you like.'

'No, when you get here I'll telephone the place in Galashiels which is much better. When will you be back?'

'I've just got to meet someone. Then I'll set off.'

'Well, make it quick. Adam will need you to lend a hand with the milking!'

There was silence at the end of the line.

Charlie walked past the Abbey and saw Eilidh beginning to close down for the day. They waved to one another, though her time with Anaïs had made Charlie wonder what duplicity was going on in those she had met. She crossed the bridge in front of the café and sat on the bench outside. It did not take long before Andrew appeared in shorts and tee shirt. He was surprisingly muscular. She stood and called out his name.

'Please come and sit with me. I need help and you may be the only person who can provide me with it.'

Andrew came and sat by her on the bench.

'My name is Charlotte Holly, though most people call me Charlie. You described Paul as the Jedburgh freak show. At the time I didn't understand very much but now I know a little more, about Paul but there's lots more I need to know. I'm not in Jedburgh for the sake of my health nor even to enjoy the good things about which the town can rightly boast. I've been sent on a sort of mission by my boss in Wales. He's a writer of biographies, a number of which are highly esteemed. Now he's turned his attention to Archie McHugh.'

'But why has he sent you? Surely he should be here himself.'

'According to our friend Paul and Malcolm McHugh, Edward Challen was at the Grammar School here as a boy.'

'But that's even odder – not wanting to come himself.'

'Do you mean you think I'm not up to the job?' said Charlie holding back a smile.

'No, of course not, no, not all,' said Andrew utterly flustered.

The smile appeared on Charlie's face.

'It's ok Andrew, I am just teasing you, though if truth be told I really am not equipped to do this though I am beginning to suspect that my boss chose me exactly because I'm not a professional researcher though why that should be I don't know.'

'You're from Wales.'

'Yes, Swansea, but even in a short time I've taken to Scotland. I have made some friends who run a farm near Galashiels which is where I'm staying.'

'What sort of farm?'

'They have some hay meadows they've been cutting this week, but mostly it's a lot of sheep, milking cattle and Chinese pigs. They have a slight crisis this evening as Rhona who runs the show had her foot trodden on this morning and so can't do the milking this evening. She has a colleague, Adam, who will therefore have to do it all himself.'

'Can you take me there.? I can milk because my dad was a farmer and I started doing it when I was just nine.'

'Andrew you might just get a place in heaven for this alone. I'll call Rhona and if we leave right away we should be just in time.'

Rhona had heard Anne-Marie bringing the sheep down for drenching, though if the weather forecast was anything to go by, they would get drenched in another way tomorrow as well. The Boss had called in to see her.'

'Are you feeling sorry for yourself?'

'Do you mean am I sorry to have an evening off milking, or going up to gather then I'm devastated but thank you so much for doing the sheep, Anne-Marie. I know it's supposed to rain tomorrow but Sam recommended we get on with it as soon as possible, and now the hay's all in, we'll get it done.'

'You're in charge so it's your decision, but I would leave them down afterwards if the weather's going to be as the forecast says, though as we both know it has been wrong before. The grass is good and will last.'

'Oh, Anne-Marie, it will be so good when back in harness together, I miss working with you and responsibility is so scary.'

'Don't I know that?'

The door opened and to the puzzlement of Anne-Marie a man walked in wearing the white attire worn in the dairy. He looked to Rhona.

'All done. One of the ladies has udder cleft dermatitis between the two front quarters which I suspect is a result of lying down in the hot sun of the last few days. I've washed the area in cold water but I couldn't find any lanolin or ointments and Adam wasn't sure where they might be, and I don't know if you have udder supports but with sunburn they can be quite useful.'

'Is she still inside?' asked Anne-Marie?'

'I'm sorry, I should have introduced you. This is Anne-Marie who's farm this is. She's my boss but is spending some months doing nothing whatsoever having given birth to Gregor, and this is Andrew from Jedburgh who offered to come and help out with the milking, and who clearly knows a great deal.'

'Thank you, Andrew, for being here. How come you know so much about farming?'

'You might have heard of my dad, Bobby MacCaig, he farmed on the south side of Jedburgh.'

'I know of him by repute.'

'He died two years ago, and my mother and I had to leave the farm as he was a tenant. Until then I worked full-time with him. Now I'm a waiter in a coffee shop, and being back on a farm is simply wonderful.'

'Well, let's go and find the lanolin ointment and apply it, though you'll have to take off your dairy kit,' said Anne-Marie.

'I'll hang it up as we go through to the milking parlour intake area. I didn't know where Rhona would want her so that seemed as good a place as any.'

Charlie had been asleep upstairs and mostly missed the discovery of Wonder-Farmer below. She had also been on the phone to Edward Challen.

'Hello Charlie, I hope you have enjoying warm summer weather.'

'It's due to end tonight.'

'And how are you getting on?'

'Why did you send me, Edward? I gather you were at school here, but you didn't tell me.'

'You have found that out pretty quickly.;

'I met someone who was at school with you – Paul Greene.'

'Gosh, that name takes me back a long way. What's he doing with his life?'

'He's the manager of the Jedburgh Co-op Supermarket.'

'Anyone else know me?'

'I've not mentioned you to anyone else. I'm keeping my powder dry.'

There was an uncomfortable laugh at the other end.

'I return to my questions. Why did you send me?'

'A professional researcher would deal with it in the wong way and so I chose you because you will do it your way. You've been through hell, and I think you will soon see the signs of others who have and be able to build on that.'

'But to do that for you, Edward, I need more time.'

'I never doubted that and you must remain there as long as it takes.'

'How will I know when I've got to the bottom of it all?'

'A rather unfortunate phrase, I think. You will know. That's why I've sent you as you're the best person for the job. Don't doubt it, Charlie, because I don't. Oh, and by the way, I've put much more money into your account today.'

'Thanks for that. Ok, I'll trust you now though I can tell that you're still not telling me everything.'

Coming downstairs to where Rhona was still watching a DVD, the farmer enjoying a sore foot said to Charlie, 'Andrew went out some time ago with Anne-Marie to see a cow experiencing sunburn.'

'Sunburn!'

'It does happen, and the udder is particularly vulnerable. I'm impressed that he spotted it and knows what to do about it. Thank you for bringing him. I only wish we could keep him. Ed and Adam are great labourers but to have someone else who knows what they are doing and looks like he does, would be great. Ah well! Now, I'm getting hungry and the time has come to order supper. What shall we order for Andrew?'

'You can't go wrong with Chicken Tikka Masala?'

'Ah, but you can if he doesn't like curry.'

The Back Door opened and in came Anne-Marie.

'There's a story in the Bible, I think, about someone finding a treasure in a field, covering it up again and going away to sell everything he has and with the money buying the field and the hidden treasure. Well this evening I have found a treasure in the milking parlour but I wouldn't do anything about it until any decision is made by us both. I haven't asked him and I've sent him into our house so we can chat, but what do you think about taking him on, here and now?'

'Anne-Marie, you know our financial position. It's a great idea especially if he's as good as you say he is and skilled help would be a huge asset, with all due respect to Adam and Ed, but we simply can't afford another salary, and we can't expect him to work for nothing, and where's he going to live?'

'These are all good points, Rhona, but you're overlooking the fact that I'm not taking any salary at the moment and don't need to for some time to come. In terms of living we still have your old room, provided he can cope with a baby crying in the night.'

'Have you said this to him?'

'Not in so many words.'

'Anne-Marie, you are utterly impossible.'

'I know, but I have brought all the yows down for drenching, and I won't charge you. How's the foot?'

'The ice is wonderful and I'm sure that within two months or so I'll be fit to return to work again, and leave it all to Andrew in the mean time.'

'Gosh, as soon as that.'

'Anne-Marie, my darling, go home and tell Andrew we've ordered him a curry which will be on its way.'

'After that I'll take him home, and if he wants to take the job he can collect his things and I'll bring him back in time for some sleep before milking,' said Charlie.

'I'll go and make him an offer I don't think he will refuse, but seriously Rhona, I won't do so unless you are really happy about this. We are true partners and if you say No to this, then No it is.'

Rhona gave Anne-Marie a warm smile.

'I know that and I also trust your judgement totally. If Andrew wants a way back into farming, and we would have Charlie to thank for that possibility, then I think we should should give it him. Farmers aren't meant to serve coffee all day long.'

Anne-Marie went out and noticed the first sign of a change in the weather – clouds gathering in the west. She found Andrew looking at the sheep.

'When were they last dipped?'

'Three months ago as we're about to start shearing.'

'Any sign of scab?'

'You would need to ask Rhona. She is the manager, in control of everything, and it may stay like that when I get back from maternity leave, using me as a farmworker. Anyway Andrew, she and Charlie have ordered you a curry that will be here soon, and then Charlie's offered to drive you back to Jedburgh. But we're hoping you will come back with her tonight and occupy the spare room in the farmhouse where Rhona used to live, though she didn't have to endure a crying baby. The thing is, Rhona and I want to offer you a full-time job on the farm. You won't get rich and you'll work hard but you'll be doing again what you're good at. It's abundantly clear that you know what you are about and we would be very glad to have you as a member of the team.'

'I don't know if the words I want to say in gratitude have been invented yet, so "thank you" will have to do'.

His eyes had filled with tears.

'I assumed my my farming life was over. I feel such joy.'

Anne-Marie held out her hand and shook his.

'You're in luck,' said Anne Marie. As well as with Adam, you'll be drenching tomorrow with the new vet Francine from Switzerland, who's offered to come and help out. You'll see what I mean when you see her.'

Anne-Marie led Andrew back into the yard and left him at Rhona's door which he knocked and walked in.

Before they departed for Jedburgh, Andrew was given instructions by Rhona about the following day to make sure he kept a close eye on both Adam and Francine with regard to their drenching technique. Both had done it before, though Adam only once and she'd had to help him get it right quite a few times. There should be no problem with Francine as she was a vet but it might be that in Switzerland their way of doing things was different.

Charlie could see that Andrew was fully attentive even though he had drenched sheep many times before.

'Do we have three guns?' he asked. 'Mostly I've been used to doing it in pairs, which makes more sense logistically.'

'It's a good question about the guns and I don't know the answer without going out to look, and you are quite right about working in pairs. Do you think I should cancel Francine?'

'No! It will be good to work with her and good for her to do this our way.'

'And I imagine Adam never said a word about her looks when you were milking together this afternoon.'

'Oh no, not a word!'

'A likely story. Ok I'll phone Adam and let him know that after milking in the morning he can go home to his beloved Anaïs and Jerome. He'll be pleased I know, because he and Anaïs are trying write a new French course book for universities.'

'We should be going, Andrew,' added Charlie.

'Yes. I'll report to you after milking, boss.'

'Oh no, I'm not the boss. That's Anne-Marie. I'm just Rhona.'

'Ok, Rhona.'

He didn't believe a word of it!

Chapter 7

It was still broad daylight as Charlie and Andrew set off to Jedburgh.

'I shall never be able to thank you enough, Charlie, for what you have done for me today. If you hadn't come to the café when you did, I would be back there in the morning pouring milk into tea and coffee instead of doing what I love – obtaining the milk from source.'

'The person you have to thank far more than me is Adam's wife, Anaïs.'

'Oh?'

'Rhona told me that she used to work for the French Police and then as an undercover agent for French Intelligence and I can believe it. She came to Jedburgh this afternoon, allowed me to talk through everything I had been doing and then pronounced that the only person I could trust was you, and that we needed to talk.'

'Are you serious?'

'Ed and Adam are both highly intelligent, but honestly I think that in terms of understanding human nature and its functioning, Anaïs can run rings round them.'

They were now near Melrose.

'It was she who doubted the sexuality of Paul and went into the shop and proved it.'

'Really?'

'Oh yes. She did it with her hands.'

'Well, I suppose that's one way of doing it.'

He laughed.

'Turn left here and the house is the last on the right.'

Charlie stopped the car outside the door.

'Do you live alone?'

'Yes. My mother died last year, just a year after my dad. She missed him so much, and the farm, that I think it's true that she died of a broken heart as much as anything else.'

'Do you own the house?'

'Oh no, I'm a tenant and I guess I must give notice sometime. Anyway, come in whilst I grab some things.'

The house was clean and tidy and the room she was in contained several farming books, a flat-screen television and a laptop, plus furniture and some family photographs, presumably of his parents. There was another, a small one, almost tucked away behind the others that caught her attention. Whoever lived here liked order, everything in place. Andrew came downstairs with two bags of clothes.

'I take it there's wifi on the farm.'

'Ed was the senior civil servant to the Scottish government so I suspect making sure of that was the priority when they took the farm.'

'What's he like?'

'He's great, and now training to be a psychotherapist inspired apparently by Anaïs's own work. She has a practice at her home and also in Edinburgh.'

'Jesus! I think I'll say nothing at all when I'm with them.'

He unplugged his laptop and loaded it with its manifold wires into a case.

'Right! Let's go.'

Charlie turned the car round and they set off.

'Ok, Andrew, tell me about Paul, or Paula, Greene?'

'Paul. It's sad really, and peculiar too. McHugh made a particular fuss of him when he was small and although I was too young to know anything, there were rumours, though I didn't really understand them. He wasn't the first however and not the last. He apparently lost interest in them when they reached 12 or so. I've seen photos of Paul when he was at the age McHugh took him in hand, and he was a lovely looking lad. When he reached his late teens he got caught up with the Piskies.'

"What on earth are they?'

'The Episcopal Church, though I know nothing about it, other than that there was a Rector who did a lot of work with young people. Paul became very much under his influence and announced to all and sunder that he wanted to be a minister too in which the Rector encouraged him greatly. He hadn't been much of a scholar at the Grammar and to be able to train to be a minister he had to go to night school and take some exams. I think he worked hard and after that they allowed him to go forward for selection. Paul swings the other way, if you understand my meaning, and apparently something happened during his selection panel which I think had to with his sexuality and they rejected him. He was utterly dejected and I even wondered whether he might commit suicide. It was then that someone said he should try again but this time as a trans because it would be almost impossible for them to turn him down because in the current politically correct atmosphere. So Paula was born.'

'And is he still pursuing his desire?'

'Changing sex takes a long time and subject to a lot of psychological testing. Paul went through the first stage, even though it took over a year to get that far and began taking hormones and dressing as a woman. Alas, for him, at this point the people of the Church rejected him. Piskies are well-known for being respectable and morally upstanding, and like you to know it. Paul was in effect forced out by prejudice and the superiority of the religious classes. However he decided to go ahead with his change which would lead to surgery. Before that he had to have further psychiatric assessments, and he was told he couldn't go forward with surgery. What I'm about to say is probably prejudiced, but in my, albeit limited, experience of trans people, is that in addition to being what they are, and that's up to them, they mostly seem to need to talk about it, sometimes endlessly. And that's what happened to Paul. He couldn't keep his mouth shut.'

Charlie thought a change of subject appropriate and managed to ask something about Chinese pigs, which Andrew admitted he knew nothing about and soon they were laughing as they turned up the lane and crossed the cattle grid and pulled up in the yard. By now it was a little darker but not completely so. And Charlie felt the first drops of rain as she went towards Rhona's door.

Looking out of her window Charlie could see that it was raining with intent! No doubt Rhona could derive some satisfaction from being able to stay in bed, away from milking and drenching the sheep and getting soaking wet in the process. Francine phoned to say she would arrive at about 8-30, ready to make a start. Andrew, after milking, filled himself with cereal, toast and marmalade whilst holding Gregor, allowing Anne-Marie to get dressed. Ed then came into the kitchen, introduced himself to Andrew and they began chatting about farms and farming, Andrew all the while holding Gregor who was sleeping peacefully in his arms.

Anne-Marie came back into the kitchen and looked at her son resting peacefully in the arms of her latest employee.

'Ok, Andrew, the deal is that I go out into the rain and spend the day drenching the yows and lambs and you can stay in here nice and dry looking after Gregory as he's obviously taken to you in very big way.'

'He's quite lovely but I wouldn't have the first idea what to do if he woke up.'

She laughed.

'If it's any consolation, neither did I until just a few months ago. Give him here and thank you for holding him. Francine has just arrived so you'd better go and meet her and get going. There's a lot of mouths to drench.'

'Yes I saw. What tups are you looking to get at the Kelso tup sales?'

'Blue-faced Leicesters.'

'H'm. Are you open to discussion?'

'Rhona might be. She's in charge and you and she will be going to buy, so have a word with her.'

'Blimey,' said Andrew as he made for the door and the pouring rain beyond.

Francine and Andrew worked steadily throughout the morning with hardly a word between them. Rhona hobbled out mid-morning to bring them coffee which was diluting by the second in the rain.

'I think they hate the rain so much,' said Andrew, 'that they're making it easy for us.'

Rhona laughed.

'They have to stay down here for a few days so when you're finished come and dry off and have some dinner.'

'Thank you,' said Francine. 'I chose my day well!'

Francine had arrived at much the same time that Charlie had set off for Jedburgh. She had arranged to call in on Peter McDonald and Jonty Dickinson who had been Archie's literary assistant or amanuenses (a new word to her which she liked). Peter still lived in Jedburgh but Jonty was to be found in Selkirk which was not too far away.

Peter McDonald was, she imagined, in his late 70s and lived with his wife, Marlene, and their labrador bitch. There were many books in the house, befitting his previous occupation as an assistant to a literary man, thought Charlie. Marlene had already heated the kettle prior to her arrival and soon a mug of tea was in her hands. They both had broad Scottish accents, so she had to make extra effort to listen attentively.

'So, you've come about Archie,' said Peter, 'and his poetry?'

'Yes, I've come about Archie, but not so much about his poetry. I am employed by a man called Edward Challen who once lived here and was at the Grammar. He is a well-known writer of biographies.'

'So you're his researcher?' asked Marlene.

'I think that's my job title, yes.'

'But you're not so sure?' continued Marlene.

'The thing is I'm not even remotely qualified as a researcher. I've not been to university and most of my life so far has been something of a mess, more than you might imagine, but I assume Edward must have seen something in me of use to his work.'

'I for one am glad about that, Charlie. We get, though fewer and fewer as the time since Archie's death grows longer, researchers and writers who come to discuss the minutiae of every poem because they're working on a new edition or a new commentary. So your coming is different.'

'I received no guidance or instructions from Edward as to what he wanted me to do here, other than just to come and see what I could pick up from just being around the place. Perhaps he thought that as a young woman I might be unthreatening and that people might talk the more freely to me.'

'And have they?' asked Peter gruffly.

'Disappointingly, my conversations with locals have only

revealed what they would reveal to any visitor expressing an interest in Mr McHugh.'

'Perhaps there are two reasons for that,' said Peter. 'The first is that even after this time he is still a local figure of note and no one will want to suggest anything to damage that. The other reason, and much more likely, is that there is nothing to discover. I can't imagine why your employer might think there is, but I feel your time here might be enjoyable as a holiday in the Borders, but I can't think you'll be taking anything back other than a souvenir which you should get from Heath's shop next to the Simply Scottish food place, just off the High St. Make sure you get to talk to Alex, the manager. He'll be able to help you.'

Charlie felt she was being dismissed but determined not to give in so easily. Marlene stood and left the room, soon returning with a tray containing freshly made shortcake which Charlie thought perhaps the most delicious things she had ever eaten, and they chatted about their family. Clearly they had communicated to her all that they were likely to give.

'Do you have a family, Charlie?' asked Marlene.

'No. I never knew my parents and was brought up in care by a series of foster-parents and was not altogether a good experience.'

'Children? There's plenty time for you to settle and marry, I would imagine.'

'Unfortunately I had a terrible accident and as a result can't have children, which I suspect would make most men not want me.'

'I'm sorry about that, Charlie. Aren't their ways around that these days? IVF and surrogates?'

'I would need a man first,' said Charlie, thinking to herself in the words of the old feminist saying that a woman needs a man like a fish needs a bicycle.'

Peter left the room.

'At once, Marlene said to Charlie, 'Give me your phone number.' She did so before Peter returned.

Charlie set the satnav for Selkirk and as she followed the instructions she wondered why Marlene asked her number in so secretive a manner. She would wait and respond if Marlene rang. The longer she was here the more she sensed she was drawing nearer to something important. At some stage she would have a further conversation with Paul, though she needed to remember that learning the truth about his non-surgery from Anaïs, confirmed by Andrew, was information Paul didn't know she possessed. Did she "come clean" about what she knew or not? There was also a possibility that just as Paul had lied about completing the gender transition process, was it also possible that he had also done so about his experience of sexual abuse at the hands of McHugh?

Selkirk in the pouring rain was probably not seen at its best. She turned into the road in which Jonty lived and ahead of her Charlie could see an ambulance with a open back door. She stopped the car and realised that the two paramedics were coming out of Jonty's house and manoeuvring him on a wheelchair but she could see that he had on a facemask attached to a large cylinder placed on the base of the chair. They placed the chair on the lift and as soon as he was inside they closed the doors. Charlie realised she'd had a wasted journey when at the front door there appeared a woman who waved to her. Risking a soaking, Charlie left the car and approached the door just as the ambulance set off, its blue light flashing.

'You'll be Charlie, I imagine.'

Yes, but I've obviously come at a terrible time.'

'To see Jonty that's true, but come in anyway and have a cup of tea and a bit crack.'

Charlie had no idea what "crack" was, hopefully a Scottish

delicacy.

'Do you not need to follow the ambulance?'

'If I did it would serve no purpose. I'd not be allowed near him while they were doing things with him and to him. No doubt they'll ring and inform me when I can go.'

'Is that because it's not the first time?'

'My brother has been a very heavy smoker all this life. He has what they call Chronic Obstructive Pulmonary Disease, COPD for short, and I'm afraid he's not long for this world and he knows it too. I realised some time ago that there would come a time when the ambulance would come and he wouldn't return. It could be this time. Coffee or tea?'

'Tea please, milk, no sugar.'

Charlie looked around her. There were some books though fewer than at the McDonalds but the realisation that in neither house was there a copy of McHugh's poetry suddenly struck her.

'I forgot to introduce myself when you came in,' said Jonty's sister as she returned with the mugs of tea, 'but I'm Betty Aldrick, that being my married name, though I was widowed ten years ago and came to look after Jonty.'

'I'm sorry to hear that.'

'Thank you, though I knew before we were wed that it might not last long. Donald, my husband had a congenital heart problem about which nothing could be done permanently. He had endless open heart operations and to be honest he was well served by the doctors and nurses in Glasgow, with the result that we managed twenty-two years together, many more than we had assumed at the beginning, and I am grateful for every one of those years. He was a good man, and never once did I hear him moan or complain, other than about my absolute failure to cook haggis to his liking.

'I think that's greatly to your credit.'

'My brother never married and make of that what you will.

And I so wish he had never got himself involved with that horrible McHugh man, who is, I think the person you're here to talk about.'

Charlie recounted the story of her mission and the considerable confusion she was encountering within herself after almost every conversation. She said she instinctively felt that something was not right in relation to McHugh but as yet she was unable to put her finger on it.

'Jonty was an English teacher at Jedburgh Grammar when he first came across McHugh. His initial feelings about him were not at all positive. The exterior he presented appealed to some who admired his poems, but my brother was not convinced and remained so even after Jonty met with him after school one day and invited him to come and work with him. Somehow he seemed to know about my brother being queer and used this to influence him to accept the job.'

'Was he the same way himself, do you think?'

'I would be very careful going there if I were you.'

'I will note your warning but is there a specific reason you say it?'

'McHugh's son is still alive and although he's affable at one level, he's more than capable of being unpleasant where the good name of his father is concerned. You might hear of a man called Bertie MacCulloch. He made some ludicrous claims that McHugh's work was not his own, though wasn't able to back it up with any evidence. Malcolm moved in like a terrier on a rat and began legal proceedings against him, though they settled outside court.'

'Was this when Archie was still living?'

'Oh no, it was just about eight or nine years ago. I know it was not a kind thing to suggest, but Malcolm pursued him and even employed men to find such dirt as they could to be used against him, and as we all have some dirt in our backgrounds, or skeletons in the cupboard, they discovered an affair from years earlier and had it referred to in The Scotsman. It caused his marriage to end and it is said that he's a broken man now.'

'Is he local?'

'Oh no. He abides now on the Isle of Man, and I can guarantee he won't be troubling Malcolm again.'

'No, I imagine not. You didn't like Archie McHugh, did you?'

'I did not – what I've just said about Malcolm, I feel even stronger about his father.'

'Was Jonty paid well by him?'

'Strangely enough he was. Archie was not mean and Jonty said he was was also generous in his support of the young people of Jedburgh. He seemed to have enjoyed their company more than that of any others. So there is that to be said of him.'

Generous? thought Charlie, but what did they have to do to earn it?

The phone rang and Betty got up to answer it.

'It's probably the hospital telling me I can go in,' she whispered to Charlie.

She wasn't on the phone long before returning it to be sideboard on which it rested.

'It was the hospital, to tell me that Jonty passed away about ten minutes ago.'

'Oh Betty,' said Charlie rising and putting her arms around her.

'Thank you, Charlie. I knew it would happen one of these times so it's not actually a surprise but is definitely a shock.'

'Come and sit down and if I may, I'll make you a cup of sweet tea.'

It had finally stopped raining, which Francine and Andrew thought typical as they were down to the last few yows, and despite their waterproof outerwear both were soaked to the skin. Once completed, and the flock moved to where they would be remaining for three or four days, they made their way to Rhona's front door and began removed the outer layers before going on into the kitchen where Rhona was standing before the cooker preparing their food.

'I can't thank you enough for what you've done today,' she said. 'And in such appalling weather after weeks of sunshine. If you want to get changed, please do so.'

Rhona, Anne-Marie, Adam and Ed thought nothing of changing before others when each day, and twice over, they had to move from the milking parlour into the sterile setting of the dairy, and did it without thinking, just as Rhona and Anne-Marie often stripped down to bra and jeans for a calving and thought nothing of it whoever might be there with them. As a vet Francine equally took it for granted as perfectly normal. Andrew had only ever worked with his dad, and was stunned when Francine removed all her clothes before replacing them with the dry and clean she had brought. He wondered if he would ever recover from the glorious sight, having never seen a woman completely naked before and even he could see the attraction. Now, he knew he had to follow suit, and feared it would be a disaster for he was aware that his willy had disappeared in the cold and wasn't yet minded to emerge, and he didn't know whether he was more pleased than disappointed that neither of the women seemed to take not the blindest notice of what he was doing anyway!

Chapter 8

As they sat eating and warming themselves up, the kitchen door opened and in came Adam, ready if also very early to do the evening milking with Andrew.

'Adam, would you like some food?' asked Rhona.

'I have to save that the smell of it makes me want to say yes but my lovely wife is preparing something special this evening and I shall be in great trouble if I tell her I have eaten here and can't manage what she will have prepared for me. But how did the drenching go?'

Andrew looked to Francine who looked back with a nod which told him that he would answer.

'It was drenching in every meaning of the word. The yows didn't seem to object to the rain even if we did, but we got them all done.'

'I expect you're both exhausted.'

'Doing the drenching itself is not too difficult,' said Francine, 'what is exhausting is holding each sheep in place. But I am so glad that I was able to come today. I wanted to come to a rural practice, not because I don't like castrating cats and dogs all day long in a small animal practice, but I adore the open-air. At this time of the year of course that means sheep and cattle, both of which I enjoy working with.'

'Trust me, Francine, you will make some farmers very happy.'
They all laughed.

'Anyway, I'm here a little early because knowing what you have been doing today will have made you very tired, I've come to do the milking by myself and give you, Andrew, an evening off. We're still not milking a full herd so it should not take me much more than two and a half hours. By the way, I'm not normally so nice so make the most of it. How is your foot, Rhona?'

'I shall be back functioning tomorrow on what Anne-Marie calls light duties. And do you know? I really missed working today. I love my sheep very much indeed and missed being with them, though knowing my sheep as I do I know full well that they would not have missed me!'

Adam left them and set about bringing in the milkers. It would not be long before there was a full herd and that would take a lot longer though traditionally Ed always did the milking by himself on a Sunday morning. Adam enjoyed the intimacy he had with the animals and spoke to them call as he disinfected their teats and placed the suckers on them. When he was working alone he allowed himself the luxury of listening to music. Although he would have preferred Radio 3, it was clear that the cattle were happier with classic FM and he wondered if that was because they liked to hear the adverts with the exception of those selling beefburgers!

Once the last of Rhona's ladies was gone, he had to set about shovelling what they brought with them and left behind. Tomorrow, the yard would require the tractor to scrape away today's offerings. If Rhona was returning on her light duties then she might find herself doing that before going with Andrew, he supposed, to the sale at Kelso, a location and event with which Adam was sure he was familiar.

The final act of milking took place in the dairy for which

Adam had shed his clothes and was now wearing a white overall. The evening milking required less work in the dairy than in the morning when everything had to be prepared for the milk lorry, but he certainly was not one to cut short the work that had to be done and he ensured he had completed it in a way that Rhona or Anne-Marie, who had originally taught him, would have approved of.

As he left the dairy he could see that the sun had emerged from its day-long hideaway. He noticed too that Francine's car had disappeared. Once again he entered Rhona's kitchen and found her reading a novel and she showed him the cover.

'Is it good?'

'I don't think I could possibly know that, but what I do know is that I'm enjoying it more than some of the endless police/crime programs that are on the television.'

'Oh well that may not be saying a great deal.'

What has been good, however, is to have had a day of reading because I couldn't do what I wanted to do.'

'Had they done a good job today, or what you would call a satisfactory piece of work?'

'I didn't see them at work very much, but on the one occasion that I went out with a hot drink, they were working very hard and doing what had to be done properly. Andrew has gone next door and probably for an early night. What a week it has been for him but I'm so delighted that Anne-Marie feels we can take him on because he's obviously very experienced and that will inevitably make things a little easier for us. I think it's going to be ages before she comes back to work, even part time, so besotted is she with Gregor, but I feel certain she will. That's when we shall have to look more closely at finance as I'm sure Andrew must realise. What he has to do is to make himself completely indispensable. Whilst Charlie is staying, Andrew will have to put up with Gregor at night, but once Charlie's finished, the best arrangement would be for him to move into my spare room. Anyway, we'll see.

'I'm sure the question of finance is affecting farmers everywhere, especially now the EU money is disappearing after Brexit and if those engaged in conservation are the ones to receive government money in their place, how will that affect farms like this on which, with the best will in the world, conservation is just not possible.'

'Independence, would hopefully make it possible again if Scotland were to join the EU again, but it's not going to happen any time soon, much to the dismay of Ed's former boss in Bute House. Which reminds me Adam, have you noticed that Ed's lost weight and sometimes doesn't look too grand? Anne-Marie mentioned a winter cold but I'm not convinced by that.'

'Anaïs said the same to me the other day. I think we should keep an eye out for him and perhaps ask Anne-Marie if he's ok.'

'On the subject of Charlie, have you any idea where she has been today?'

'Yes, she mentioned something about seeing the two men who worked with Archie McHugh as his scribes or whatever, one of whom lives in Jedburgh and the other in Selkirk. I'm far from convinced that she has even the first idea what it is she's looking or even listening for and all I can say is that I hope that if it's there, she will find it.'

'Anaïs is helping her a little or, if I know my wife, a lot, and although she says very little she has told me that she thinks there is something serious beneath the surface, something that possibly a professional researcher might discover straightaway but miss the heart of it. She thinks that Charlie was chosen because, although worldly in so many awful ways in terms of the filth thrown at her in her life so far, she has a wonderful naïveté which might enable her to accomplish whatever it is with greater skill than a professional.'

'It's certainly true that she's more worldly than I am, though probably not you, given all you had to go through before you met Anaïs, but I feel she is entrancing – and it's a strange word to use – because she is that mixture of knowing exactly how the world works and what the human heart contains together with an unusual innocence or maybe it's an apparent innocence which she might well be able to use to her advantage.'

'Well, do tell her that Anaïs will be at home in the morning if she can endure the presence of Jerome with them as they talk. She's got a satnav and will easily find us.'

'Of course I will and I'm quite sure she will welcome the opportunity to see Jerome who is quite gorgeous and, happily for him, looks exactly like his mother.'

'Aw, thank you Rhona for those words of encouragement.'

'Oh come on Adam, you know I only mean them!'

Adam laughed.

'And what of you Adam? Are you going to find it extremely difficult if we integrate Andrew into the life of the farm and thereby push you and possibly Ed a little further out? I fear that Anne-Marie when she was making up her mind to take Andrew on did not give sufficient thought to how it might affect you.'

'I very much enjoy what I do, whether it's milking or on the tractor baling hay, even muck-spreading and I shall be always delighted to be invited to do what you might require of me every time you hurt your foot or whatever, but when we came to live here I was not wanting to be a full-time farmer, or, to be honest a part-time farmer. I have been doing this because it's good fun and has given me some purpose. But things change and we now have a son and I suppose it's not entirely impossible that there will be another given that, being French, Anaïs has got it in her mind that we should try every night though I shouldn't complain after my years of marriage to lesbian Alice. I have been greatly helped and supported by Anaïs as I have tried to recover from the terrible traumas of the past couple of years and now, I feel ready to pick up the reins of my career once again. I have wanted to write a major work for university students of French for some time. I am now in a position to do so and that's what I'm planning to occupy myself with in the next year.'

'That's great Adam, but I could have wished you had been consulted before the decision to take Andrew on was made.'

'Truly Rhona, I'm totally at ease with it, though I do love the ladies and they are clearly at ease with me, so please make sure your foot hurts regularly and I can and spend happy time milking them.'

'Don't worry, Adam, I will, and don't overlook that you're on early in the morning and probably with me because I can't spare or bear, another day off. It's hurting less this evening but doing nothing is sending me out of my mind.'

'Well, look after your foot. Injuries to farmers are a serious matter, though you'll be perfectly safe milking thanks to the herring bone parlour we use.

They could hear the sound of a car arriving and stopping in the yard.'

'That might well be Charlie,' said Rhona.

'Yes, I can see her through the window. I'll be off and see you in the morning.'

'Ok. Give my love to the sexpot in your life, and a kiss for Jerome.'

Charlie and Adam exchanged words outside the door, Adam repeating the invitation to come and see Anaïs in the morning.

'Hi Rhona, how's the foot.'

'Much better than watching DVDs or daytime tele, I can tell you. I shall be back at work tomorrow. And what about you?'

'It's been an usual day to say the least. A mysterious phone call from the wife of one those closest to McHugh, followed by the death of the other. I arrived to witness him taken off to hospital and less than an hour later he was dead, so I then accompanied his sister to the hospital mortuary and saw my first corpse. His sister was full of information and I'm going to see both women again. And then for light relief I decided to call on Paul/Paula in Melrose who was surprised to see me.'

'I bet he was.'

'I decided to cut out the niceties and went straight for his genitals, in a manner of speaking. I asked him why he had lied to me and many others that he had undergone their surgical removal and acquiring a vagina when he had not, and was actually a gay cross-dresser who enjoyed sex with men whilst wearing women's clothes? It's interesting that he was not in his female attire when I called. I knew the answer of course but I wanted to see if he would tell me the truth.

'Slowly and bit by bit he told me exactly what I had learned from Andrew. I have no doubt that Andrew did not lie to me, but I recognised the possibility that both he and I were fed the same lie by Paul, so I was wary of what he said.

'He said he had been turned down for surgery by the psychiatrist he had to see, but that he wished to have another go if it was possible. In the meantime, and not least because he had now been on oestrogen for a long time which was markedly changing his body, he was determined to continue living as a woman. It was then that he told me that how some stupid French woman had challenged him over his sex at work the other day and groped him to find out. Gosh, isn't that terrible? Whoever could it have been?'

Rhona laughed.

'And were you satisfied that you got to the truth in the end?'

'I don't know and I'm not sure at the moment I will be able to discover it, though perhaps Anaïs may be able to guide me in the morning.'

'Well, I have some food for you keeping hot in the aga.'

'Thanks Rhona, and how did things go here today?'

'Andrew and Francine are both experienced professionals and they got soaked to the skin but just got on with it. Poor Francine, it was quite a shock to her system but I still think she enjoyed it. Andrew, I'm sure, has had many days like it.'

'Does his coming mean that Adam is being cast aside?'

'No. We've spoken about it and he wants to give more time to writing a book he's been planning for some time, and he wants more time with Anaïs and Jerome.'

'You have intimated that he came here after trauma.'

'Yes, he was a Professor married to Alice, who was not only a lesbian but also an agent of an extreme right wing group in France. She died of cancer but then her identical sister, Simone, a doctor, wanted to marry him instead. She too, and her father, were also members of this neo-fascist group. She alas, had a mental collapse and had to be hospitalised. Then he met Anaïs, who had been the investigating officer into Alice and Simone, and although their initial encounter was hilarious in that within moments of meeting him in her house in Cornwall, she made him take off his clothes, the reason being he was utterly drenched and not wearing a coat. It was love at first sight, however, and to me they seem so very happy, though I wonder if she is missing the excitement of her former life.'

'I'll have to see if I can do something about that when I see her.'

Andrew was out of practice and therefore very tired by his exertions of the day. Anne-Marie's supper was delicious and afterwards Ed took Gregor for his bath and prepared him for his last feed of the day.

'What does tomorrow hold?' asked Anne-Marie.

'What my boss tells me to do.'

'Correct,' said Anne-Marie with a laugh.

'She's given me a morning off in the parlour and told me she's returning to work tomorrow.'

'That's not surprising. She is so good and a natural with animals. She would be a brilliant vet but she won't countenance the idea. I always thought I was good with livestock but Rhona is utterly intuitive in how she works. It's meant that we have needed fewer veterinary visits for calvings, other than for caesareans, though I'm sure she'd be willing to give that a go.'

'You've a lot of yows, as I know from drenching today, so lambing must be a lot of fun, and how many tups will you be using?'

'Last year we used four easycare Blue-faced Leicesters and had only 14 empties which is good going. Rhona will decide anyway, not me.'

'You have great confidence in her.'

'Not at all. I have *total* confidence in her. I'm a very able farmer, but she's the best I've ever come across. And you'll come to see that if you work with her long. She won't expect you to agree with her, and she likes arguments as long as they're well thought-out, but time and again I've found that she's mostly right. The other thing is that she relishes hard work.'

'I'm terrified already,' said Andrew with a laugh.

'The irony is that I'm the owner of the farm and technically the boss, but I would almost always defer to Rhona.'

Andrew yawned and said he thought he'd go up to bed.

'Good idea. The true boss will be back at work in the morning and don't expect her to give you a lie-in every morning.'

Rhona woke at about 2.00. There had been an unfamiliar noise and immediately she was out of bed and at the window. She could see two figures in the yard clearly opening each of the sheds in turn. She knew at once that they were after the quad bike. Despite her foot still hurting she put on her boots with a dressing gown and quietly crept down the stairs. She made a very quick call to Anne-Marie's mobile and then went to the gun cabinet and opened it, withdrawing the shotgun but without cartridges. The two figures had found what they were looking for and both were in the shed preparing to drag it out and then push it down the lane to where they would no doubt have a vehicle waiting.

Rhona opened the door and quietly closed it behind her and stood still. The yows, recovering from their drenching seemed to have sensed something was not right and were in full voice. To her right she realised that Anne-Marie was now out with her, also carrying her shotgun (and Rhona could well believe that the boss did have cartridges in it). They could hear the sound of the quad bike beginning to be moved back and it began to emerge, the two figures pushing from the front. It was heavy but bit by bit it appeared, and now Rhona wished that she had brought cartridges. Now it was fully in the open and the two figures with balaclavas could be heard laughing at their triumph.

Both the farmers now edged their way forward. In the distance Rhona could see a flashing blue light (summoned, no doubt, by Ed) which gave her the courage necessary to speak.

'That looks hard work, lads. Can we give you a help?'

A bright torch lamp now shone into the shed where they still were, struck dumb. The lamp, a very powerful one, was held by Andrew.'

'I think you two had better sit down where you are, not least because on either side of me are two farmers with loaded shotguns and frankly I wouldn't trust them as far as I could throw them. I said "Sit Down".'

It occurred to Rhona that they were thinking of making a run for it until Anne-Marie pointed her gun into the air and pulled the trigger. Now, everyone in the area, including Jerome and Charlie would be wide awake. But the two men sat down quickly enough.

The flashing blue light, once in the distance, now drew near and came into the yard, From it came two officers, one of each.

'Farming's not what it used to be,' said the female officer, a sergeant, 'in my day, farmers wore overalls, not nighties, when working outside.'

'You should come in the day time when I do the milking in my bikini,' replied Rhona.

'What time does that happen?' said the male officer.

His senior college brought the two out of the shed, removed their balaclavas, and said to one of them, 'Good morning, Alec. I thought I hadn't seen you for ages and then I remembered you'd been away for a while, but now released on licence. We'll be taking you straight back to prison where you'll have now to serve the rest of your sentence, plus a little extra for this nighttime excursion. Turn round please.'

She handcuffed him.

'One of the mad bitches fired her gun,' yelled Alec.

'I find that highly unlikely,' said the sergeant. 'We never heard anything, did we, constable?'

'Nothing at all, sarge.'

Alec spat at the junior officer, and missed. He led them to the car, and gave Alec a push as he was getting in.

'Someone will need to come and make a statement in the morning.'

'I can do that,' said Anne-Marie, 'my boss here will be in her bikini doing the milking!'

The police and their prisoners departed.

'Hot chocolate?' said Rhona, 'though if we've no milk I'll don my swimwear and get some!'

They laughed as they went into Rhona's kitchen where they were joined by Ed, Gregor and Charlie.

Chapter 9

Adam found Rhona bringing the milkers in from the fields, having already walked through the sheep looking for any signs of illness or injury..

'You're bright and early, Rhona.'

'That's because I've been up since 2 o'clock.'

'Was your foot giving you a hard time?'

Rhona laughed.

'No, we had some night visitors who wanted to borrow the quad bike without intending to return it.'

'O God. What happened?'

She told the story of the night.

'You were very brave,' he said when she'd finished.

'Do you know how much a new quad bike costs? You won't get much change from 10k and the insurers have premiums so high, it's cheaper to buy a new one, so I wasn't going to let the bastards get away with it.'

'Even so, the pair of you in your nighties must have impressed the thieves, it would have done me. But Rhona, aren't you tired out? Leave the milking to me.'

'Thank you, Adam, but one day idle has made me miss the ladies and they're looking round and waiting for us.'

Adam turned and saw that Rhona was quite right. They

laughed and headed towards the parlour.

To her surprise, Charlie had fallen asleep almost as soon as she returned to bed after the rude awakening brought about by the shotgun. Rhona was milking and wouldn't be in yet, so she got on with making herself some breakfast. She would then leave to meet Anaïs from whom, she hoped, she might find some help in making sense of what utterly bewildered her. Although she didn't know the way she had been assured that it was easily found, but would nevertheless rely on the satnav. Adam's car was in the yard confirming that he and Rhona were busy with the ladies, as the boss insisted on calling them, and which she rather liked. She approached her own car and noticed how filthy it was following yesterday's atrocious weather. Today had brought a return of sun and warmth.

As she drove down the long lane to the main road, she sensed that something was not right and wondered what it could possibly be. On the road ahead there was a lay-by and she pulled in and stopped the car because she knew there were tears coursing down her cheeks. Once she had stopped, the tears gave way to uncontrollable sobbing and a feeling of such wretchedness the like of which she had never known, even when she had been the victim of the most savage sexual assault and rape at the hands of the policeman in Swansea. She feared that she might never be able to stop crying and that possibly she would die here in the car. It was proving difficult for her to breathe, and still the tears came. Gradually however, though still shaking, she was able to breathe a little more easily and then her tears dried up, although she felt that was because there none left. At this moment she would have given anything for a cigarette but having given them up she had none with her.

She took her time, opened the front car windows and allowed what breeze there was to pass through. She considered abandoning everything, returning to the farm to collect her things, and setting off back to Wales, defeated, and perhaps like Andrew working in a coffee shop in Builth Wells or some such place, but a greater instinct made her start the car again and continue to see Anaïs and Jerome. She found the house easily enough but was appalled by how she looked in the driving mirror. All the same she clambered out and walked towards the front door which opened as she approached it with Anaïs standing in welcome, and looking so very lovely. It wasn't necessary to be an experienced psychotherapist to read the face and demeanour of Charlie. Anaïs said nothing but took Charlie in her arms and drew her inside. Tears returned with force.

Anaïs led her into a room and sat her down, passing on to her a box of tissues. There was a great deal of sniffing and sighing before she could raise her eyes but doing so she could see that the eyes gazing at her were the same loving eyes she had seen gazing on her husband and son. She felt that she too was being mothered and cared for.

'I'm so sorry, Anaïs.'

'Oh Charlie, if you only knew how often people feel the need to apologise after tears. I want to put a notice on my door proclaiming that in this house we welcome tears because they are a sign of life. I've seen quite a few dead people in the course of my previous work in the police, and though they might have good reason to do so, they never cry.'

Charlie smiled.

'Believe it or not, I saw my first dead body yesterday. I had gone to talk to him as someone who had been amanuensis to Archie McHugh but I arrived as he was being taken into hospital by ambulance where he died about an hour later. At her request I accompanied his sister to the mortuary and there he was, not only not crying but refusing to answer my questions!'

'I'm afraid the dead are like that, though I'm told that a good pathologist can learn a great deal from them, albeit indirectly. Adam once had to visit a mortuary in Marseille to see my body which he had been told could be found there, but as you can see, I got away. But Charlie, if you wish we can talk about the reasons for your tears. Adam rang me earlier and told me all about the excitement in the night, but somehow I don't think your tears are related to that.'

'Not at all and I wasn't actually involved in any way. Anne-Marie and Rhona were equipped with shotguns and I felt it best to stay inside. Apparently Ed continues to have certain privileges from his previous job in government, one of which is an emergency access to police protection. They came in what must have been a record time.'

Her head dropped and she went quiet, and Anaïs let her do so without a word, feeling that she was probably needing to summon up her courage to say what it was that was going on inside her.

'Only you and Rhona are aware of my history. To be brought up in care or by foster parents, some of whom want to take advantage of you, and then drifting into drugs and prostitution and to be treated more appallingly by men than you can possibly imagine. Even now when it's over, I continue to be overwhelmed by feelings of worthlessness and the pointlessness of my life. Being here, even in so short a time, has brought me face-to-face with a world so very different from that which I have known, a world to which I have had no access, and cannot see how I ever could.

'Because of the vile and disgusting actions of the South Wales detective sergeant, now mercifully dead, I cannot even hope to be a mother, and indeed I would say that the very word hope is not in my vocabulary. I have nothing to hope for. In Rhona, Anne-Marie and you, I have met women with everything to hope for. You are all highly skilled and able and my admiration for each of you knows no bounds. And the contrast is made even greater by the fact that I have been asked to come here to do a job for which I'm totally unequipped and haven't the first idea how I should now proceed after my initial conversations with the obvious people to whom I've spoken.

'Without any warning, and quite suddenly, as I was driving up the lane from the farm to come here, I started to feel that something was not right. I don't know what I mean by that, but as I drove it got worse and when I pulled into a lay-by the floodgates opened and to be perfectly honest I wanted just to escape, to go back to Wales, to go back to the life of misery I knew before, but which was at least familiar. I had seen in you three something unattainable and it made me feel despair because I'm nothing, nothing at all.'

Charlie once again began to cry and Anaïs once again decided to say nothing until Charlie was ready.

'I would like, if I may, to call you by your name Charlotte. It is such a beautiful name and very feminine. I don't think you should accept a male name, especially in light of the way you have often been treated by men which I know full well will have been quite despicable. Are you happy with that?'

'Eilidh at the Abbey in Jedburgh calls me Charlotte though it will take a little bit of getting used to as no one ever has called me Charlotte.'

'Well, Eilidh and I shall. You are probably aware, but possibly not, and people in my profession never, under any circumstances, tell clients what they should do. It is called being non-directive, and on the whole I totally subscribe to that. Fortunately, you are not my client and you are not required to pay me, so actually Charlotte, I can say anything I like to you and if it works, I might start adopting it with my clients.'

They both smiled.

'Please don't tell Adam how much I actually adore him as it

will only go to his head, but he continues to be in touch with a lot of people at Edinburgh University, even on the medical side, which I discovered in pregnancy, when almost every time I was seen by an obstetrician or a gynaecologist, they would enter the room and immediately say, "Hi Adam"and engage in chatter with him long before they turned to me. For revenge, because I'm very childish, I took to only speaking to them in French! But what I'm working up to say is that there is a woman gynaecologist whose particular speciality is repair of what has happened in a catastrophic childbirth or in other ways not dissimilar to your own. I think you should have the opportunity at least of consultation with her. I'm sure your doctors in Swansea were superb, but this lady is the best.'

'To be honest, Anaïs, I'm not sure exactly how superb they were. I was seen and operated on by a senior registrar on duty at the weekend and I got the feeling, and of course I may be wrong, that they were dealing with a whore who had almost certainly brought this upon herself as a way of making enough money to get drugs. Otherwise I think the consultant on-call would have been brought in, but there's a problem with what you say. However could I get to see this lady. NHS waiting lists for just about everything are enormous and I certainly couldn't afford to see her privately. On the other hand, if there is just the slightest hope, unlikely though it might be, that would be for me a source of joy. You will think me utterly stupid, but, on a farm there is always talk about breeding, about artificial insemination, about tups and lambing, about calving, and of course the gorgeous sight of Jerome and Gregor, so possibly that is a great deal to do with what has happened this morning.'

'Charlotte, please would you allow me to make some enquiries on your behalf? Of course I cannot promise anything, and if you see Mrs Muldoon, perhaps she will say exactly the same thing as you were told in Swansea, but I would entrust all my female bits and pieces to her in a way that I would no other, other than Adam of course.'

'What else could I do but to accept your offer? It is unbelievably kind. Thank you.'

'That I think is the most important aspect of your grief this morning, but there is considerably more to it and perhaps we can begin to address some of that as well. I think it might be wise to take a day off walking in the hills.

'Then, tomorrow would be an ideal day to telephone Edward Challen and resign, but tell him you will sell him what you are already finding. Don't take no for an answer. He has lied and misled you enough and there is something here he wants, something he needs you to uncover for him that he is hoping to use to bring him money and repute.

'By all means see the two women again because my nose is twitching where they are concerned. Then there is the question of Andrew.'

'Andrew on the farm, do you mean?'

'Yes. The thing is, he is involved with all this, and in a big way. I'm absolutely certain he knows exactly what he's about in terms of farming, and I can see straight away why Anne-Marie should want to take him on even though Rhona knows that financially it makes not a great deal of sense. But, trust me, Andrew knows a great deal that you need to know. He is not untrustworthy and you are at no risk from him, but you've got to find a way of digging deeper though you really would be well advised not to try doing so by getting into bed with him, not that for one moment I think you would.'

'How do you know all this? You've barely met Andrew.'

'Meeting him is not important. His behaviour, reported to me, tells me a great deal.'

'I didn't read a lot when I was at school as I spent a great deal of time rebelling, but one thing I did enjoy reading were the stories of Sherlock Holmes. I didn't read them all by any means, but it seemed to me that he had great gifts, not magic, which were about understanding people at a level far deeper than the superficial way we tend to do on a day-to-day basis.'

'He was of course a character in fiction but did you know he was based an actual person who seemed to possess some of the talent the author gave to Sherlock Holmes?'

'No, I didn't.'

'He was called Dr Joseph Bell, and he was one of Conan Doyle's professors.'

'Gosh. I rather suspect going to see Dr Bell as your GP might have been quite scary. I'm pleased that I no longer have to work with criminals of various kinds. They are always challenging and can be extremely resistant to the help I might have been able to bring them.'

'I have to say that I've always found Andrew to be a kindness personified, even when he said what he did to me about Paul.'

'Were you surprised by the way in which Andrew invited himself to come and help on the farm?

'Not really. When I learned his family history and realised he was born and bred a farmer, it made perfect sense that he would want to get away from working in a café back to the farmyard .'

'Charlotte? Has there ever been a movement in the past two or three years say, when considering your existence in Swansea, you might have imagined a different world in which to live, a different life for yourself, and possibly a life shared with another?'

'I've always had a longing to live in the country, to find myself at ease with the natural world and its beauty. I'm sure you will understand what I mean when I say I saw no beauty in and around me in the early years of my life. It was all darkness and corruption and perhaps inevitably led me to drugs. In fact I suspect it's something of a miracle that I have lived to tell the tale. Others, some of whom I knew quite well, never made it.

'Until I came here a little while ago, I had never considered the possibility that I might leave Wales and settle somewhere else, but you've already given impetus to the thought that it might be a good idea to give up my job with Edward Challen and remain here to try and find out for myself just what has been going on, but now I feel my whole life is being turned upside down by what you're saying.'

'If you think I've said too much, and you feel you want to continue on the path you were on, then I will do everything I can to support you in that, but I would be sad if Charlotte returned to being Charlie, just as I'm sad about the terrible confusion that has come upon Paul or Paula. I think you need to have time in the countryside you love, to reflect on all this.

'Psychotherapists, and I hope Ed is already learning this, can themselves get everything catastrophically wrong in their work. We hope that it doesn't happen very often and it explains why we do not work alone, but answer to someone with greater wisdom about ourselves called supervisors, and who we have to see regularly. So, if you leave and come to the realisation that I've got everything wrong, then it's quite possible you're right. But I don't think so. And there's something else.

'I'm thinking, and Adam agrees with me, that we should employ someone to live in with us to help with domesticities and also to look after Jerome, but only for part of the day and never at night. We would pay you well and the house would be yours at all time, and the rest we would work out in detail together. If you're interested, and having thought about some of the other things I've said, and concluded that I'm not totally crackers, the job is yours, and I would willingly join in your investigations with you into Archie McHugh, not least because I'm increasingly intrigued by what you're discovering.'

Charlotte had arrived shivering with the pain of mental agony.

Leaving, she was shaking for quite different reasons and knew that Anaïs had been wise to recommend a day off spent walking in the countryside. She was, however, expecting a call from Marlene in Jedburgh wanting a meeting with her and Betty, and if she needed it to be today, then the country walk would have to wait.

Although nothing had been said to any of the others (though both Anaïs and Rhona had noticed something amiss), Ed had not been feeling well for some time. He had lost weight and was regularly subject to night sweats. When he and Anne-Marie had first visited the doctor some weeks earlier there were a number of tests of various kinds that Ed had to endure and on his return to see the doctor a week later was told that the results of his blood tests warranted seeing an oncology consultant at the hospital. Ed and Anne-Marie were aghast at this development and hardly able to talk about it on their way home. Ed needed to talk to someone though, and chose his closest friend, Alex, his former philosophy colleague at Cambridge and the man who had been made the Lord Bishop of Truro and abandoned it after only two years because he couldn't stand it anymore.

'Did your doctor indicate what it might be?'

'He wouldn't commit himself, and I can hardly blame him. He wouldn't wish to speculate when I shall need more tests but his whole demeanour was somewhat solemn.'

'How's Anne-Marie?'

'Preventing herself thinking too much and is fully engaged with Gregor.'

'Farming?'

'No, though she probably wishes she was.'

'Have you an appointment yet?'

'There's little point in having money if you don't use it when you need it, so I have made a private appointment.'

'Good.'

'How is the poet in your family and the twins?'

'All three are well and growing up fast. Emily has a new volume coming out soon. Some of them are extraordinarily good, though I suppose I'm biased.'

'Surely not, Alex! A man like you. Biased?'

They laughed.

'What is certainly the case is that she has taught me a great deal about why poetry does and does not work. She is a fabulous teacher,' said Alex.

'I won't ask you to pray for me Alex, not least because having treated the Church so badly, I know there is a veto in heaven on any prayers you offer.'

'Sh, that's meant to be a secret. Seriously though, you know I couldn't do that but I already think of the three of you so much.'

'Thanks Alex.'

'Give our love to the Boss and Gregor.'

'Love to you too.'

Alex put the phone down.

'That sounded like bad news, 'said Emily in far-off Derbyshire.

'Yes. It's Ed. He's not been well and has been referred to an oncology consultant.'

'Oh no, that's awful. Should I call Anne-Marie?'

'I think that would be a very good idea, my love.'

Andrew had spent most of the morning on the tractor. All the bales Rhona and Adam had done two days earlier had also been brought in by them a couple of days before the rain and the bruised foot event! However there was another meadow, the last one, where hay had been cut but was soaked through. To begin the drying process, Edward used a waffler, which whipped the fallen hay and spread it about in the hope that sun would do its work. This was where Rhona had to hope for good weather and she had checked on the internet. It might be touch and go, but Andrew would be spending a lot of time in that meadow today going up and down, though he loved the cab and all it had to offer (apart of course somewhere to wee!). Otherwise she was keeping a close eye on one of the heifers showing clear signs of wanting to calve her first born, and achieving very little so far. That was not unusual in a first birth and heifers were normally a little smaller than older cows. There was no need whatsoever to call a vet as she was sure she and Andrew could more than manage but she didn't want to miss anything important so popped into the barn regularly.

Marlene was on the phone to Betty.

'I'm so sorry about Jonty, Betty.'

'Thank you, though you know how much he smoked and wasted literally thousands of pounds on it.'

'Have you got a date for the funeral yet?'

'No. I have to return to the hospital later today to collect the death certificate and then register the death. I imagine it'll be at the crem next week, but I'll let you know. But I imagine that the other reason you're ringing is to arrange for us to meet that nice Charlie.'

'Yes. Do you know, although at first she came over as a bit innocent, almost naïve, by the time she left I felt I was with someone who was very shrewd and I even thought if the innocence wasn't just a ruse, and, do you know, that might just work as things begin to emerge.'

'You might be right about that. What I do know was that she was wonderful and caring over Jonty's death and even came with me to see him in the mortuary.'

'That was good of her.'

'Afterwards I wanted to tell her everything we know.'

'Everything?'

'Jonty's dead, so it doesn't matter.'

'You've lost your brother so that gives me a good reason to tell Peter I'm coming to see you. Is tomorrow morning possible?'

'I need to register the death then meet the undertaker, but I can do the afternoon.'

'It's my flower club but if I leave slightly early, I can be with you by 4:00. How would that do you? I'll give Charlie a ring and if she can manage I won't call back. Ok?'

'That will be lovely.'

Before lunch Rhona had asked Andrew to give the heifer the once over.

'She's straining and getting nowhere, so perhaps after lunch we should give her a hand.'

'I agree, so let's tuck in.'

Rhona's sandwiches were always an entertainment because you could never quite work out their content even when you'd eaten them, though whatever it was you were eating, it certainly did not lack taste.

'How has your morning been with Anaïs been?'

'Let's say it has given me a great deal to think about and after lunch I shall go out across the fields to do precisely that. She's quite a woman, a strange combination of beauty and scary, but I was left with knowing one thing more any other, that she utterly adores Adam.'

'I think it's quite mutual.'

'What about you Rhona? Most men would find you very attractive. No secret boyfriends?'

'Oh I had close men friends at agricultural college but not what you'd call a boyfriend, and I never had a great deal of such before that. You may not have heard, but there was one who was imprisoned for drug offences, for which he blamed me. On release he came here to get even but I was away selling lambs. He had a knife and attacked Anne-Marie before he was chased off by her and the driver of a delivery lorry. He ran round the corner of the dairy and going much too fast to stop, fell into the slurry tank.'

'God, what a terrible way to go,' said Andrew.

'But couldn't they get him out?'

'You don't survive in a slurry tank,' said Andrew.

There was the noise of a vehicle arriving outside.

'It's yet another police car,' said Charlotte looking through the window.'

'Ok,' said Rhona, in which case I'll go and get my shotgun.'

They all laughed and there was a solid knocking on the door.

Chapter 10

Rhona opened the door to find two solid police officers standing before her.

'There's no one next door, so possibly you can help. We would like a conversation with Mr Andrew Sinclair who lives in Jedburgh but who we have reason to believe is working on this farm'.

'Tell me,' she replied with a smile, 'when you're in training do you have to include learning to speak in cliches?'

'I'm not sure what you mean.'

'It's alright, she's just trying to be funny,' said the other who now revealed by her voice that she was a woman.

'Andrew is right behind me and please keep your conversation brief because he and I have to go and deliver a calf we think may have got stuck. If you've time, please come and watch, and I'm not being funny. I've delivered loads and I never cease to be amazed by it.'

'If we could come in and see Mr Sinclair, please?'

'By all means. Tea for both and I can make you a sandwich.'

The officers looked at one another, and nodded with a smile. That was the moment Andrew felt that whatever was coming he might just survive.

'I there somewhere we can go?' said the police woman.

'I'd prefer to stay here with my boss and friend.'

'As you wish. Your name has been given to us as the perpetrator of a hate crime, words spoken in the Abbeybridge Cafe in Jedburgh where you were working.'

'And to whom am I alleged to have spoken these hate words? The complainant presumably.'

'No, to someone we haven't as yet identified.'

'Did the complainant or anyone else hear the words I'm meant to have said?'

'No.'

'I imagine that she won't be wanting to take this to court given the almost total non-existence of a witness and any other evidence.'

'We're just trying to find out what happened and discover if a crime has been committed.'

By this time the officers had almost finished their sandwiches and Rhona had gone to look at the heifer.

'I was the mysterious visitor you have been seeking,' said Charlotte, 'but no, I'm not a witness. Andrew served me and said he would bring my drink over to me. He said my table companion was called Paula but once had been called Paul but said nothing derogatory about her.'

The door burst open.

'Andrew, you've got to come,' said Rhona.

He rose at once and followed her to the barn.

'Well,' said Charlotte to the officers. 'Get on your feet and come to watch the sort of thing that makes life worthwhile.'

They got up and followed her to the barn. On arrival they found Andrew stripped to the wait and Rhona in her bra and waterproof trousers, her arm lost to view somewhere inside the heifer that even the police officers could tell was in distress.

'I had to have a caesarean for my third,' said the woman officer unhelpfully, whilst her colleague had his mobile out recording the event.

'I'm trying to attach a rope,' explained Rhona but I'll let Andrew have a go as his arms are a bit longer than mine.

Andrew said he'd got somewhere, first with one front leg and the other, but that they would need a calving jack to get it out. Rhona had anticipated this and now took over. To Charlotte and the police officers this was something they had not seen before and they watched in amazement as Rhona began ratcheting the jack and then there was the eventual appearance of two feet and a nose. Andrew completed the job and eventually out came a large black and white calf hitting the straw with quite a thud. Rhona turned into a midwife cleaning out the mouth of the calf and encouraging it to breathe. Meanwhile the mother look round wondering what all the fuss was behind her, though obviously relieved that all that pain had stopped.

If the policeman had been hoping for a sexy photo of Rhona he was to be very disappointed as she was covered from head to toe in blood, afterbirth and what the mother had chosen to discharge from her bowels and bladder whilst she was using the jack. Charlotte was lost in wonder and admiration, and even more surprised when she saw the calf struggling to its feet, after two or three attempts, and already attaching itself to it's mother's small teats which which would already be bringing forth colostrum.

'This costs me a fortune in underwear,' said Rhona.

'I want a baby,' said Charlotte to no one, and no one heard.

The police left having profusely thanked Rhona and Andrew for what they had experienced. Rhona was already fully dressed and had the kettle on.

'He knows what he's about,' said Charlotte.

'He's brilliant for a waiter in a coffee shop,' came the reply and both laughed. 'Adam has certainly played a blinder and I take nothing away from him, but Andrew is the real thing.'

'Do you fancy him?'

'If I did, don't you think that I would be wasting my time?'

Charlotte nodded but already her mind was working overtime and she knew that she needed to talk with Andrew, and soon.

Andrew came down the stairs into the kitchen kitted out in an overall that was far too small for him.

'Do you need me to buy overalls for you, Andrew, when I am at the farming suppliers this afternoon?'

'That might be a good idea and because the rest of my clothes are next door, I'm not wearing anything underneath. Are you going to Agriparts Borders by any chance?'

'I am, but I don't think they sell clean underwear for men. On the other hand I've got a key to next door and you can go and put anything you think you need on and then, smelling sweet and clean, you can undo all your good work mucking out and feeding the pigs. Oh, and they need new straw today.'

Andrew smiled and nodded, and took the key from Rhona, disappearing next door.

'Rhona, might I be allowed a short time to speak with Andrew before he gets to grips with the pigs. It won't take long but I think it's very important.'

'Of course you can.'

The door opened once again and Andrew appeared, this time looking much more comfortable. Rhona raised a thumb and Charlotte gave him a broad smile of approval. Rhona made her exit.

'Andrew, can you spare me a few minutes, please? I did ask Rhona if that was ok, and it won't take long.'

'Hey, I owe being here in the first place to you, so how could I refuse?'

'I have a couple of questions I need to ask you, the answers to which might help in my quest of Archie McHugh.'

'Ok. Ask away.'

'Andrew, how old were you when you realised you were gay?'

He blushed immediately, and then smiled.

'How did you know?'

'Trust me, I have absolutely no difficulty with it and I've often wished I was a lesbian because my life might have been different and less awful, but it came to me gradually, not least when I realised you and Paul have been close, far closer than I realised, and while you were getting your things together at your house, I couldn't help but notice among the photos you had on show a small photo of Paul. And it was confirmed for me just before the calf was born earlier.'

'That I don't understand.'

'Oh, it was quite simple. Rhona appeared wearing only a bra and waterproof trousers. I'm not attracted to women but even I could see what a lovely body she has. The poor policeman couldn't take his eyes off her, but you didn't seem to notice. It wasn't just that you had to get on with calving, you weren't interested. It was the same when Francine undressed completely in the kitchen.'

'Yes, but farmers do that all the time in one way or another. After milking we have to strip down to our underclothing before we enter the dairy.'

Charlotte said nothing and just gazed at Andrew with a gentle, almost loving, smile on her face.

'Please don't tell anyone.'

'I don't need to. Rhona has already worked it out.'

'If I wasn't gay, I'd go for that woman in a big way,'

'And if I was, so would I.'

And the second question?'

'Oh don't worry. It's much simpler, just a straightforward answer to a straightforward question. I know what happened to Paul, if that is he told me the truth'

She paused.

'Go on,' he said, almost certain by now he knew what was coming.

'Did McHugh ever sexually assault you?'

'Yes, often.'

'Oh, Andrew, I'm so very sorry, and if you think my sympathy contrived, I can assure you it's not. You see, I know from my own experience what it was you were subjected to.'

'I've lived with this since I was about 13 when McHugh had moved on and finished with both Paul and me, and we simply fell for each other. I don't know whether I'm gay because of McHugh or because I'm made that way, but I know for certain that I am. But it has never stopped me being a bloody good farmer.'

'No one doubts that. In fact Rhona thinks you're outstanding.'

'Really? Even though she knows I'm gay.'

'Andrew, prepare yourself: What the fuck has that to do with it?'

Andrew laughed.

'Charlie, you're wonderful. If I wasn't gay, perhaps you're just who I'd like to marry. You're in pretty good shape yourself, if you don't mind me saying so, and that policeman noticed.'

They hugged one another.

Charlotte spent almost two hours alone in the hills. Her mind began in a whirl as everything from the day all demanded a hearing at once. What might, even at this late stage, be possible for her? Was there any hope after all? She sat down on the grass and once again cried, but whether tears of sadness for what had been or tears of joy for what might yet be, she couldn't have said.

The men working in the agricultural supplies shop in Kelso were also a little confused this afternoon. They all lusted after Rhona whenever she appeared, but all, to a man, were terrified of her.

She was not unaware of this and always strove to make it work to her advantage. It was rare for her to leave having paid the full price on anything. Although unable to join in the banter of her colleagues after Rhona had left the shop, the one woman working there, a young girl from the town who dealt with the till, would have given a great deal to hold and kiss Rhona. It remained her secret longing.

In addition to avoiding kisses at the till (something Rhona suspected) and ribaldry from the men, she was there to obtain green overalls for Andrew, food for the Chinese pigs she hoped Andrew was feeding and cleaning at that very moment. Most of all she wanted something she had seen in the Farmers Weekly, a new alarm system for protecting equipment kept outside or in a shed. With so many thefts of quad bikes it was selling well and didn't rely on padlocks which can be broken as had happened last night, but of course, they had sold out but told that they were "on order"! Driving on to Hawick would be a fag and might produce the same result, so once she was back in the landrover, she telephoned them, only to find that they had one left in stock.

'I forbid you to sell it before I get to you,' she uttered with all the force she could muster.

A voice which had grown more timid by the second made her a promise that he would put on it a label proclaiming Sold at once.

'I shall hold you to it,' she said again, this time with a laugh.

It was a further 20 miles or so and would add at least an hour to her journey but it couldn't be helped. She started up the engine when she received a call from Anne-Marie.

'Hi Rhona. Andrew told me you were in Kelso and I just wanted to tell you not to buy one of those new fangled alarm mechanisms with an electric cable. Ed, Gregor and I went to see one of Ed's former colleagues who works in security for the Scottish government. We told him what had happened last night and asked his advice. The first suggestion was a permanently armed guard patrolling all night, and I said I might offer to do that. The second would involve closing the gate into the yard and equipping it with a very powerful alarm and synchronised lights. When I mentioned the other alarm and cable, he said that thieves already had found a way round it, so it was pointless.'

'I've just set off home, Anne-Marie, and got all I came for and you will be relieved to know it doesn't include the wired alarm.'

'That's great. I'll see you later.'

Now Rhona had to telephone Hawick and eat humble pie which never tasted good!

After her time walking, Charlotte (as she was trying to think of herself) knew the time had come to call Wales and resign from her job.

'And just what other sort of job do you think you'll get with a past like yours? And you still have the car which you need to return, and for which I'll take from your money and each day's hiring fee after today.'

'Edward, I'm not altogether sure I'm getting through to you. Quite why you sent me here I don't know but what I have already discovered and the evidence which I'm now in a position to produce is, I believe, what you were wanting to know but which you would not have been able to unearth because of your time here. So well done you for sending me. I need more time to complete everything but it's big, and I am certainly willing to sell it to you when I'm done. As to my future. I am staying here and this morning I was offered a very good job which means I must now work especially hard to finish what I've begun.'

'I see.'

'I've discovered that I can hand over the car, if you insist, to a local branch of the hire company. I also have two questions for you. Did you know Andrew Sinclair when you were at school?'

'Yes, he was a farmer's son. I always thought him a little besotted with Paul Greene.'

'With whom you yourself were more than a little besotted.'

There was no reply.

'I don't think my second question will come as a surprise, Edward, but I suspect you won't want to answer it. Were you sexually assaulted by Archie McHugh?'

There was a long silence.

'Yes.'

'In which case everything I discover and support with evidence I will hand over to you for an appropriate payment, and I will do my best to deal with this once and for all.'

'Once a whore always a whore, I suppose.'

'The price may just have gone up.'

'Charlie, please forgive me. That was a truly horrible thing to say. It was simply that I feared this wouldn't now get done. I shall pay you now a proper daily fee, and a good one, and expenses on top, and I should continue to use the car while you need it.'

'One other thing, Edward, I have developed a serious short-term memory problem, and I can't remember a single thing that we have have talked about, and it will stay that way.'

'Thank you, Charlie.'

'Charlotte.'

'It's a beautiful name, Charlotte.'

In addition to having to grovel to a delighted shop assistant in Hawick, Rhona knew she would need to repeat the process to Andrew in the milking parlour because she would be late. She stopped the landrover and pelted round the side od the dairy towards the entrance of the parlour where those awaiting their turn looked away from her in disdain.

'Sorry ladies,' she said and made her way in. All was

functioning smoothly and two figures were at work in the well of the dairy. She could tell Andrew because his overalls were too short, but who was the other? And then Anne-Marie stood up and turned round with a huge grin on her face.

'I'm just keeping my hand in until you got here, but please take over.'

'I'm sorry Anne-Marie, sorry Andrew. Almost certainly I set off too late, but I'm back. The ladies won't forgive me I know as cows like to bear grudges, but I hope you two won't.'

'I think that might be possible provided you've brought overalls that fit me.'

'I quite like seeing you as you are,' said Anne-Marie with a mischievous look.

'Women!' said Andrew, 'my dad and I never had conversations like this when we were milking.'

'Sad.' said Rhona. 'Oh Anne-Marie I saw some lovely things in the lingerie shop in Kelso.'

'One of you please, go away,' said Andrew laughing, 'or the ladies will all be asking for frilly knickers.'

Unable to stop laughing, Anne-Marie made way for Rhona and left.

As they were changing to go into the dairy, Andrew cast a furtive glance at Rhona in her underwear, and had to admit that even from his perspective she was a bonny lass.

'Have you a boyfriend, Rhona?'

'Andrew, don't be daft. There is no way I can run a farm like this and have any kind of social life and at night I'm usually asleep not only when my head hits my pillow but usually before that. As I'm sure you are, I'm dog-tired. I have one great love in my love, greater than any person, and that is my farming. Why are you asking? Are you offering?'

'I gather you know that such would be highly unlikely. It's just that even a queer like me can't help but notice how attractive you must be to most men.'

'This is a very odd conversation for a dairy.'

They both laughed.

'Thank you for the compliment, and I could quite easily return it. Farming is everything to me and the truth is I don't hanker after anything more.'

Chapter 11

Charlotte continued her thinking long into the night. She now knew she wanted a baby and she hoped that when she saw Mrs Muldoon what she might offer would be positive. She had already decided that she would accept the offer Anaïs had made of working for them and caring for Jerome which might eventually help her were she ever to have a baby of her own.

She was due in Selkirk in mid-afternoon and wondered what the two women were wanting to say. Before then she wanted to return to Jedburgh itself and see if she could persuade the manager of the Supermarket to spend his lunch break with her. As she drove into the town she was aware that the return of the sun had brought out out the tourists, some of whom might be coming because of their love of the poetry of Archie McHugh. It was clear that a lot people did like it and perhaps it always been like that, poets and writers and other creative artists producing great art, but whose personal morality was highly suspect or worse. She had heard of a famous British composer, though couldn't remember his name, who was known to be gay and adored being surrounded by little boys, but was sure there must be others, including poets, though again she could not recall their names. However she had mentioned to Andrew but never admitted to another soul and almost certainly never would, that it had happened to her as she had told Andrew. He was a teacher and she knew she had flirted with him but she was just 14 and surely he ought to have been the one to take responsibility for what happened, not a flighty silly girl, however old for her age she might appear. Now, she felt angry about what had technically been rape, and which may have led her into the life of prostitution. And how many other girls had there been after her, and was he still a sexual predator? Going to the police would be utterly pointless because it would be his word against that of a former whore, so he would almost certainly have got away with it. She was feeling very confused and wished she could speak to Anaïs.

She parked in the Supermarket car park and went into the shop which was very quiet. She wandered up and down the aisles and placed into the basket a couple of items she knew Rhona could do with, but all the time was on the lookout for Paul. Not seeing him she assumed he was in his office and so approached the door and knocked, and hearing a noise assumed it was an invitation to enter and did so. What she saw was Paul on his knees performing a sexual act on a man she did not recognise.

'Good morning,' she said cheerily, as if she hadn't noticed. 'What time is your lunch break, Paula?'

He spluttered an attempt at a reply, which Charlotte thought truly funny.

'12.15,' he eventually managed.

'I'll wait outside for you. Nice to meet you,' she said to the man, and turned and quickly made her exit but said as she did so, 'I should always make sure the door is locked if it was me.'

She paid for her purchases and left the shop, before bursting into fits of laughter. It was probably a good job she hadn't been the Regional Manager, and then had the thought that maybe the other man was the Regional Manager!

She walked down to the Abbey, but there was no sign of Eilidh

Hart, as she made her way on the pathway to where the wonderful stones stood. Monks, she knew, were not allowed a wife, but were they like some of the supposedly single priests across the world who had been arrested and imprisoned for sexual offences against the young. She hoped not and wished she knew more.

'Hello Charlotte,' said a voice, and turning she saw Eilidh equipped for gardening pushing a wheelbarrow.

'I'd offer to help,' Charlotte said, 'but I have a lunch appointment.'

'What a pity, and how are you getting on in your involvement with McHugh?'

'Alright, I suppose. I think there are a lot of visitors at the Museum today, so there must be a lot of people who like his work.'

'Do you?'

'I read some last night in bed. I don't really understand poetry so it was rather lost on me. You probably know much more than me, so what do you think of it?'

'It's good and some of it is very good.'

'Can I ask you an odd question?'

'Yes, of course.'

'The glam rock performer Gary Glitter was highly successful for quite a time. He sold more than 20 million records and his music was loved by many. Then his sexual offences took him into prison in Cambodia and Vietnam and when deported he went to prison here. My question is this: Do his offences mean his music was not that good after all?'

'The difficulty is answering the question lies in the way our thinking about sex has changed in my lifetime. Young people now demand no constraints on their wish to have sex with whom and whenever. Pornography is now freely available on the internet. Gay sex, of whatever gender, is to be allowed special status, and now we have men and women deciding that they are the opposite sex and are called trans. To challenger any of these things is a hate crime. I think people are more sexualised than ever before. Those without inner stability become susceptible to the forces this generates within them, and some engage in activities which are so frowned upon that they become absolute hate figures even though they are merely on the receiving end of an obsession in society with sex.

'I cannot pass judgement on Glitter as a person, but the music he produced was loved by many. If it really was good, then it remains good.'

'No doubt there are others in the music and literary world of whom this would be true.'

'Lots, but as time passes we tend to overlook the negative.'

'Do you think Eilidh, that all this was a problem for the monks here hundreds of years ago.'

'Human nature being what it is, then and now, there will have been sexual problems even for those living in the cloister.'

'So we idealise them?'

'Probably, but don't forget what the poet T S Eliot wrote about humankind being not able to bear too much reality.'

'After what I witnessed earlier, I'm inclined to agree with him.'

'What was that?'

'Oh nothing really, but it has made think.'

Charlotte waited across the road from the entrance to the supermarket and, a little late, Paul appeared and crossed the road to her looking somewhat sheepish. She was determined to remain upbeat and didn't need to refer to the earlier event because they both knew it was there and would only turn into an elephant in Jedburgh if either of them let it. She led him down the street to *The Belter's Bar* in Castle Gate and offered to buy him a non-alcoholic drink as he was working though he would have given a great deal for a pint and whisky chaser.

'I spoke to Edward Challen and he told me that what had happened to you had happened to him too. Did you know and if so why didn't you tell me?'

'I should have done so, and I apologise. It's just that you work for him and thought I should protect his good name.'

'That's very noble of you, Paul, and it's also total bullshit and we both know it. The fact is that once he had been discarded by McHugh, which means there was already another, younger and prettier, boy in the queue, you and Edward began a sexual relationship which later also involved Andrew Sinclair and possibly others.'

She didn't ask him to affirm what she had said, because it was nothing more than a guess on her part and she hoped she'd got it right.

'You have to understand that Archie was the local celebrity and to be in the presence of one who had met royalty at Holyrood a number of times and been awarded a CBE was a real thrill for each of us. When he came to the school we all cheered and thought to ourselves that he was a great man who had put Jedburgh on the map. When we were singled out by him, it was exciting, and what happened to each of us we accepted as a sign that we were special.'

'What about Jonty? He died a couple of days ago, by the way.'

'Good riddance to the repulsive bastard.'

'Tell me, Paul.'

'Sometimes when we were called by McHugh, we arrived to find Jonty there as well. That was always bad news. What he wanted and McHugh allowed was horrible and always he reeked of cigarettes. I could gladly have killed him, and perhaps my longing to be a woman is because of him.'

'If you go ahead with this and always you need to keep asking yourself if you do, whether in the hope of being a church minister or because you enjoy wearing lace undies I have a suggestion and one you should heed, and it is that you take care about what you eat in your office at work. Don't bite off more than you can chew.'

This set them off laughing. People turned and looked.

'I must get back to work,' said Paul, standing. 'You're a pretty good person, Charlie.'

'Charlotte! I'm a woman and I'm going to reclaim my woman's name.'

'Me too. Charlotte and Paula. Come and see me again soon, please.'

After he had gone, Charlotte went to the bar and ordered some lunch from the menu for which the place was highly regarded, and when it arrived it more than lived up to its billing.

After her lunch Charlotte walked up the town. It was an attractive place and she was enjoying her time here. She decided, though had never done so before, to take a look inside the Catholic Church of the Immaculate Conception, which she assumed was the updated version of the Abbey. The notice board outside indicated that it was now joined up with two other towns, Hawick and Selkirk and judging from his name, that the priest was clearly foreign, perhaps Polish. Approaching the door she expected it to be locked but was pleased to find it open which she felt must be right so that anyone could come in when they needed to.

It was not of course even a tiny bit like the Abbey, and in some ways rather garish, even tacky, with its decoration and statues that didn't quite work, but from the first she liked it and felt totally at ease there. She sat down and looked around her. It was only then that she noticed she wasn't alone. There was a man sitting at the front and he had not made a movement since she had entered. She thought she should leave and not disturb him and was just about to stand when the man did so. He made a bow and then stood still before turning and coming up the centre of the building to where Charlotte was sitting. He was perhaps a little older than her but not a great deal, rather dishy, and with a warm smile as he approached her.

'Hello,' he said with a slight accent that might have been Eastern European.

'Hello.'

'Are you a visitor to Jedburgh?'

'Sort of. I'm doing some work here for a few days, and I was taken with the Abbey and thought I would like to see how it compares to what the Catholic Church is now. But I fear I have interrupted you.'

'Not at all. I'm Father Radoslaw Zolkiewski, and this is one of my three parishes.'

'You're hardly a Scot.'

'No. Do you think it would help If I wore a kilt?'

They both laughed.

'I'm Charlotte Holly and not a Scot either. I come from Wales.'

They shook hands.

'I spend one full day a week in each of my parishes and come on other days as required, so you have been most unlucky to meet me.'

'I don't think so, but tell me please, were you praying when I came in.'

'Like the monks who were once in the Abbey, as a priest I am supposed to pray formally a certain number of times each day. This book I'm holding is one of three volumes for use throughout the year.'

'I didn't know that and I'm really impressed by it. Do all priests do the same?'

'We are supposed to do so. Sometimes of course circumstances prevent it, but I truly believe most of my brother priests do so. Of course I regret to say that the actions of a small number of priests has tended to bring us all into suspicion over the question of child abuse, but I go on striving to be faithful. In the UK there is a considerable amount of residual anti-catholic feeling so recent scandals are grist to their mill.'

'Child abuse is what has brought me here. I work for a writer of biographies and I've been sent as a researcher to see what is to be found.'

'And have you found?'

'Yes. You will know more than me from your work, but I'm beginning to think it's endemic in our society.'

'My feeling, Charlotte, is that it always been happening, just unrecorded, and I'm not sure that our modern desire to have whatever we want, when we want it, helps that.'

'You have a tough job, Father.'

'I'm not a moralist and I only rarely would ever preach about such matters, even though many people assume that we are primarily concerned with that.'

'Then what are you a priest for if not keeping people on the straight and narrow?'

'God, pure and simple. What else is there? I felt I was called to be a priest by God and I choose above to give myself to God, above all in prayer. Not church services so much as in the silence of my heart where God dwells. I'm not all that far from those monks who did much the same long ago in the Abbey.'

'I've never heard words like those you've just used and in my life I've been about as far away from the God you've just mentioned as it is possible to be.'

'I very much doubt it, Charlotte, but the God you've felt far away from, and very often that God is the God of the Church community from which we both might feel alienated from time to time, or even a lot. What I seek to live, and as yet I haven't arrived, is the God that is, metaphorically speaking, in my heart, but also in your heart. Now Charlotte forgive me for I'm preaching.'

They both smiled.

'Ok, here's a question for you Father. Why is it that whilst you were speaking just now, did I feel as if my heart was on fire and it felt I was drinking deeply on pure water?'

'There are two possibilities and you must consider both. The first is that I am a Polish confidence trickster and I shall be asking you for money next. Don't discount that possibility. The second possibility is that there is something going on in your heart Charlotte, and it is a matter of urgency that you discover what it is.'

'H'm. It's turning out to be the sort of week when two people have said to me more or less the same thing in different ways, and both of you coming very from very different perspectives. She's a French psychotherapist and you're a Catholic priest from Poland.'

'Almost certainly she wouldn't approve of me.'

'Would you approve of her?'

'Why not? Psychotherapy helps a lot of people and can make a real difference to their lives. On the whole, however, they very much disapprove of religion.'

But you seem to me to disapprove of religion too. What you live by is God, in words I have never heard before and which move me greatly.'

'In your researching, might you ever come to Hawick, where I live?'

'If I was to be invited I just might say yes.'

She grinned at him.

'Charlotte, will you come and have some lunch with me tomorrow?'

'I would love to.'

He gave her a card with his address on.

'12ish?'

She nodded and just for a moment wanted to kiss him, but held back just in time. It was as if he sensed that, and took hold of her hand and gave her a wonderful smile.

As she walked away, back to her car, knowing she had stayed longer than she intended she couldn't stop thinking about all that the priest had said, something utterly new to her, but neither could she stop thinking about just how totally gorgeous he was. Arriving back at the car she knew she had to reorientate herself, stop thinking what she had been thinking and fantasising about and turn her mind back to Archie McHugh and the two women she was on her to meet in Selkirk.

After the deluge, the weather had recovered and was warm and she drove with her windows down and BBC Radio Scotland on the car radio. She had been listening regularly as she drove around over the previous days and found it so very informative about the country she was in. She had not broached the issue of independence at the farm, and remembered that Ed had until recently been senior civil servant to the First Minister. But the longer she stayed here the more she felt she really could understand why a lot of Scots thought independence to be so positive. She too was from the Celtic fringe but felt that Wales would not be ready to consider independence for a long time to come.

More by luck than judgement, Charlotte arrived five minutes early. What was she going to learn from Marlene and Betty? It could be nothing and it could be a great deal. Either way she knew she had to say next to nothing about what she knew. She wasn't using a tape recorder of any kind, and she needed to reassure them of that, but it also meant she would need to depend heavily on her memory.

Chapter 12

Marlene herself had just arrived and was still in the process of taking off her coat, one which Charlotte thought was far too heavy for such a warm day, but wondered if it might mean that older people felt the cold more than the young. Betty had prepared tea and shortbread for them and as they ate and drank Marlene reported on the activity of the Flower Club she had come from. Everyone, she said, was most excited at the prospect of a visit from *Gardener's Question Time* in the Spring. Charlotte had never heard of it but learned that is was broadcast on BBC Radio 4.

Refreshments over, it was to get down to business, and Charlotte allowed Marlene to set the ball rolling.

'By now, you almost certainly will know that Archie McHugh was a child molester. The word I now hear used is "groomed", which is a silly word to use if you know anything about caring for horses and pedigree dogs. Archie McHugh groomed young boys he drew to himself on his visits to the Grammar above all. He was celebrated and feted and this provided him with adoring ten or eleven year olds, those on the verge of puberty. What is worse is that he got away with it. My husband believed this was going on but claims he never saw it in action. Betty's brother Jonty, however, not only knew about it but often participated in what was debauchery.'

'I'm sorry to say that what Marlene has said is true. When I was widowed and came here to look after Jonty he told me all about it, though I can assure you I didn't want to know. There were photographs too, some of them so obscene you cannot imagine. I burnt them all in the fireplace. It might strike you as odd that I didn't leave him, but he was my brother no matter how despicable I found him, though he told me once that it had happened to him as a lad, the victim of a sheep farmer near Ettrick. I don't know but perhaps that is what caused it all in him, but that's no excuse, is it? We have to take responsibility for what we do, and if this had come out some years ago, he would have been sent to prison, and rightly so.'

'Marlene,' said Charlotte, 'you indicated that Peter was not involved, but did he not think that he should do something about it, such as informing the police?'

'I could never understand why he didn't, until I discovered something about my husband. He was running an illegal gambling racket right across the Borders, which included bare-knuckle fighting, prostitution and animal fighting. I'm told people came from a long way away, and as in all betting, it was the bookie who made the money – in this instance, Peter, and we made a lot of money whilst others lost what they had, and what they hadn't, which is where Andy Dickson comes into it.

He was from Cumbria, a place by the sea, called Maryport. His full name was Anderson Samuel Taylor Dickson after the poet Coleridge. He was a lovely looking lad and clever. He went to university and wrote poems, some of which were meant to be very good, though I wouldn't know as I just don't get poetry. He married and had a couple of kids and worked for the post office.They lived in Langholm and she was a teacher in Lockerbie. He continued to write poems but had a secret vice, about which his wife knew nothing, and that was serious gambling, something which has ruined many a good man and many a good marriage.

'How he first heard of what Peter was organising I don't know, but when he started attending he was allowed a winning streak, which is normal apparently, and only after that do they begin to turn the screw. In his case they turned and turned, and like all gamblers, he kept coming back for more in the hope that his luck would change any day soon. Peter told me that the idea that he should be set up for a big hit came from Archie and for a very definite reason.

'After an evening when they made sure he did well and was cock-a-hoop, one of the girls (a word I use advisedly) made him an offer he was too high to refuse, and when they got wherever it was, there was a second girl waiting. I hope it was worth it because they were being photographed. What Archie wanted was not money, but poems, which must be one of the oddest forms of blackmail ever.'

'Couldn't he have gone to the police?' asked Charlotte.

'Oh, quite easily, because a number of policemen were there almost every time, taking part.'

'How long did this last?'

'Until Andy took his own life. His wife had left him ages before. He had no money and had to put his house on the market. His superb poetry had all been stolen by Archie McHugh and claimed as his own and he must have felt he couldn't go on. He chose the Glasgow to London train just south of Lockerbie.'

'Why have you stayed with your husband after knowing all he had done?'

'I've asked her that time and again,' said Betty.

'I shall be a widow in three months, and I have made sure everything comes to me and it's a great deal. With it my own final years will be fun.'

'Three months? How sure are you?' asked Betty.

'I'm not because it might be less. He has cancer, and although he has been told that, he hasn't been told how extensive it is and I have no intention of telling him.'

The three women sat in silence for a while.

It was Charlotte who broke the silence.

'So all of Archie's works were written by Andy Dickson?'

'Correct,' said Marlene. 'He wrote not a word.'

'And when Andy died, what then?'

'He made an announcement on the tv, on the programme that Melvyn Bragg used to run, that he had decided to end his writing and concentrate now on living, having said all he needed to say, which brought him even more publicity and television appearances. He loved it.'

'And he was living a lie throughout. Do you think Malcolm, his son, knows anything of this?'

'It's difficult to think he doesn't.'

'Did he inherit his father's estate?'

'As far as I know, but it's worth noting that he plays no part in the promotion of his father's name.'

All three of them admitted that a stop was now necessary to allow them to attend to nature, and when Charlotte returned there was a fresh pot of tea on the table. As they drank there seemed so little to say.

'Charlotte,' said Marlene after quite a while of silence, 'when your employer asks you for an account of what you've found, will you be wanting to tell him everything?'

'Jedburgh is a lovely place and some of the people I've met are just delightful, so I don't want to be the cause of any sort of serious damage to the good name of the place and certainly not to any of those who were victims of McHugh. These sexual crimes are regarded far more seriously than many others, but I think the theft of the poems, the blackmail of Anderson Dickson and his subsequent suicide, all lie at the door of McHugh and it was he and no others that I was asked to come and research. Others will be referred to anonymously and I shall give my boss no names. But tell me, is the gambling business still operating?'

'If it is there's no involvement on the part of Peter or anyone else I know. You may laugh but the Borders are pretty lawless.'

I'll remind you of that when I'm stopped for speeding.'

They laughed and Charlotte prepared to make her exit.

Getting into the car she noticed the time was 6.15. It had been an afternoon like none other and when she had time to process it all she felt she would be exhausted. More important now was staying awake as she drove back to the farm, so she turned to Radio Scotland, trying her best to put out of her mind everything she had heard. But there was one conversation and one person she kept returning to in her thoughts.

On the farm it had been a day to forget. The milk lorry somehow managed to destroy the gate between the lane and the yard. Rhona was expecting two men after lunch to install the new alarm system which was centred on the gate now like matchwood before her.

'Any thoughts, Andrew?' she said as they stood together having been drawn by the noise of the crash.

'Not ones that are fit for you to hear. The only hope is to be in touch with Mitchell's and see what stock they've got. We'd need to take the trailer but if we're to leave and be back in time for the security guys we should phone now.'

'Ok. Do they know you, because if so it would be better if you called them. Agree to what they want to charge, because the milk company insurance will have to fork out for it.'

Andrew disappeared inside the farmhouse whilst Rhona began clearing away the wood of the former gate with the driver who had already phoned the depot to let them know what had happened and to ask for assistance as the lorry was damaged.

Andrew returned and said that they had in stock a metal gate of the required size, which would of course cost considerably more than a replacement wooden gate. There was now a crowd gathering, Ed, Anne-Marie, Gregor and Adam had been sitting drinking coffee and had rushed to see what the noise was.

'It's your decision and no one else's, Rhona, but I'd say get it and make the milk company pay for it out of their insurance.'

'There's no question. I'll just shift the rest of the wood and then help you Andrew with the trailer. I've not been to Mitchells, so how long is it likely to take you?'

'Oh, it's not at their office, but on a farm near Peebles.'

'Not too bad, I suppose. Let's go and hitch you up. What about you, Fraser?' she said to the milk lorry driver.

'I'll be fine, Rhona. Probably get the sack,' he said with a forced laugh that made Anne-Marie wonder whether he was serious.

Rhona and Andrew left, returning only a few minutes later.

It was now Rhona's turn for a forced laugh.

'The trailer has a flat tyre,' she announced.

The assembled gathering were unsure whether to laugh with her or cry. Even Gregor seemed unsure.

'I'll give Gordon a call and see if we can borrow his if, that is, he's not using it to bring in hay. What a wretched nuisance.'

'Farming is a wonderful life,' said Adam.

Again they laughed.

Rhona already had her phone in her hand and moved away from the ribaldry in order to be heard.

'Gordon, it's Rhona.'

'I take it you're on the scrounge.'

'Gordon, I'm horrified that you have such a suspicious mind. However, in this instance you're quite right, I am on the scrounge.'

She recounted the events of the previous ten minutes.'

'If the driver was Fraser, you can tell him from me he should be breathalysed .'

'But he's teetotal, isn't he?'

'Aye, but that's why he should be asked to blow into one of those machines the police carry 'cos I bet he's been on the wine gums again. I have warned him.'

Rhona was wanting a yes or no quickly, but couldn't stop herself laughing.

'Has anyone ever told you what an idiot you are?'

'Och, it happens so often now, I've begun to take no notice. Anyway, I got the last of the hay bales in yesterday, so come and get it.'

'It won't be me, Gordon, but my new colleague, Andrew Sinclair.'

'The one from Jedburgh?'

'Yes. Do you know him.'

'Only by repute. I knew his dad well enough. Good family. You've done well to get him back on the land. I'll be pleased to see him.'

'Yeah well, don't keep him gassing, and I'm sorry you'll not be seeing me in my bikini. Next time maybe?'

'It's in my diary already!'

'Thanks, Gordon.'

Depending on how long Andrew got caught up with Gordon, Rhona expected him back within 2½ hours or so. She now needed to seek assistance with the flat tyre. She was accustomed to using strings to repair all sort of tyres, including those of tractors, but she couldn't see where the puncture might be and instinctively felt it was a puncture given the speed with which it had gone down, and of course the trailer was very heavy, and she would need a compressor working with a large jack to lift it so she could find and repair the tyre. Without Andrew this would be more or less impossible as it was a job for two.

Rhona walked back to the yard considering her options, when she saw Fraser sitting in his cab with the door open letting some breeze in on what was already a warm morning.

'Fraser! Having wrecked just about the whole of Anne-Marie's farm in one fell swoop, I wonder if you like to come and give me a hand changing a tyre?'

'Certainly, neither my wife nor my daughters can do so and I have to change theirs.'

Rhona smiled, ignoring the slight on the sisterhood, and followed by Fraser led the way to where the trailer stood looking rather forlorn.

'Ah. I've never done one like this before.'

'As you can see it's not really much bigger than a car tyre, but the weight of the trailer is considerable, so we have to use a compressor with the jack. Have you ever done that?'

'Er, no.'

'They are superb but very expensive and Anne-Marie apparently managed to get ours second-hand by fluttering her eyelashes. It's in the barn over here, It's an Industrial Screw Compressor and exerts pressure up to 10 Bar and I'll use it in combination with a special jack we've got. It's only weakness is its weight. It's nice and compact to look at but you'll have to be careful carrying it, though it's not far.'

There was no way Fraser would have agreed to this had it not been for the fact that he had just destroyed their farm gate. Really it ought to have been lifted on its pallet by a tractor but Rhona didn't seem to be offering that – at first, for Rhona knew there was no chance whatsoever of his being able to lift it. So after enjoying, and wishing his wife and daughters had been with her also enjoying the sight of Fraser straining, struggling and failing, she told him to leave it for a moment and that she would be back in a moment. True to her word she reappeared in a tractor with a fork-lift attachment. He marvelled at the ease with which she handled the machine and had the pallet and compressor in place by the trailer in a matter of a few minutes.

'I saw your mate go off in the Fastrac, a wonderful machine, but can it do anything that this old Fergie can't?'

'43 mph on the roads and in testing it has apparently gone even faster, and it's superb on the land. But this old boy can still prove his worth as you have seen.'

'Old boy? Don't you mean old girl?'

'I know what I mean.'

Fraser unwound the cord back to a socket in the barn, and returned to find that Rhona had already lifted the tyre clear of the ground enabling her to turn the wheel for close examination.

Rhona saw the nail at once but thought she would give the privilege of pointing it out to Fraser.

'Thanks Fraser. Oh yes. It looks like a three inch nail from its head. Do you agree?'

'I would say so.'

She marked the spot with chalk and then continued turning the wheel, looking closely at the tyre.

'As I'm sure you do, I always look for more. It wouldn't be the first time I've mended a hole and then realised I've missed another, but this time I think we're limited to just one.'

There was a loud squall, the sound of pigs fighting.

'I don't suppose you have any Mandarin?'

'I have an orange in the cab for my dinner.'

'I was thinking of the language, Mandarin, which they speak in China. It just might have stopped the Chinese pigs squabbling.'

'Good heavens! Are they really Chinese?'

'They're definitely Chinese pigs but came here from a pig unit in Coldstream, which is perhaps the furthest east they've been. Some will be leaving us at the end of the week.'

Rhona removed the nail and applied the extremely sticky

string with its tool.

'I'll attach the compressor to the tyre now and then we can lower the jack and see how we've done.'

As he returned to his lorry Fraser, who had in fact done nothing, was feeling pleased with himself. Though he knew Rhona had also been making gentle fun of him, which he had enjoyed, he was impressed by her skill and the ease with which she did things. This farm was the only one on his round run by women and perhaps the best run. Both Rhona and Anne-Marie asked no concessions but simply got on with it, and the thought occurred to him that he would like to ask Rhona if he might sometime bring the family to meet them.

A pick-up truck arrived followed shortly after by an identical lorry to that driven by Fraser, and then a car from their head office, the driver of which first of all set about taking photographs and then made notes during a conversation with Fraser. Rhona could hear some of the questions which were mostly about the fault of the farm causing the accident and decided to intervene.

'Hello, I'm Rhona McKenzie and I'm the farm manager. I think if you have any questions about how the farm is run, they should be addressed to me, not Fraser.'

'I was just asking Fraser about what happened . . .'

'No, you weren't. I heard your every word and you were trying to exonerate yourselves from any liability by looking for our failures that might have brought about what happened. There were none, and the situation with the gate was this morning as it is every morning when Fraser is here. He will tell you what happened which was failure of the steering mechanism. Perhaps it would be as well for us to ask for an independent inspection of the vehicle in case this gets to court and I assume that is why you have been taking photographs. Now, your best bet is to drive back to your office taking Fraser with you and leave your other chap to complete the transfer of milk to his vehicle and then let the pick-up truck do its business. This is a working farm and very soon a tractor and trailer will be arriving with a new gate, for which of course I shall be letting you have the invoice. I will also be charging for the cost of travel to and from Peebles to collect the gate, but that's what insurance is there for. I shan't however, be charging for the cost of installation as the hinges are still in place as you can see.'

'Well, I've finished what I need to do here which was primarily to make sure no one was hurt and I hope you're able to get the new gate fitted soon. We will of course send a couple of our men to help if necessary.'

'Why on earth might we need men? Thank you anyway. Now I must get on.'

Rhona turned and thought to herself: Please no calving today!

When, a little later, Rhona sat in her kitchen with a cup of tea and the biggest sandwich imaginable which could well have served as the proverbial door wedge, she had a call from Andrew.

'A problem, boss.'

'Why doesn't that surprise me?'

'They've told me that the insurance company will only pay like for like, and they don't have a wooden gate in stock.'

'Get it anyway. Ed's home today so I'll get him to ring NFU Mutual. They always seem to listen to him.'

Ok, and don't forget to see to our Oriental friends.'

'I've got everything ready but I can't weigh them without you, so I'll wait until you're back, so get going.'

Before she had the chance to pick up her mug of tea or sandwich, she heard a vehicle arrive in the yard. It would be the people coming to install the new yard alarm system, and she went out to welcome them, but it was a police car containing the same two officers who had been a couple of days back.

'Not that it's not nice to see you,' she said, once they had emerged from their vehicle, 'but which one of us has committed the hate crime this time?'

'The younger (male) officer said, 'I'm afraid Ms Mackenzie it's you. I overheard you saying to my sergeant "I hate having to call the vet" and we ought properly take you into custody for that statement.'

'Actually, after a morning like mine, I'd be very agreeable to that. But what are you really here for.'

'The Countryfile king here,' said the sergeant, 'wondered how the new calf was getting on and wondered whether we might see it as we were nowhere near!'

'She's doing fine, feeding well and seems to be enjoying life in the world. I'll show you, though I fear you might get your shoes a little mucky.'

'Don't worry about that.'

She led them across the yard and towards the paddock behind the house where there were a number of cows with their calves, and she pointed her out to them.

'Between you and me,' said the sergeant quietly, 'I think he really wanted to come and see you again. He's taken a fancy to you.'

'Well, that's very nice, but he has competitors in the form of all those sheep over there. For some reason they adore me and treat me like Little Bo Peep and do so without first seeing me half-undressed.'

The sergeant laughed.

'It's alright, I don't think he's lived much but he hasn't stopped telling everyone all about your calving.'

'He needs a lass.'

'He does, but he is doing extremely well as a copper and he'll get the confidence to ask someone out in time.'

He came back to them.

'It's amazing that she's already up and about, feeding herself from her mum. So why do human calves take so long to do it?'

'Ask your sergeant. She's had three calves of her own.'

'Right little animals they are too sometimes,' she replied with a grin.

A vehicle could be heard arriving.

'Time to go but do tell me your names.'

'Thelma and Drew.'

'Well, whenever you're passing or in this case not passing . . .'

Rhona turned and made for the yard where she saw a van with wording on the side proclaiming security systems. Rhona reflected that she was unlikely to finish her sandwich.

Chapter 13

Charlotte had hoped to be in time to stop at the Teviot Smokery near Kelso in time to buy some fresh fish for her and Rhona, but she was much too late. She pulled into the car park all the same and used her phone to call Anaïs. It was Adam who answered,'

'Hi, it's Charlotte. Are you not supposed to be milking?'

'I've been given a day release for covering for Andrew whenever it was.'

'Do you miss it?'

'I hate to admit it but I do especially in the light of summer mornings. I'm not quite so keen in the winter.'

'I bet.'

'Are you wanting to speak to Anaïs?'

'Briefly.'

'We're not quite at Jerome's bath time so I'll call her.'

'Hello Charlotte.'

'Please forgive me for not getting back to you sooner.'

'I didn't expect you to do so.'

'I've heard some astonishing stories today from the wife and sister of the two men who worked with Archie McHugh. With my far from blameless past I certainly shouldn't judge anyone but what I learned has appalled me, and it might even do the same to you, but I'll save it up for when we meet. The other thing to say is that I would love to accept your offer of working for you.'

'I would prefer to describe it as working *with* the three of us. I'm free early rather than late tomorrow morning as I have to take Jerome to the baby clinic, but could you be here by, say, 8.30?'

'That would be fine. Earlier if you like.'

'No' 8.30 will be ideal. I look forward to that.'

Driving up the long lane the first thing Charlotte noticed as she neared the yard was a new metal gate which she was sure hadn't been there this morning. Entering the house she found it empty as she had anticipated, Rhona would still be milking. There was however something new in the kitchen, a metal box that had been attached to the wall near the door. On closer inspection she realised it was the control panel for the new security system and it looked extremely complicated and she decided to leave it to Rhona who, it seemed to Charlotte could do everything, and even one or more things besides.

There was no sign of food having been prepared and the fridge offered her little, which meant an inevitable take-away. Either they could order when Rhona came in or she could drive into Galashiels and pick something up for them while Rhona was in the shower.

Charlotte made herself a mug of tea and then sat down, picking up the Farmers Weekly which Rhona had worked her way through systematically. Her mind was not on the paper, however, but on the priest she had met today and whom she was visiting for lunch tomorrow. Charlotte had no religion at all but something of what he said had touched her deeply, or was it less what he said and more that it was he who said it? She was soon asleep.

Rhona and Andrew came into the kitchen and woke her up

smelling of something definitely not of the milking parlour or dairy.

'Ooh, what's that smell?' complained Charlotte.

'Chinese pigs,' said Andrew.

'We've been selecting those who are leaving us. We weigh them and paint a Red Cross on the backs of the unlucky ones, which it makes it easier when we separate and take them,' added Rhona.

'Do they go to market?'

'No, we have a contract with a butcher, so it's straight to the abattoir.'

'Well, do you want me to go and get take aways for the three of us?'

'Oh just phone. They'll be here by the time we've showered, and I mean separately, though that policeman here earlier would gladly have shared a shower with me, or so his sergeant informed me.'

'Until you were covered in afterbirth and worse he couldn't take his eyes off you. I was quite jealous because I rather fancied him myself! Perhaps for the next calving with an audience I'll appear in just my underpants.'

The tests in hospital lasted a large part of the morning so having taken Ed in, Anne-Marie returned home and returned with Gregor at noon for the appointment with the consultant Dr Mehta. The staff could not have been nicer as Ed was ushered beneath and through various pieces of machinery He was in awe of those operating such equipment, for they were all such young women and completely at ease with what they were doing. The experiences of the morning had made him feel quite exhausted but it had to be done if the doctors were to begin to treat whatever it was they found.

He was hugely relieved by the return of his wife and son.

'How has it been?'

'Everyone's been so kind but it has left me quite exhausted.'

'I imagine we shall be soon on our way home.'

'A young doctor came towards them and invited them to come with him. He led them down a corridor and through a door where Dr Mehta was waiting for them.

'Please take a seat, and how nice to meet you Dr and Mrs Hunniford, and a junior Hunniford.'

'Gregor,' said Anne-Marie.

'I'm a great fan of Scottish rugby and their coach Gregor Townsend, so your son has a great name.'

They smiled.

'I have now received all your results. One of the wonders of new technology is that you have had many tests this morning and here are the results already. It is clear Dr Hunniford, that you are suffering from a condition known as Non-Hodgkins Lymphoma, which is a form of cancer of your lymph system. This has been confirmed by the bone marrow biopsy you had when you first came in this morning. The senior pathologist herself attended to it and was clear about the result. This is serious as I'm sure you probably realise but there is a great deal we can do and great strides forward have been made in the treatment of Non-Hodgkins Lymphoma. I have not delivered you a death sentence, but the treatment won't always be pleasant, and what we really need is a bone marrow transplant, but the chances of that are not great because you have a blood group, AB-Negative, that is shared by only 0.6% of the population and then there would have to be a tissue match. We have an international register of those willing to be potential donors. We will put out an appeal at once. Without a living parent or sibling the chances of a match are less than they would be but we shall make every effort and sometimes people who share your blood group offer to be donors precisely because they know it is rare.

'I think we should begin treatment as soon as possible. You will need both chemo and radiotherapy, but the best news I can give you is that what I and Dr Evans here are agreed on is that you are at Stage II and not III or IV. All the same I want you to begin chemo next week.'

'Is there a known cause, Dr Mehta?'

'One of the factors that may have led to this is exposure to pesticides. Do you use them on the farm?'

'No, not all,' said Anne-Marie. 'We only have animals and no crops where pesticides might be used.'

'I am pleased about that though it leaves shrugging our shoulders as to cause. Some believe that stress lies behind many types of cancer, but we really don't know why it happens to some and not to others.

'However there is something I must mention. During therapy you will be particularly vulnerable to infections which would not be good news. Is it possible for you to be away from the farm, all three of you, throughout the treatment period which may last quite a while?'

'In my life,' began Anne-Marie, 'there are two things I care for more than anything else in the world, and my sheep and cattle would be appalled to know there not first in my affections, but Ed and Gregor are. I happily accept that Ed must move away from the farm because of the high risk of infection. As I'm sure you know farmers build up resistance as they work, and although Ed milks the cows every Sunday he is not anywhere nearly as protected from infection as the rest of us are. So here and now he is fired. Now we shall look for somewhere to live, not so far away that I can't keep my hand in and do the work I love, but where Ed will be able to feel he's safer.'

'Will you dispose of the farm?'

'Oh no. One day it's going to be Gregor's and whoever else comes along. I've stopped breast feeding and make Ed work hard every night in bed, which might of course account for his weight loss.'

'I'm pleased to hear it, but I think you should arrange as a matter of urgency, before chemotherapy begins, to store sperm, as the treatment can ruin your fertility.'

'How do I do that?'

'My secretary will arrange it for you, probably for tomorrow. It will seem odd that I say you are lucky when what we are talking about is cancer, but in this instance you are. Doctors should never under any circumstances, something I stress to our medical students, advance a prognosis to a patient, but although it is going to be uphill, you have grounds to be hopeful that you will see your son on a tractor one day.'

'You have been wonderful, doctor. Thank you so much,' said Anne-Marie.

'One final word of warning. During chemotherapy you will sometimes feel terrible but persist. I shall of course see you regularly and Angie, next door, will make all the arrangements with you for tomorrow and next week, as well as confirming your entry on the bone marrow list.'

Winding their way through the Edinburgh traffic, Anne-Marie said to Ed, 'I am happy to give up everything for you Ed. I need you to know that. I love you totally.'

'Don't ever think I feel any different about you my wonderful escaped criminal.'

'O God, when I think back to that, handling stolen medieval books for uncle Oliver, I shudder. The art squad knew it was me of course, but then I turned up trumps for them when I realised what was happening with the heroin in the art studio. I might still be in Holloway and heaven knows where uncle Oliver would be but probably not married to the sexiest former police office in Sicily and a first-time father at his age.'

'A lot of fine poets owe a great deal to him. Anne-Marie, you must find someone to talk to about all this. You would be foolish to think you could keep it to yourself without going mad. You have Rhona or Anaïs who is a professional listener, or possibly from your time with the poets, Emily.'

'Emily would be first-choice but she lives in Derbyshire and that's unrealistic and in any case she has the two children, three if you count Alex.'

'Alex is a good man.'

'I know. but as a former philosopher and Archbishop of the established church he is more confused about most things than anyone I have ever met.'

'You're right. He wasn't at all like that when he we taught together at Cambridge. He was the youngest ever professor primarily because his thinking was so clear. He fell among thieves, and it's not often I quote the Bible.'

'It's a real sign that you are not well.'

The weather forecast threatened thundery rain later and it was certainly very humid and Charlotte walked to her car. Whenever and wherever she returned it to the hire company it would need a good wash. The rain the other day and liquidised most of what was on the yard and much of it had splashed onto the doors and sills.

The new alarm system had only gone off and woken everyone by mistake twice and she heard Rhona on the phone at about 3.30 am insisting that an engineer would be on the farm with her at 8.30 "and no later" she had said in her strongest tone. As Charlotte made her way along the potholes of the lane, she met a van coming the other way. Somehow they squeezed past one another and she saw that it was the van presumably containing the engineer who, she could see, was a woman. She was impressed by the company's thinking: a man just wouldn't be up to containing Rhona.

She arrived to find a most odd sight, Adam sitting on a chair at a table working on his laptop in the middle of the lawn. So engrossed was he and with clever ear pods pouring music into his ears that he neither saw nor heard Charlotte as she approached and she swore that when he did eventually, his body leapt at least a few centimetres into the air.

'I'm so sorry, Charlotte, I just wasn't aware of you until you stood in front of me.'

'Tell me Adam, has Anaïs thrown you out?'

'Not Anaïs, but Jerome. I suspect he's teething though Anaïs insists he's too young for that, so she's intending to take him to the doctor's this morning.'

'And isn't he due at the baby clinic later?'

'Yes, single-handedly he's using up the NHS budget. Much more important is the news that I rang my friend Angela Muldoon and asked how we might get you to her as soon as possible. As best I can I described what had happened to you and she said you needed immediate attention and she will see you on Friday at 2-00.'

'Adam, that's wonderful. Thank you so much.'

'My lovely wife says she'll take you as you won't be allowed to drive afterwards, so make the arrangements with her. Now, I must try and do a little more work and see you later.'

Charlotte went into the house and could hear Jerome, and found his mother in the kitchen folding washing.'

'I'll do that if you want to be with Jerome.'

'Thank you but I'm ok. I have always been told that it's when babies don't cry that you should worry, but would you come to the doctor's with me and we can begin talking on the way.'

'Of course.'

Within a few minutes they were ready to set off, Charlotte sitting in the back with Jerome. Although Anaïs was trying to give the impression of being blasé about Jerome's condition, Charlotte could tell that was anxious and concentrated on Jerome rather than trying to recount anything from the previous day. As it happened they were there in a very short time.

'I'll stay here, shall I?' said Charlotte.

'I'd really prefer you to come in.'

'Of course.'

They made their way to the reception desk.

'You must be Mrs Clément with Jerome. I'll let Dr Horrocks know you're here.'

She picked up a phone and spoke to the doctor, who in a very short time appeared at the desk.

'Hello, Mrs Clément, I'm Alex Horrocks. Would you like to follow me?

Anaïs was clear she wanted Charlotte to come in with her.

'This is Charlotte, a friend who's about to come and live with us and help with Jerome's care.'

'That sounds good. Now then little man, let's see what's hurting.'

Anaïs and the doctor took his clothes off and the doctor set to work, gently touching, taking his temperature, listening to his chest and tummy and looking in his ears. She also asked Anaïs questions about how much milk he was taking and the content of his nappies.

'Let's get him dressed again, and the good news is that Jerome is suffering from colic, something one in every five babies gets. It's a sort of indigestion. He doesn't have a temperature and his ears are fine, as they can often cause a lot of pain to babies. He's breathing ok and his heart is quite normal. That's the good news. The bad news is that this can go until he's 3 or 4 and can't be treated by medication. What he needs more than anything is handling with his head up. Changing to bottle feeding wouldn't help. You'll notice him bringing his knees up to his chest which he was doing a few moments ago if you remember. The other important thing is that mum, dad and live-in help make sure they get rest.'

'What's a live-in help?' asked Anais, 'it's a phrase I've not met before.'

'It means me,' said Charlotte.

Anaïs and Charlotte smiled at one another and for the moment Jerome was silent, having drifted off to sleep.

'Alex,' said Anaïs, 'Charlotte has an emergency gynaecological appointment with Mrs Muldoon on Friday but as yet is not registered with a GP as she's about to move in with us. Is she able to register with you?'

'Of course. Mrs Muldoon is probably the best there is so I hope it goes well. Collect a form from Reception and fill it in, and when Mrs Muldoon is done with you, make an appointment to come and see me as we like to do a check-up on all new patients.'

'Thank you, doctor, I will,' said Charlotte.

Once back at the house, Anaïs made a cup of coffee for Charlotte, Adam and herself.

'You didn't come to see the doctor with us,' said Charlotte to Adam pointedly.

'No. I was banned. Whether I picked it up from the cows and calves, I don't know, but I've been struck by the runs. It wouldn't have been right for me to go but I'm so glad you went with Anaïs. Thank you Charlotte, and welcome to your new home, whenever it is you intend moving in.'

'Charlotte has come to talk with me and so far we haven't been able to, so we'll disappear my darling and see you later. I have to go to the baby clinic later.'

They went into Anaïs's study and sat down in extremely comfortable chairs.

'Tell me.'

With the exception of her encounter in the Catholic Church

she recounted all that had happened and she had heard from Paul, Marlene and Betty. She was determined to do so as unemotionally as possible but by the end she could no longer conceal her feelings of anger. When she had finished, both she and Anaïs sat in silence for at least three minutes.

'When Edward Challen sent you up here, how much of this was he aware of, do you think?'

'Your guess is as good as mine. He has admitted to me since I've been here that he was one of the victims of McHugh, and perhaps that is the extent of his knowledge, hoping that I would find more former victims with the intention of destroying his reputation.'

'H'm, that's possible but I don't buy it.'

'Gosh, fancy you knowing a phrase like that.'

'I have sometimes watched American films and learned all sorts of colloquialisms. You see I have to assume that he was well aware of those of his peers who had experienced the same as him. That he didn't is more than unlikely.'

'There is a word I've heard but can't remember, which means claiming as your own someone else's writing.'

'Plagiarism, but what the women in Selkirk described to you is very much more than that. Charlotte, you have reached a turning point. You can stop now and be proud of what you've discovered.'

'Or?'

'You could try to find out where the son and daughter of Andy Dickson are and get to speak to them. At some stage you must also return to see McHugh's son, Malcolm. It is inconceivable that he is ignorant of all this.'

'I know where I can find him, but how do you suggest I set about discovering the whereabouts of Dickson's children when I do not even know their names?'

'Peter McDonald may well hold the key but you must do what

you can to protect your source, meaning his wife Marlene. I suspect however, that getting out of him what he will not want to give will be extremely difficult. The other way of course is to ask your boss, Edward Challen, because he knows.'

'How do you know that?'

'You and I once spoke about Sherlock Homes. I read him first in translation and you said you loved his stories. I think it was in *The Sign of the Four* that he said to Watson by saying: "How often have I said to you that when you have eliminated the impossible, whatever remains, however improbable, must be the truth?". Well, so it is now. Challen sent you because he thought you would be able, being an innocent young woman, to creep in under the radar. He couldn't come himself but you were the perfect person, perhaps, and mistakenly, because he thought you would be naïve. But he knew everything already: the gambling set-up, the blackmail of Anderson Dickson, the involvement of McDonald and Dickinson and possibly even more. I did a search on the internet last night and it wasn't difficult to discover that Edward Challen is married to Eleanor Challen, née Dickson. Believe it or not it is there for all to see on Wikipedia. I printed it out for you.'

'But if he knew all along why send anyone? Whatever he's going to do with that knowledge he could do without me.'

'I fear I have another American gangster movie phrase for you. I think he was setting you up to be the "fall guy", the one who can be blamed for everything coming out into the open, the person responsible for destroying the reputation of the great Scottish poet Archie McHugh and making disgusting and unprovable insinuations about his sexuality. For Challen and his wife it is win-win but for you it is existence as a pariah not only in Jedburgh but in Scotland as a whole. Challen knows about your past life in Swansea, I take it?'

'Yes.'

'Then I expect he didn't trouble himself too much about making use of you, as you had been made use of by men many times before.'

'Jesus!'

'I doubt that!'

They laughed,

'Have you any thought about how I should proceed?'

'I think you should arrange to go and see Malcolm McHugh to forewarn him that the story may be about to break as I imagine that Challen and his wife may be on the verge of publishing the complete works of Anderson Dickson blowing apart completely the alleged work of McHugh as stolen by blackmail, a huge act of plagiarism. He ought also to know that this publication will be followed by a large-scale exposure on television and in magazines and the newspapers, in the course of which McHugh's serial abuse of young boys will emerge. He may choose to get right away, or prefer to tough it out, but all you are doing is giving him information with which to make a decision.'

'Poor Malcolm.'

'Yes, indeed. But Charlotte, I must get Jerome ready for the baby clinic. There is one other thing we must do, and it involves both of us. I can't go into it now, but I must become your literary agent, and negotiate a substantial fee for you as we on the verge of signing a contract with a newspaper for you to tell the whole story including his part in it. If he wants to use you as he has, he must pay and I shall make all that we have spoken of perfectly clear to him.

Jerome had been quiet for a while and Anaïs was reluctant to wake him. She and Adam considered the options. There would be another clinic in two weeks' time they knew, but in the end decided to go now.

Charlotte was upset about all that she heard from Anaïs, not least because she suspected that it was accurate. Edward simply regarded her a prostitute of a different kind to be used as he wished. Well, she was determined to get her own back. The pain remained as she drove on towards Hawick, and it was the past rather than what lay before her that dominated her mind. For now.

The shearers from New Zealand had been on the farm for a couple of days. They worked extremely hard and fast, and drank in much the same way. They had been here before and made remarkably light work of it. Rhona had become used to the occasional naughty comment and was told by Andrew to give back as good as she got but that only encouraged them the more!

Once they had received their brand new haircuts the yows and lambs were set to return to the hills, but the remaining tup lambs who were kept back from shearing as they were not to make their way to market and most likely afterwards to the abattoir. Rhona was happy to let Andrew deal with it. He had done it many times when working with his father, and Rhona already knew him canny enough with regard to prices. It was important too for his face to be seen there once again, now working for the "two lasses" as they were often referred to in their absence because if they did so when they were present, those doing so would regret it. "We are two farmers just like you, only better", Anne-Marie had once informed someone or other.

'Evolution hasn't yet twigged on that what we want are gimmers, not an equal number of tup lambs, almost all of which are good for nothing but eating,' said Rhona.

'It's odd, isn't it? But it's exactly the same with calves. I'm sure it's the same with you but my heart always sinks when we get a bull calf. They're useless.'

'And I always hate having to take them to the Buccleuch kennels in Melrose to be shot. Ok, enjoy the market and please don't buy anything unless they have some alpacas. I'll drive the sheep out, or at least the dogs will and then I'll see how the lass from the Security company is getting on.'

Newly-shorn the sheep were very happy and needed little encouragement to take to the hills once again, so Rhona was back in good time to make and enjoy a coffee and a bit crack with Anastasia, which had to be the most unlikely name for an electrical engineer.

'Does your name get shortened to Annie or something like it?'

'It certainly does not. I adore my name and the sound it makes, so it's the full works or not at all, though my boss is allowed to get away with "Oi, you".'

'What a concession. I should think you're quite a draw to work with.'

'I'm ever so bossy so I'm sometimes given a very wide berth by the men when two of us are sent out on a job. It suits me as I prefer working by myself.'

'Are there other women in your team?'

'Not engineers, and what about you? Do you have other women to work with?'

'The farm is owned by Anne-Marie and she's a brilliant farmer, but at the moment she's on maternity leave meaning that I'm in charge as Farm Manager. I have one full-time colleague and two who come and help with milking.'

'Men?'

'Yes, but they're perfectly clear about who's in charge.'

'I'm glad to hear it. Now, your security system is the best so I'm sorry the men didn't manage to install the wiring properly. The problem was a short circuit in one of the lamps outside so I've changed the lamp and rewired it back to the box here. I've also done a full system test and if they had done that before they left, your miscreant lamp would have shown up but that's men for you.'

'Thank you Anastasia, and with luck I'll get a full night's sleep tonight.'

'Are you married or with a partner?'

'Most of the time I'm filthy dirty and smell of animals. I can get clean in the shower but the smell lingers, so the idea of anyone wanting to share a bed with me is highly unlikely.'

Anastasia stood up and collected her tools.

'I would,' she said as she opened the door and looked back at Rhona who was blushing. 'My card is on the table. See you soon, I hope.'

She closed the door behind her leaving Rhona flabbergasted.

Chapter 14

Charlotte had absolutely no idea of what was coming. She couldn't recall ever having been invited to a lunch by anyone, let alone a Polish Catholic priest she had only met on the previous afternoon. On arrival she rang the door bell almost expecting it to play a hymn tune. "Oh God, she thought, I'm totally out of my depth".

The door was opened by a lady in her late fifties.

'You'll be Charlotte. How lovely to see you. Welcome and come in. Father will be with you soon. He's just got back from a funeral and he's changing. I'm Gloria, the housekeeper. It's a good name for a catholic.'

Charlotte laughed but had no idea what had been meant by it.

'Now, I've been told to get you a glass of wine. White or Red?'

'White please.'

She had been led not into the parish room at the front but to the priest's own sitting room which, she noticed, did not have any religious pictures or statues, but pictures instead of what she assumed was Poland.

Gloria returned with the wine.

'I finish at 12 so I hope you have a good visit. It's so nice to meet you.'

Gloria made her way to the door, turned and shouted up the

stairs, 'You're very bad-mannered Father. Charlotte is sitting by herself down here.'

'I'll be less than a minute,' came the reply and Charlotte heard the front door close.

Seconds later an amazing sight greeted Charlotte's eyes. At the door stood a really good looking man wearing a t-shirt with a Polish Logo and a pair of shorts. She was, to say the least, taken aback.

'Apologies for not being here to greet you. I was hoping you might be a little late and Gloria already gone. She would hate to see a priest dressed like this in the presence of a woman. The important thing is that you're here and you've got some wine. Welcome Charlotte.'

'Thank you. I have to admit that I hadn't anticipated seeing a priest dressed so.'

'Actually in summer I wear shorts under my soutane as much as possible but have to wear a clergy shirt. I have to be careful if it's windy though, just in case I reveal more than is good for me or them.'

He held up his glass.

'Sto lat!'

'What does that mean?'

'Bottoms Up!'

'It seems to me that priests are much more interesting people than ever I had thought, but why is a Polish priest in Hawick? And are there Scottish priests in Warsaw?'

'The basic reason is a fall in numbers. We have many in Poland because it remains a catholic country but in the UK things are pretty desperate. Because I speak English I was volunteered to come for a few years. I don't of course speaks Scottish, so I have usually little idea what they say to me in confession, which suits them.'

'Why did you become a priest?'

'Technically because of God. Priests have all been called by God.'

'That's kind of him, but what about the rest of us? Do we just have to work it out for ourselves? I ask because I could have done with God calling me to something. As it is I was completely overlooked from the very beginning. I think I have lived most of my life as one of God's out and out rejects.'

'I am truly sorry to hear that, Charlotte, though if you don't mind my saying so, looking at you now it is not how you come over to me. But I would love to know about you and why you speak as you do, but of course only if you want to.'

Charlotte picked up her glass and drank, put it down and looked towards him.

'What am I to call you? I can't call you Father.'

'Zolko is what my family and friends call me and I would love you to do likewise.'

'Ok Zolko. I can assure you there were no angels around me when I was born, because my parents, whoever they were didn't want me and the Social Services took me into care until I was 16. I had a series of foster parents, good people whose life I made a misery. The last foster-father attempted to rape me and that was the end for me. I had already started using drugs when I was 15 but now began to do so in a bigger way, including, I'm ashamed to to say, supplying others with them in order to pay for mine. I came to the attention of a horrible guy called Ollie who suggested there was good money to be paid working for him, and all I would have to do was to open my legs down by the docks. It wasn't quite as easy as he had suggested and all the girls experienced physical assault from time to time, myself included. I came to despise all men, especially Ollie, who took away about 75% of our earnings for himself.

'Some of those who came to me had important positions in the city though of course I pretended not to know them. My name was Rosa because I was determined to preserve something real about myself. There was nothing glamorous about it. It was disgusting and I felt humiliated by it, even though that was true of my whole life.

'There was a policeman who came down to see us from time to time, He was a detective sergeant in the South Wales police and a brute of a man. One night he came to me and subjected me to the most horrible attack internally and then raping me. I was taken to hospital by ambulance and operated on the following day. Shortly after that he raped his own 14-year daughter and was arrested and placed in prison awaiting his trial. No one knows what happened but one morning he was found dead in his cell. The coroner said it was suicide, but I'm sure it wasn't. Either way, I'm glad he's dead.

'I left hospital and assumed that I'd be back on the streets soon, when two women officers called to see me and offered me witness protection outside Cardiff. Since that day I have not smoked, taken any illegal drugs, and made no contact with anyone from the past.'

Charlotte was grateful that Zolko had not interrupted her and he, as a priest, was determined not to do so. That sat in silence, looking at one another. At last Zolko spoke.

'I have no doubts that all that you have told me is true, even though I suspect you have edited it for my tender ears. I suspect that there has been worse. But what I see before me is a hero, someone who has triumphed against the odds and come out on the other side. You are shrewd and thoughtful, and highly intelligent, someone who would have used higher education to your advantage, and done great things with it. As yet however, I don't know what it is that you are doing here in the Borders, and it's obvious to me you are doing something specific. I fully understand you may not want to say but after all you've told me about your past I'm intrigued.'

Although she felt she could trust Zolko, she decided to tell an edited version of the story.

'What you're saying is that not all of the poems of Archie McHugh were his work but something stolen from someone else, and that you are employed by a writer in Wales married to the daughter of the man who wrote the stolen poems.'

'Yes, but it's even more complex than that and I have to keep it concealed for the time being as there are still one or two people to see.'

'Will it cause a fuss when it all comes out into the open air?'

'Yes, and I'm not doing the town of Jedburgh any favours.'

'You must do what is right, but I think that is what you are already doing.'

'I hope so.'

'Are you staying in Jedburgh?

'No, I've been with friends on a farm near Galashiels but I'm leaving to take up a job sharing the house and baby with other friends, though I have a major personal thing to face. The surgeon who operated on my insides told me I could never have a baby but on Friday I'm going to the Royal Infirmary to see the gynaecologist consultant Mrs Muldoon, to see what might be possible.'

'That's good news, Charlotte, and is there a man you have in mind?'

'I think I've got to wait and see what the gynaecologist says first. I'm trying hard not to fantasise.'

Zolko suggested they have some lunch and led Charlotte through to the dining room where the table was set out with pies and various forms of salad. Charlotte refused further wine.

'Tell me,' said Charlotte, 'how does your backstory compare with mine?'

'Oh, I've been so blessed with good and loving parents, that if I tell you about my upbringing I shall feel guilty.'

'Oh, Zolko, there's no need of that.'

'I was born in Gdansk, the port in the north of Poland where the collapse of communism began when Lech Walesa an electrician and union organiser began the Solidarity union with an extraordinary amount of support from the Catholic Church. This was before my time but it is now part of Polish history. He became President and won the Nobel Peace Prize. I was one of six children and becoming a priest seemed inevitable. I was sent to England for two years to teach in a seminary, a place where priests are trained, near Guildford in Surrey. I was the pastoral director, not an academic post as such, but having responsibility for the well-being of those preparing to be priests. I had studied English at University in Warsaw and being at Wonersh Seminary in Surrey for two years meant that I became fluent, and when the Catholic bishops in Scotland asked for help, I was sent here.'

'You must miss home?'

'I miss my parents and my three sisters and two brothers but living in the Borders is a particular joy.'

'Are either of your brothers priests?'

'Heavens, no!'

'When we spoke yesterday, you talked a language about the possibility of a meaning of God that I thought I could make sense of at the time.'

'But God's not to be made sense of. A medieval writer said that God may be caught by love, but by thought never. So much religion in all its forms gets stuck on the things that are of no consequence whatsoever and I find myself increasingly frustrated by it.'

'What can you do about that?'

'I don't know at the moment. Now, let's go back to the other room and I'll make some coffee.'

'Thank you for a lovely meal, and that trifle was delicious.'

'It's from the supermarket.'

'I never thought otherwise, but it was still good.'

Zolko soon came through with the coffee.

'I take it that after your operation, assuming it happens, you'll be returning home to Wales.'

'I have no home to return to, so I shall hopefully stay here.'

'Oh that would be good. I'll tell Gloria she's fired.'

Charlotte laughed.

'You will find it odd, as I do, but you are the only person who understands what I am talking about when I speak of the God who is beyond the God of religion and its systems, and the irony is that you have no experience of Christianity whatsoever.'

'Or anything else. But I take it that it's not meant to be like this.'

'Increasingly Charlotte, I have become aware of just how little I know, which when I preach to my congregations three times each Sunday is causing me more and more great distress.'

'Isn't there someone you can talk to?'

'There is no way I would talk to a fellow priest about this and in any case I know none of them well enough to to be able to trust them. As for my Archbishop, my boss, I suspect I would be on the first plane to Warsaw if I spoke to him as honestly as I am to you. My Archbishop has a theory that doubts in a priest can only lead to child abuse, so no one in their right mind would admit such thoughts.'

'Would you be better off in Poland?'

'The thought has been in my mind certainly but . . .'

'Yes?'

'I have quite unexpectedly met someone very special, a young and lovely young woman that has caused me to think otherwise. It's early days of course, but I have never felt like this before.'

'Is she from one of your churches?'

'Occasionally a priest will discover that a young woman, or man, whom he sees in church, has a crush on him. You learn to cope with that, but I have only ever seen this woman in church once and I have already discovered that above all she ministers to me rather than other way round.'

'Zolko, I think you should take hold of this with woman both hands. If you were to leave the priesthood you would not be abandoning God in any way and perhaps in a funny way you might have more time for God without having to spend so much time engaged in the religion you are becoming more and more uneasy with, and I say this not least for the sake of your mental health.'

'Have you ever heard of the American writer F Scott Fitzgerald?'

'No.'

'He wrote something to the effect that an artist is the one who can hold contradictory beliefs and not be destroyed by it. The trouble is I'm not an artist and you are right about mental health.'

'Is your new friend aware of these things?'

'Oh yes. The problem is that I have never had a girlfriend. For obvious reasons they weren't permitted either at Junior Seminary or University when I had to live in Senior Seminary. It means that not only am I a virgin but neither have I ever kissed a woman properly.'

'At least you're not used goods like me..'

'Ah, but have you ever made love rather than been used by men.'

'No, never, and not once did I ever have an orgasm, but what of your friend? Would you want to be with her and have children with her?'

'Unquestionably.'

'In which case, Zolko, the way forward for you is clear. You really need to speak with your friend about all this as soon as possible and make your mind to act, and I mean exactly what I say, you must do so for God's sake, but more than ever for the sake of your own happiness. Lots of people change their minds about what they once set out to do in life, and that includes me, and I bet your friend hasn't spent her nights with drugs in prostitution. To change before it's too late to start again seems to me what you should do and you must tell your future partner that you are ready to do it and want to live with her.'

'You think so?'

'Definitely.'

'By the way, Charlotte do you think love at first sight is a possibility?'

'I met a man recently whom I have not been able to stop thinking about. Good looking, intelligent but more than anything he has a soul. If that is love at first sight, then yes, I know it is a possibility.'

'Might anything come of it? Will you be meeting him again?'

'I sincerely hope so.'

'What is his name?'

'It's difficult to say.'

'Oh I'm sorry. Of course you wish to keep it private for now.'

'No, you idiot. It's difficult to say because it's Polish, and the name of the woman of whom you have been speaking?'

'It's Mary,'

'What?' said Charlotte deeply shocked.

Zolko laughed.

'Who is the idiot now? It is of course Charlotte.'

Zolko stood up and walked over to where Charlotte sat on arguably the most lumpy and uncomfortable sofa in Scotland, took her her hand and sat next to her.

'Is there any chance that I might at long last experience what it is to kiss a woman? You've had more experience than me.'

'No, I haven't. Girls in my former profession never kiss. It sounds ridiculous I know when you think of what else they might do, but there is no kissing, so we learn together but I think we make use of our lips and tongues to do so.'

They did. Charlotte could tell how nervous Zolko was, but what most delighted her was that he did not in way attempt any kind of sexual approach. They did however what lovers do which was to whisper all sorts of warm and loving words, "sweet nothings", to one another.

Rhona insisted that it must have been her fault and though Andrew was more than happy that she should accept the blame for which he himself felt guilty and assumed it had to have been his mistake. But the fact remained that when Rhona popped her head over their yard wall as she was passing on her way to something other, she discovered they had all the pigs gone and their gate was wide open. Her first act was to check inside their large hut to see if there were any members of the "escape committee" still resident but all had disappeared, no doubt led by one called Steve McQueen!

The job she had been going to do had to be forgotten because what had to be done now was going to take simply ages. Andrew and she looked at one another with a telling smile. Rhona had already equipped them with buckets containing pot-bellied pig cubes which they shook and hopefully drew them out from where they might be hiding.

The pigs had spread far and wide and it took until milking was due to begin to entice the last back into their unit. They were both tired out by the swine-hunt but that would not be an acceptable excuse to the ladies who were already waiting by their gate to come into the parlour. An hour earlier Rhona had decided to see if the cavalry in the form of Adam and Ed just might be able to help out but had luck contacting either. Perhaps she should have given Charlie some lessons, but she had no idea where she was or what she had been doing.

Charlotte and Zolko had moved barely at all and just gently cuddled one another. Charlotte found it a wonderfully healing experience. There had been one moment when she suddenly wondered if she was just the latest in a long line of Hawick maidens Zolko has drawn to have his wicked priestly way with them. So if this was going to be real and to happen, she decided to tell him her thought.

He laughed gently.

'Oh dear, how did you guess?'

'I'm sorry Zolko, and I didn't think it for one moment but it may take me a little while to recognise that what we are offering one another is love and not exploitation, and I will need you to help me with that. The other reason is that at the moment in my work in Jedburgh I seem to have hit a massive wall of lies and deceit plus a terrible history of child sexual abuse.'

'Charlotte, please may I call you my darling?'

'I would love that.'

'We are both going to require a lot of mutual support. I will give you all that I have, my darling Charlotte and I believe you will too.'

'I will. I will.'

'But what are you going to do about you have uncovered?'

'I can't go to the police for the man who did this is dead, but there is something else, something perhaps even bigger. I have proof that the poetry of Archie McHugh was written by a man called Anderson Samuel Taylor Dickson from whom he stole it by means of blackmail following his involvement with an illegal betting and prostitution group somewhere in the Borders.'

'I have heard of it, though I am not allowed to tell you how because of the seal of the confessional which I cannot break. Nor can I tell you where and when it is, but provided you do not ask where we're going, we might have a drive out into the country and see the sights. Is Dickson still alive?'

'He took his own life.'

'This man McHugh was a criminal and a phoney, a cheat and a pervert, and still the tourists come to honour the man and the poems he didn't write. What can we do to stop this?'

'We talk to Anaïs.'

'Who?'

'Anaïs Clément, who has offered me a job, helping with the home and the baby, Jerome. Anaïs works as a psychotherapist in Edinburgh, is undeniably beautiful, married to Adam who once was a professor of French at Edinburgh University, and in France was an undercover agent for the French Police Service. She has been my adviser and counsellor in all this. She has a mind like that of Sherlock Holmes – do you know who I mean by that?'

'Yes. He is popular in Poland.'

'I'm sure she makes a brilliant psychotherapist.'

'Is she the one of whom you said yesterday that she wouldn't approve of me?'

She smiled and hugged him tighter.

'She'll love you. But there are three words I have never spoken to anyone including all those who were supposed to look after me when I was young. I want to take the huge risk of saying them to you if you will let me.'

'Before you do, please remember that I have said those words to my parents and my family many times, but when I say them now there has never been a moment in my life like this.

'I love you, Zolko.'

'I love you, Charlotte.

Chapter 15

A quick call to Adam confirmed that Jerome was a little better, and that she could move in with them on the following day. Charlotte said nothing else. By the time she was back at the farm Charlotte found Rhona fast asleep on the sofa in her sitting room. Charlotte looked at her and felt deeply envious of how it was that Rhona could do the job she did and manage to look so incredibly gorgeous, though she smiled at the thought that she had today passed the beauty test with one person.

Rhona had left out a ready meal for her to put into the microwave which she did. Having had a good meal at dinner time she didn't really mind that the ready meal tasted of nothing, and most of it went into the bin. Rhona wandered into the kitchen, the beeps of the microwave having brought her back to consciousness.

'Thanks for the food though it was horrible.'

'I had the same and you're right.'

'Rhona, you look unbelievably tired.'

'Either Andrew or I failed to lock the pig gate properly and they all escaped. It took us three hard hours to get them back. I ought to have made Anne-Marie do it, as they were her daft idea in the first place. Then there was milking and three heifers had to be introduced to the parlour, so I'm going to have an early night hoping for no alarms malfunctioning.'

'Well, you won't have to put up with me after tonight. My work's just about completed.'

'So it's back to Wales.'

'Er, well, no. I have no reason to do that. I have no home there and no family. I love it here.'

'But I thought you said you were leaving tomorrow.'

'I am but I have secured employment and somewhere to live.'

'Really?'

'Yes, I'm going to move in with Anaïs and Adam and work for them looking after Jerome and sharing in the housework.'

'Oh that's brilliant, and it'll mean we'll be seeing lots of you.'

'There is something I need to ask you, Rhona, a favour, er, a very big favour.'

'Of course. Tell me.'

'I've met someone who as a matter of urgency will need somewhere to stay for a while from tomorrow. It would have to be somewhere where his face will not be known and away from the public eye. He is about 30, highly intelligent and would be willing to work for you without pay and would be willing to learn whatever you might wish him to. He is gentle and kind and although he is actually Polish speaks English perfectly well. He is called Zolko and lives in Hawick at the moment. Tomorrow morning he is ceasing to be a Catholic priest, and wishes to make a clean break.'

'Shouldn't he go back to Poland?'

'Poland is a very Catholic country, as are all his family and he thinks they will require some time to come to terms with it. He loves this part of the world, and who could blame him for that?'

'How on earth did you meet him?'

'In the Catholic Church in Jedburgh. He was praying when I walked him and we began to speak, and then we met again in the Presbytery in Hawick. Some might describe it as a religious crisis, something I don't really understand, but he speaks of it as a need to continue to relate to God without any of the paraphernalia of religion.'

'Blimey! And would the Catholic Church make things difficult for him if he remained in Hawick?'

'Difficult – no. Impossible – certainly.'

'When might we get the chance to meet him?'

'I have a meeting in the morning, but after that I shall go and collect him.'

Charlotte could see Rhona thinking and weighing up ideas in her mind, and smiled, because she had exactly the same look on her face when trying to decide matters to do with pigs, yows and her beloved ladies.

'It would have to be on the basis that if he rose in the middle of the night and celebrated High Mass he would have to go.'

'I don't even know what that means, but I rather suspect he won't.'

'I also wonder whether he might be better living next door with Anne-Marie and Ed, and Andrew moving in here. We're the ones, at least for now, living the anti-social hours. I'll call Anne-Marie and see if we can pop round and see them, including Andrew.'

As they walked in through the kitchen door, they were sitting at the table having eaten something that looked infinitely better than Charlotte had brought out of the microwave.

Rhona did the talking, very much as if it had been her idea all along, for which Charlotte was more than grateful.

'Will we have to construct a priest hole?' asked Ed to laughter which Charlotte joined in though had no idea why it was funny or even what a priest hole was. If she and Zolko were to be together she was going to have to do a great deal of reading.

They discussed it for a short while but inevitably talk quickly turned to the swine hunt of the afternoon, itself now a different source of merriment.

'Ooh, I wish I'd been here,' said Anne-Marie. 'Was it like a wild boar hunt? Or more like going on a bear hunt she said, mentioning the title of a much love children's book.'

'My knowledge of wild boar hunts is rather limited,' said Andrew, 'but by the end Rhona and I would happily have massacred the lot.'

'You'll get your wish on Friday, if I remember aright, and when I had a look at them this morning I could see some marked with a red cross. Gregor loved seeing them.'

Andrew and Rhona looked at one another.

'When are you coming back to work, Anne-Marie?' asked Rhona.

'In the late autumn, though only working part-time at first.'

'That will be great, though I wonder when you do you'll be willing to go on a "back to work" course which will include basic things such as making sure you properly bolt the gate on the pig enclosure?'

Her hand shot to her mouth.

'Oh fuck. Do you mean it was me?'

'I prefer to think it was Gregor.'

'I am so sorry,' and none there could ever recall seeing Anne-Marie blush so.

She changed the subject quickly.

'Will our new priest require us to call him Father.'

'His name is Zolko and he wouldn't want anything more than that. He's really quite lovely.'

It was now her turn to blush.

'He's also one of six children so he's more than used to family life.'

'Gregor can't wait,' said Ed.

Charlotte called Zolko when she was in bed.

'I get the impression that they're looking forward to having you joining the family,' she said having recounted the conversations of the evening, and the food will at least be better than here in Rhona's.'

'Charlotte, you are a wonder, and my whole evening has been spent thinking about you or talking about you to my mum and dad.'

'You've told them?'

'I adore my mum and dad, and you will too. However could I keep from them the news that I have met the woman with whom I hope to spend the rest of my life?'

'But weren't they shocked when you told them she is called Gloria and works as your housekeeper.'

'Actually, my darling, that happens more than you might imagine. They were at first somewhat stunned when I said I was abandoning the priesthood but when they heard about you, that I was leaving celibacy for the joys of married life, they were clear that they only want the best for me. Perhaps even in Poland there are changes in attitude, though it may just be my mum and dad.'

'Have you done anything about informing your Archbishop?'

'I rang him about an hour ago and he almost set off to come and see me at once. He thinks it's just a passing phase such as many priests experience and says he will be here to see me tomorrow afternoon at 3.00. I tried to tell him that I won't be here but his hearing is obviously failing so I have asked Gloria if she will be here to let him in and make him a cup of tea and show him where the loo is.'

'Zolko, you are wicked.'

'Yes, probably and by five past three I'm sure the Archbishop will agree. In the morning I shall go to buy a new sim card for my phone.'

'I will collect you as near twelve as possible. What will you do about your car?'

I'll leave it in my Jedburgh church car park and I will put the keys through the letterbox of one of the people there.'

'You are making a huge sacrifice to be with me.'

'I love you, Charlotte, and I am both terrified and overwhelmed by the thought that you also love me.'

'Well, my own darling, try and sleep well on your last night in Hawick. Tomorrow you're sleeping on a farm and probably entertaining a lovely little boy called Gregor.'

'You sleep well too, my love.'

Jerome once again was troubled with colic but at least there had been a break in the night allowing Anaïs and Adam some sleep, and when he had to sit with Jerome, it afforded Adam the opportunity to work quietly at his computer. He also discovered that Jerome quietened a little when his dad played Haydn quartets. When Anaïs came down shortly after 5.00, her breasts uncomfortably full of milk, she found both Adam and their son fast asleep as Haydn continued to work his magic. She would have loved to have left them but nature was demanding she woke Jerome up, and like son like father. Their conversation continued as usual in French.

'Telling you how much I love you, Anaïs, in French is even, more wonderful than saying the words in English.'

'I shall never forget, I hope, my first glimpse of you standing at my door in Newquay in the pouring rain first thing in the morning. You had no coat and you were soaking wet, and I thought to myself you must be a wonderful man to do that, or a total idiot. Well I was right in my judgement.'

'And . . . which was I.'

'I'm pleased to say that you were a little bit of both, and I am delighted that I think you are still so now.'

Thank you, my darling, and I am also the luckiest man in the world. People turn when you pass and just check how totally beautiful you are.'

'Don't be silly. It's because I wear expensive clothes.'

'And isn't that strange, because I most delight in you when you take them off.'

'Adam! You must be careful what you say in the presence of your son, or he will grow up with an Oedipus complex.'

'Wasn't his mother very beautiful?'

'Yes, but Jocasta was mother *and* wife remember.'

'I can see a mouth begging for attention.'

'Yes, he is. Just like his father.'

They kissed and then Jerome was rewarded for waiting. Adam would have to wait a little longer before he was called into action. Whether that would change with the arrival of Charlotte he would have to wait and see, but he was besotted with this French woman. She wanted another baby and determined to take every opportunity to try. He smiled to himself. He might have joked to Rhona about it, but when push came to shove he really wasn't complaining, and after his catastrophic marriage to lesbian Alice and then in relationship with her identical twin sister Simone, life with Anaïs was exactly that – life.

Neither of the new lovers slept well. Zolko had packed everything and would be ready for Charlotte when she collected him in Jedburgh. He was of course sad to be leaving some of his flock behind but hoped they would understand and, come to think of it, he hoped he himself would understand what he was doing. It was quite impossible for him to stop thinking about Charlotte and he wished she was here in bed with him now. He looked back to his years in seminary. It had been five years of intensive study, first of all philosophy, catholic philosophy from Aristotle to Aquinas where philosophy, they had been told, ended. Then came Theology, and now the recognition that despite all that study, the use he had made of it was nil. Neither in Poland nor the Scottish Borders had anyone ever asked a single theological question. What a waste it had been. At least he had taken the opportunity here to read some modern philosophy and novels forbidden in his seminary. It was as if he had been preparing all along for the day that lay ahead, and that day had now finally arrived.

Charlotte too kept thinking and hoping that Zolko was probably the only person who could accept and heal her past, though she was also longing for Mrs Muldoon to have some good news on Friday. Healing was also going to be required soon in Jedburgh, and tomorrow she had to return there and tell Malcolm McHugh that his great father was a serial paedophile and never wrote a poem of his own, but achieved his reputation by a cruel and terrible blackmail which pushed a man to suicide. It would be the final act of the drama, thank God, though just thinking those two words first made her smile and then caused her to laugh aloud at the wonderful thought that she had fallen in love with a catholic priest from Poland. Oh my goodness, she thought, just what is Anaïs going to make of this? And again she laughed aloud.

Once milking was over and they were enjoying breakfast, generously cooked on her last morning on the farm by Charlotte, Rhona and Andrew began speaking about the forthcoming tup sales in Kelso. There were two stages. The first was preparing their current tups for sale, which meant washing and drying them, manicuring, and giving them fancy haircuts, and of course checking that their nuts were in fine fettle, as potential buyers would want a feel of any they were intending to buy. And that was the second essential, that of initially agreeing on what they were going for and how many. There would be large crowds present as farmers from the whole of Scotland and much of the North of England made the journey each year. Tups had to be changed every year to avoid the possibility that they might mate with their own offspring. At Agricultural College someone had shown photographs of just what might happen if they did, and Rhona knew of no farmer who would ever ignore this absolute rule. Rhona still favoured blue faced Leicesters.

'I know they look stupid and haughty, but they produce good solid mules and in my experience they all know what to do and how to do it without killing themselves.'

'You may well be right,' said Andrew, 'but I think a good case, maybe even a better case, can be made for a cross bred. I've worked with Charolais-Beltex cross, though I don't think I'd especially recommend them, but my dad started buying Texel-Suffolk cross which produced some fine lambs, even if towards the end of the season the tups noticeably lost weight.'

'That's what comes of too much sex,' said Charlotte as she washed up the breakfast things.

'I wouldn't know' said Rhona and Andrew in perfect harmony.'

They all laughed.

'And you start your new job today,' said Rhona.

'Not quite. I still have the toughest encounter this morning to which I'm not at all looking forward and then I shall to make my report for the my boss. I have to go and collect Zolko and deliver him here. Only then will I go to my new abode and tomorrow it's a trip to hospital which I'm hoping will soon be followed by an operation. So I'm not beginning paid work until the dust has settled.'

'Gosh, good luck with your meeting this morning. I would rather do a tricky calving than something like that. And thank you for having been a good housemate. Sadly you're now condemning me to living with someone who prefers cross breeds to real breeds, but there we are, I can't have everything.'

'I explained my reasoning to Anne-Marie who admits she can see why I might think the cross bred have advantages over

Pedigree tups, but then told me it had nothing to do with her because you and you only are in charge.'

'Anne-Marie is such a wise person.'

'It's a female conspiracy, you mean.'

Rhona smiled.

'I should hope so,' said Rhona.

One of the things she most liked about her hire car, which alas she would have to hand in soon, was the hands-free phone. Resisting the temptation to call Zolko again she asked Siri to call Anaïs, more in hope than expectation for she didn't know what hours she was working today and it might well be Adam oe even Jerome who answered, though she loved them both.

It was Anaïs.

'Charlotte! We are so excited about you coming to live with us.'

'So am I, very much indeed. There is, however, a slight complication, well, a big complication from Poland actually.'

'Go on,' said the psychotherapist.

'When you showed me my room, am I right in thinking that the bed there was a double?'

'No, I'm afraid not. It's a kingsize.'

'Anaïs, do you tease your clients as you do me?'

'If they keep away from the real thing they need to mention, I do.'

'Gosh, how on earth does Adam manage?'

'Because we adore one another. So tell me about the Polish friend you want to bring home with you.'

'Have people ever accused you of being a witch?'

'I have heard it said,' she said laughing, 'but to me it is a compliment. Some of those women who suffered so much at the hands of men were more than able and wise, but you are still avoiding the question.'

'I have fallen in love with Zolko whom I met in Jedburgh and then again at his house in Hawick. I don't mind if you snigger but for both us it was love at first sight, and for both of us the first experience of a boyfriend or girlfriend. I have hidden nothing from him about my past, absolutely nothing, and I know all about his. And this is the bit you'll really like. Until nine o'clock last night he was the catholic priest for Hawick, Jedburgh and Selkirk.'

'I'm interested that you think I might snigger which under no circumstances would I ever do, but perhaps indicates on your part a hesitation about what has happened. You may not know but one morning I opened my front door in Newquay and fell instantly in love with a soaking wet idiot called Adam.'

'Oh that's wonderful, but you're right not about my hesitation about Zolko, but my hesitation in telling you.'

'Oh never feel that again. My clients sometimes say something like it so I shall take it to supervision and discuss why I seem to do this. Not you, Charlotte, and not Zolko – what an amazing name – when you arrive here later in the day. We shall eat after Jerome has eaten me. It's time for weaning to begin. And where are you going now?'

'To meet with Malcom McHugh again.'

'Be gentle, Charlotte, and don't forget I am now your literary agent.'

'That only means you are after 10% of my earnings.'

'Of course, but don't forget that 10% of nothing is nothing. Mr Challen has to pay first.'

Charlotte was in Jedburgh by now. She would miss it in a funny sort of way but whether Jedburgh would miss her was a different matter once the truth entered the public domain, which she was sure was the intention of Edward Challen and, his wife, the daughter of Andy Dickson. She made her way out of town and then turned into Malcolm's drive, turned off the engine and took the deepest of breaths ever. As she sat there Malcolm opened the front door and waved. Charlotte opened the door and advanced towards him.

Chapter 16

'Hello Charlie, thank you for coming again. Do come in. There's someone I want you to meet.'

Charlotte followed him into the sitting room with the wonderful view from the window. On this occasion there was another person present: a smartly dressed, nice-looking lady in her mid-40s'

'Charlie, this is Justine, the lady who I shall be marrying in a few weeks' time.'

Charlotte shook her hand and offered congratulations to both. Malcolm left the room, presumably to bring the coffee.

'You have good taste, Justine. I like Malcolm. Where will you be marrying?'

'Thank you. In Christ Church, Oxford. It's the cathedral for the Oxford diocese and wonderfully, the Archbishop is coming to marry us.'

'That is indeed wonderful and will you be living here?'

'Oh no. I work in the City so we are intending to live in St Albans.'

Malcolm had arrived by now.

'Are you going to work, Malcolm?'

'Yes, at the Foreign Office. And what about you, now that you've completed your work here?'

'I have a new job working as a sort of au pair working for a family I know well.'

'Well that's different to what you've been doing.'

'It is but I'm very much looking forward to it. There have been good moments in what I've been doing and I've met some good people, as well as some less good. I gather you were troubled at one time by someone called Bertie MacCulloch. Is he still being a nuisance?'

'Justine is a corporate lawyer and some of her colleagues were most helpful in seeing off MacCulloch and I gather he now lives on the Isle of Man, but to answer your question: no I have not heard anything from him in quite some time. Have you?'

'Not at all. I was given his name. And I was given a number of names and advised that this or that person might be able to provide me with information.'

'And were they? More coffee?'

Charlotte shook her head.

'It's a strange sort of conspiracy in which everyone thinks someone else knows things they don't, or at least won't, mention and thereby involve themselves.'

'But what have they to fear?'

'Justine's colleagues and associates I imagine. When you've seen the big stick being waved you will make sure you stay out of its way.'

She smiled, covering up her realisation that cleverly, by ensuring he introduced his fiancée to her, he was also introducing his lawyer.

'How are you intending to present your findings assuming there are some?'

'My task was never to make any kind of report. I'm simply a researcher and I accumulate stories and opinions, and am always listening for lies especially those wishing to bad-mouth others as some sort of revenge. I shall publish nothing and what may appear in print will be decided by the person who pays me and his lawyers.'

'I think you mean his publishers.'

'I know what I mean.'

Malcolm looked uneasy and caught the eye of Justine.'

'That would suggest there might be legal issues involved.'

'Aren't there always? Surely that's what pays your wages. And it will be up to Edward and, I imagine, his wife, Eleanor, who according to records is the daughter of someone called Anderson Dickson, who committed suicide.'

It was clear that Malcolm was shaken by this name.

'I have found a number of people in Jedburgh ready to swear to their experience of being sexually assaulted by your father who was often joined by Jonty Dickinson, whose sister and Marlene McDonald have confirmed that, as has Edward Challen himself from his own experience.'

'These are serious accusations and would require a great deal of defending in court,' said Justine.

'Of course, but those recounting their experiences can use other ways of communicating them in the community and I suspect it will enable the conspiracy of silence here to come to an end and it is very real.'

'That sounds like a threat of blackmail.'

'Don't be silly, Justine, I'm not bright enough to blackmail anyone.'

Again Malcolm and Justine exchanged looks.

'I've learned all about the Borders gambling circuit (including where and how it still operates) and how, as in all such set ups, there were targets initially allowed a winning streak but then to experience considerable losses including their homes and then held further by photographs of them with prostitutes. One such was Andy Dickson, an outstanding poet, in a set-up operated on your father's instruction by his employee Peter McDonald.'

'If people gamble they risk a great deal. No one else is to blame.'

'There was a very good reason why your father did this, and you know what it is.'

There was silence.

'The thing is, Malcolm, only now have I grasped that you knew everything already, and that you, Justine, almost certainly know as well. I have not been bringing you any semblance of news. I also believe you have no responsibility for any of it. The suicide of a poet whose wife had left him and who had lost all his money is tragic and the poetry magazines and television will want to make something of it, calling it something like the greatest theft in the history of literature.

'I dare say it will be possible for you to plead ignorance and to tell the story in such a way to make your father seem like a kindly old rogue, who helped Dickson out financially in return for his poems, especially as it was always your intention to come clean about the the authorship once it had been revealed to you by an interfering Welsh woman, or something like that. Allegations of historic child abuse are now two a penny, difficult to prove and in any case it was all a long time ago. But I have no idea what Challen and his wife will do with it, though I don't believe it will be nothing. It's with them and not me that Justine will begin to earn her corn.'

'Do you think they will want a financial settlement?' asked Malcolm

'Darling, Charlie can't possibly know that,' said Justine.

Malcolm looked towards Charlotte.

'I'm afraid you will be wasted as an au pair. You hide your considerable intelligence behind a naïve exterior unbelievably well. You have also been most respectful to us and I thank you for that.'

'You will be leaving here when?'

'Next week I'm relieved to say. We shall recover but whether Jedburgh will I don't know.'

'Oh I do. They're good people and communities are often remarkably resilient, and if there's notoriety it might even bring even more tourists to be boost the economy or is that too cynical of me?'

She looked at her watch.

'I must go. Someone rather special is waiting for me.'

They stood, shook hands and she wished them a happy married life together, before driving back towards the town.

'I was very tempted,' said Justine, 'here and now to offer her a job that would be infinitely better paid and more satisfying than being an au pair, and I might yet do so. Not only is she good at her job, she seems to me totally fearless.'

Zolko had been far from her mind during the session with Malcolm and Justine but now it was they who were forgotten. All of a sudden her anxieties were present in force. Would he be there? Might he have changed his mind and could not break with the Church? Might his parents have called him back and talked him out of being so stupid. Thought after thought came faster than ever as she made her way to the pick-up point – the Supermarket car park. As she approached she couldn't see him and she was only 10 minutes late. Surely he had not done a runner. As she drove into the car park itself she saw him sitting on a wall in his t-shirt and shorts, looking as if he didn't have a care in the the world. He looked like someone who was happy and utterly content with his lot.

She stopped the car, steadied herself with a rapid glance at the driving mirror and opened the door. Zolko had seen her from the first moment she had pulled into the car park and immediately began shaking with terror and joy. Here she was! Here was the beginning of his life and watching her leaving her car he was spellbound by her beauty. He could hold back no more, leapt off the wall and ran towards her now running towards him. The former priest could not help thinking of the disciples running to be with Jesus when he first called them.

Charlotte and Zolko arrived at the house just outside Melrose where Adam, Anaïs and Jerome lived. They had stopped for lunch at a pub and spent most of the time telling one another how much in love they were, though they also managed a Ploughman's lunch each, though neither ate their onions!

'Do these ploughman's lunches go back to medieval times?' asked Zolko.

'I'm sorry to say my darling, that they were first invented in the 1960s.'

'Oh, those poor medieval ploughmen, they would never know what they were missing.'

As yet Charlotte had not got round to informing Zolko of their sleeping arrangements this evening and thought that now was as good a time as any.'

'I have something to tell you,' she began, 'something important, wonderful and frightening.'

'Ok.'

'The initial arrangements I set up with regard to you being at the farm with Anne-Marie and Ed have had to be changed, though I'm not quite sure why, and Anne-Marie said she would explain later, with the result that we shall both sleeping tonight at Anaïs's and Adam's house, and that means doing so in one bed together. Of course if you are uneasy about that, I am told the floor next to the bed is very comfortable.'

'You put me in an extremely difficult position,' came the reply. 'The floor or with you? However shall I decide? I know. It would be wrong of me to leave you all alone in a strange bed in a strange house, so I will take the risk of sharing the bed in the hope that you might be willing to lead and teach me.'

'You know I will and remember we are learning and loving together. I have only ever been treated as worthless. Love, such as I feel for you, will be patient with us both.'

Adam and Jerome opened the door, both of them smiling.

'Hello Zolko, welcome, and of course Charlotte. Have you got luggage to bring in?'

'Just these two bags. I've packed away my books and they are being stored though mostly they are theology and philosophy and I can more than do without them.'

'I can well imagine. Anyway, come in and make yourself completely at home. I shall make some tea.'

Adam left Jerome with Charlotte and Zolko but he made straight for Zolko and was completely at ease with him, and he with her. He also talked to him in a strangely effective way to which he listened and laughed. Charlotte was impressed and left them to help Adam with drinks.

'Is Jerome ok?'

'Yeah. He's with Mary Poppins.'

'Sorry?'

'A side of Zolko I didn't know about: the natural child minder.'

They took the drinks into the sitting room to find Zolko and Jerome both stretched out on the carpets on their backs giggling for all they were worth.

Jerome wanted to stay with Zolko whilst he had his tea and Adam answered the landline. He returned to the room and was completely ignored by his son who was only relating to Zolko.

'That was Anaïs to say that she's had a cancellation and instead of coming here she wants us to meet her at the farm where we shall be eating. She also said you should both bring your bags and that there will be a full explanation at supper.'

Charlotte received a text, her mobile making a sound immediately interesting to Jerome.

'Good heavens,' said Charlotte.

'Yes?' said Zolko.

'It's from Justine whom I met this morning, the fiancée of Malcolm McHugh. She is a corporate lawyer in the City of London. This is a job offer from her, to work as an investigator for her company based in Edinburgh. Pay is £60k.'

Zolko went pale.

'£60k? Is that the sort of money you're earning for what you've been doing in Jedburgh?' he asked.

She laughed.

'In my dreams, though I should be awarded a bonus for kidnapping and falling totally in love with a man I met there, and that reminds me, I imagine that your disappearance will be known by now. Do we have to place a blanket over your head as we move around outside?'

He laughed.

'As long as you don't ever cover your beautiful face. That I couldn't stand.'

'O God,' said Adam. 'You two are even sloppier than Anaïs and me!'

They all laughed, even Jerome.

They travelled together in Charlotte's car as Anaïs would bring back Jerome and Adam and the baby seat plugged straight into the car.

'This is the long lane from the main road to the farm,' said Charlotte, 'and ahead you can see some of the buildings. The sheep are spread out over the hills and most of the ladies will be inside the parlour being milked.'

'Parlour?' What a wonderful name. It's like the way in a hospital you speak of an operating "theatre".'

Charlotte smiled.

'Don't forget, my darling, that hopefully on Monday I should be paying a visit to the theatre.'

They passed the brand new gate and entered the yard where she parked the car. Adam lifted the baby seat out with Jerome asleep and headed for the back door, Zolko and Charlotte holding back.

'You may laugh, but doing something like this, having a meeting on a farm, is almost totally outside my experience. I am used to meetings when I am in charge and so this is both exciting and terrifying.'

'Oh my darling Zolko, they will love you, and although it is an overused cliché, just be yourself. You can live fully now without titles or a position in which everyone looks up to you, not least because they have to. These are very good people, and so are you, and I love you.'

'I love you too Charlotte, but where did you learn such wisdom?'

'Who knows?' she laughed. 'Now let's go in.'

Zolko was warmly welcomed as Charlotte knew she would be. Rhona and Andrew had milked earlier than usual and were already here. Only Anaïs was not yet here. Anne-Marie was preparing food for them all. Rhona reported that there was a problem with the the electrics in the dairy and would to call someone to come.

'Why don't I do it?' said Zolko.

Everyone looked at him and he laughed.

'You are obviously shocked but in seminary we were all supposed to acquire a skill which had nothing to do with theology and philosophy. And now I must name-drop I fear. I come from Gdansk which you may know of as the birthplace of Solidarity. My father, as an electrician in the shipyard, worked closely with a man called Lech Wałęsa, and when I was born he became my godfather, and later became our President and won the Nobel Prize for Peace. So when offered the chance I studied electronics and became a fully qualified electrician.'

The gathering was stunned by what they had just heard.

'That is an amazing story, Zolko,' said Ed, 'truly amazing. Your god-father is, with Mandela, someone who can truly be called great and has made a real change to our world for the good.'

'Yeah, but can you fix the electrics in our dairy?' asked Rhona.

They all dissolved in laughter and at that moment the door opened and in came Anaïs.

'My arrival is not that funny surely,' she said.

'Your arrival is wonderful as always,' said Anne-Marie, 'but we will explain later.'

'I thought at first we should eat before everything is explained but I would prefer to get it over with as soon as possible,' said Ed. 'I began feeling unwell some time ago and eventually consulted my GP who decided I needed tests. They were extensive but the bottom line, as the accountants say, is that I have been diagnosed with something called Non-Hodgkins Lymphoma, a cancer of the lymph glands. It is graded 1 to 4, the latter most serious, and as I begin treatment I am a 2. I shall begin chemotherapy on Monday which will not be at all pleasant but my best long-term hope lies in a bone marrow transplant for which I have been placed on the national register seeking a potential donor. During chemotherapy I will be especially susceptible to infection and my consultant has said that I need to be away from the farm completely. That will not mean that Anne-Marie is intending to dispose of the farm nor, after my chemo is completed that she cannot return to part-time work when she is ready to do so, but it does mean we shall need to find somewhere to live nearby. I am not in pain but at times I don't feel 100% and my psychotherapy training will have to go on the back-burner for a little while, but I have good reason to think I may last quite a bit longer.'

'Ed, that's so unfair,' said Adam.

'I wouldn't argue with that,' he replied, 'but these things are completely random and in life we simply have to accept what nature has given us. For some it's far worse, and especially so in children. I turn once again to some of the philosophers I once spent my days learning and then teaching. Ironically, those from whom I can learn most in the face of this are the philosophers of ancient Greece, the greatest of them all. Most modern philosophy has disappeared up its own backside, and that is the best place for it. Would you agree, Zolko?'

'I do. I always thought that letting us read the ancient Greeks in seminary was dangerous, for they unsettled me and like you I love them, but I'm a humble electrician so what do I know?'

This was lost on Anaïs.

I'll explain later,' said Adam, 'but it happens to be true and also an outstanding child minder.'

She looked even more puzzled.

Anne-Marie needed to speak.

'We can have lots of existential discussion over this wonderful cold meal I have prepared but there are some practicalities we must deal with. Anaïs already knows about them as we spoke a little earlier on the phone. So after we have eaten, Ed, Gregor and myself will be going to stay with Anaïs in Melrose. Charlie and Zolko will move in here, and Andrew will share with Rhona. I've made up the bed for the electrician and our intrepid investigator, so there we are. Now let's eat and if any of you need to know more about Ed's illness, look it up on Wikipedia. Now tuck in as this may be the last meal I serve you here for some time to come.'

Chapter 17

Charlotte insisted that the clearing away and washing up be done by her, though Andrew helped as Zolko was going with Rhona to look at the electrics in the dairy.

'Did you know all about Zolko's heritage?'

'Not at all. I was as amazed as the rest of you.'

'I wonder the catholic church will cope with his leaving the priesthood and, even worse, getting together with a Welsh girl. Obviously they would have fully approved of a Scot,'

'Unless she was called Paula!'

'Yes, I can't imagine Uncle Lech would be wild about that.'

'Do you know anything about being gay or lesbian in Poland?'

'As in many countries which once were strongly catholic, it isn't illegal in any way at all, though same-sex parents can't adopt. I'm sure Zolko will be able to tell you very much more about it, but the influence of the Catholic Church remains considerable, whether for good or bad. I'm told there is still a strong after-shock from the Polish pope John Paul 1, who was undoubtedly a major figure in the collapse of communism, but in terms of morality was a very hard line conservative. Ironic really, given that now we know something of what his priests were doing.'

Rhona was watching Zolko at work and felt greatly reassured that he seemed to know exactly what he was doing. He pointed to something.

'It has burnt out and needs to be replaced. I can do a temporary fix for you to deal with your milk in the morning, but I shall need to go and obtain the switch as soon as possible. You will be able to tell me where I might find a good electrical shop where I can also buy some tools. My reason for saying that, Rhona, is that I regret to say that your electrics, all of them here, need attention and it is something of a wonder that they haven't crashed out before now. Perhaps tomorrow, after I have finished the repair here, you will permit me to do a thorough check. Even now with this switch blown the rest of the electrics will have greater pressure upon them, and I can imagine you and Andrew will not enjoy milking by hand.'

'I suspect you may be right.'

They laughed together.

'I wonder, however, Zolko, if you could quickly look at a new alarm box fitted in the kitchen this last week. Perhaps that has caused this.'

'Of course, but just allow me five minutes to do what I can with this and make a temporary bridge. I must get some tools.'

Once he had done it they went into Rhona's kitchen and Zolko opened the box whilst Rhona explained what it was intended to do.

'It's been put on the same circuit as the dairy meaning that you are quite right. Any problem here will find the least resistance in the circuit and overload it. I need to make some changes, not least in re-routing it. Some of the materials they have used could have been better and that will not have helped. My problem, Rhona, is I cannot do this without the tools that would make it safe for me to do so. With them it would be complex but perfectly possible.

'There is a major problem however, and it would be the same in Poland as here. I am sure you have an electrician you employ on a regular basis or a firm of electricians. I can do all these pieces or work for you and at the same time do a full-scale electrical check on the two houses and all the outhouses, and they will be done properly, but you must ask yourself if in so doing I will cause offence and they may not work for you in future when you might need them in an emergency. Oh, and I will not charge anything other for anything expensive in the way of parts.'

Rhona laughed.

'You drive a hard bargain, Zolko.'

She held out her hand.

'Welcome to your first contract in Scotland.'

Zolko and Andrew passed one another.

'Sleep well,' said Andrew.

'I hope not!'

They both laughed as they made their way to their respective domains.

Charlotte and Zolko both spent some of the night in tears, but they were tears of ecstasy and joy, and even when they had dressed and were having breakfast they clung to one other.

'We may have to explore other possibilities tonight, my darling. I don't know what Mrs Muldoon is planning but it may leave me in pain or discomfort.'

'Yes, I've realised that, and it may be even more the case if you have surgery, but my love for you is so great I shall contain myself if need be for the greater good.'

'I don't think it will come to that – trust me,' she replied with a mischievous look.

'Of course we could go back upstairs and have another go.'

'Zolko, behave yourself! Actually I would love that too, but Mrs Muldoon might not be quite as keen for us to do so.'

'I see what you mean. Besides which I have electrical work to begin here. Rhona is adding me to the farm vehicle insurance so I can go and get what I need.'

'You will save the farm a lot of money and I had the opportunity to learn something about your handiwork in the night . . .'

'I am going red with embarrassment.'

'No you're not. It struck me that you might ask Rhona if you can learn the art of milking cows. She's lost Ed from the rota and I think you'd be good.'

'For what it is worth, you have pretty impressive hands too.'

'I really will turn red in a moment.'

You must have been out in the sun.'

'I must have been with the person I love.'

They were on the verge of hugging when Rhona walked in.

'That's what I like to see my tups and yows doing. Good morning. Two items of news. The first is that you're now on the farm vehicle insurance so you can get off to B & Q or Howdens on the Industrial Estate in Galashiels. We have an account with Howdens so I've got a letter for you authorising your use of the farm credit card meaning you won't have to pay. When we get back we'll put you to work.'

'And the second item of news?' asked Charlotte.

'You Zolko are famous; well, you got a mention on the local news this morning – "the priest who disappeared" or something like that. They interviewed your Archbishop who totally denied the rumour that this was because you were hiding from the police because they wanted to interview you on the matter of child abuse, and said that the reason seems to be because he has met a young woman and fallen in love.'

'Thank you Archbishop,' said Zolko.

'I would suggest you keep your wits about you in public. The police won't take any notice because you've committed no crime, though our former electricians might not agree, but anyone recognising you from the papers or tv, might want their moment of fame by informing the press.'

'As you know my family helped my godfather bring down communism. I shall not be intimidated by a local journalist.'

He turned to Charlotte.

'My darling I will go because this new boss is very strict and I am terrified of her, but you and Anaïs will collect me at 12.30. Yes?"

They gave each other a long kiss, at the end of which Rhona said, 'If you'd only told me, I'd have brought a book to read!'

Charlotte drove the short distance to see Anaïs whilst the fugitive electrician went in search of tools. Charlotte smiled all the way to Melrose. After Zolko had left, Rhona had told her how relieved she was that their electrics were now in his hands, as she had been dreading a return visit from the electrician, Anastasia, who clearly had made a lesbian pass at her. "I may be in love with all my ladies but I am not that way inclined", she had said, and Charlotte could not keep a straight face and added, "So it's Andrew for you", to which she had replied, "I think I might stand a better chance with Anastasia than with Andrew, if you know what I mean".

Anaïs was outside in the garden with Jerome as Charlotte arrived.

'Good morning, Charlotte. You are looking good.'

'Yes and I have every reason for that.'

'Let's go inside. No Zolko?'

'Rhona has him at work already. He says the electrics are not in a good state, so he has gone to buy a set of the tools he will need.'

'Did you know about this skill?'

'Not at all, nor about his amazing heritage. What a man his godfather is and has been. Are Ed and Anne-Marie in?'

'No they have a couple of things to sort out at the hospital with regard to beginning chemo and also with saving sperm for IVF if needed. Anne-Marie, in her unique way as a farmer is well used to AI and says she will lend him a helping hand! Apparently it's not always easy for men to perform by themselves in a room in a hospital.'

They laughed.

Anaïs had prepared coffee, good French coffee. Jerome was playing on the floor.

'I hear Zolko and Jerome got on well together.'

'Oh yes. He comes from a large family and there were always little ones to be cared for.'

'You have been offered the chance by Justine to move into big time investigation. £60k is good money but perhaps we should talk about it after you have brought me fully up-to-date with the completion of your work in Jedburgh.'

Charlotte recounted all that had happened since last they had spoken together, but focussing above all on the meeting with Malcolm and Justine.

'You must have been somewhat taken aback to find a lawyer with him, even though she is also his fiancée.'

'"Taken aback" is a something of an understatement. She was very much a Sloan Ranger as once might have been said: glamorous, wealthy, well-connected and extremely posh.'

'Oh. It's not a phrase I have ever head before.'

'It's fallen out of fashion. People apparently used it when Princess Diana appeared on the scene. Justine used a little legal language but they were both honest with me, as far I could tell.'

'I'm sure they recognised what you have managed to achieve in a very short time and were impressed, hence the job offer. I must hand it to you, Charlotte, you have done a first-class job, and you recognised also that they knew everything anyway. Not threatening them in any was very important. Justine's judgement as to your quality and ability will have been obvious. I have looked her up on the web and she is a serious high flyer. So have you decided how you will reply?'

'Anaïs, I trust you implicitly, and there is no way, other than sending an acknowledgment saying I would reply in a day or two, that I would make such a decision without talking it through with you and Zolko.'

'And what does he say?'

'£60,000 made him a little dizzy, but he thinks the most important conversation should be with you.'

'You can tell him that it makes me dizzy too, given that my clients pay me less than £100 each time we meet, and often quite a lot less. I so look forward to getting to know him. Is he good in bed?'

'Anaïs! What a question.'

'I'm a French psychotherapist, so I ask such questions often in my work.'

'We've only had one night to test the mattress, and he had to be slowed down and then it was a wonder for me and also for him.'

'Does he know that if you have your operation you will have to discover diversity?'

'When I told him he smiled and said he liked the sound of that.'

Anaïs's eyebrows rose in pleasure.

'What are we going to do about Edward Challen who sent you to discover what he mostly knew already, though I'm bound to say his choice of you for the job was inspired? You will be presenting him with the evidence and certainty he lacked to completely destroy the name of Archie McHugh and give the true attribution to Anderson Dickson, as no doubt his daughter longs for. This will emerge first in the newspapers and then on television, always holding back the full account for the book, and possibly a new version of the poems of Anderson Samuel Taylor Dickson. At the very most you will get mentioned in the Acknowledgements. So we have to work out in financial terms just how much what you possess is worth to Mr Challen. After all, you have done the legwork and gathered the material, and could make a name for yourself by taking it to a publisher Anne-Marie would know, and not only a name but a hefty advance and royalties, with Mr Challen mentioned in the Acknowledgements. The latter will involve more work, writing it up in full and negotiating with publishers, though you might well risk losing Justine's job offer which I imagine is also there to encourage you not to be tempted to do this. I am sure she is enough of an actuary to have worked out the odds.'

'Are you suggesting that she might be untrustworthy?'

'No. Definitely not. Being true to her word will matter a great deal.'

'In which case, before I accept or decline, I need to know considerably more about the job.'

'Yes.'

'And in the meantime I want to shed everything about McHugh and Jedburgh, which means dealing with Edward Challen.'

'As I said to you before, we need to be canny about this – Oh, you must admit that "canny" is a good word for me to have learned – and use a literary agent to negotiate on your behalf. You must now shed your hire car but you will continue to need a car no matter what else you decide to do, so I think Mr Challen will need to know that you are worth a car to him, a new car I think. I shall ask for £35,000 and settle for £30,000.'

'Will you get it?'

'Do you know, I rather think I will.'

Jerome had slept through most of the foregoing conversation and now Anaïs picked him up from the floor, opened her blouse and put him to the breast.

'I thought you said it was weaning time,' said Charlotte.

'You are right. Tomorrow!'

They both laughed gently.

Once Jerome and his mum were satisfied she burped him and changed his nappy before dressing him for the trip into Edinburgh, by way of the farm, where Rhona and Zolko had been doing a great deal of getting mucky as he explored the antiquated electrics in the milking parlour. They chatted a great deal about her love for farming, and he tried to describe something of what he knew about agricultural life in his homeland.

'Will you miss the life of the Church?'

'No. I will try to tell you why, but if you think I am only speaking nonsense, then please accept the possibility that I probably am. Last night I made love for the first time ever. Charlotte was wonderful, gentle and understanding. As a priest I was supposed to know about such things to advise and teach those who of course know infinitely more than me. The Church makes fools of us all especially in ways related to sex, whether gay, lesbian or trans.

'I also hated preaching, telling people to live as we directed and we were now supposed to do it at every Mass, which some idiotic Pope decided. Nor did I ever like being called Father, especially by those many years older than me.

'But most of all I'm glad to be away from it because I came to realise that religion was totally obscuring God. That couldn't be right.

'Finally, I was lonely and wanting to share my life with another but I knew it couldn't just be anyone. You might imagine that someone with her past couldn't possibly be the right person, but immediately I knew she was and when told all about her past,

I felt even more that we were made for each other.'

'And will the Church hierarchy be after you?'

'It will great fun if they try. Oh no, Rhona just look at this junction box. It could go at any time and then you would have to milk by hand for a few days.'

'Can you do anything about it?'

'Rhona, is the Pope a Catholic?'

And they both dissolved in laughter.

'As you know I have to go to hospital in a few minutes' time. I will make it secure on a temporary basis now and when Andrew gets back from his trip to the abattoir with the pigs, you could go into Howdens and get a couple of things, then tomorrow morning I will do a permanent job.'

'Zolko, you're a wonder. I am a bit confused about the religion-God issue, but all the rest I fully understand. Having you here with us is an unexpected wonder.'

When Charlotte, Anaïs and Jerome arrived they had a quick sandwich made by Zolko and set off into Edinburgh, with Zolko clean and smelling sweet. He and Charlotte sat in the back with Jerome in his front baby seat. As with every hospital in the United Kingdom, trying to find somewhere to park was hell, and eventually Anaïs opted for a multi-storey, a five-minute walk from the hospital.

With Anaïs attending above all to Jerome in his buggy, Charlotte and Zolko walked a little ahead, hand in hand, something new for both of them, as Charlotte pointed out.

'Are you nervous?' Zolko asked Charlotte.

'Well, if you are a woman you have to get used from an early age to medical procedures downstairs, if I may describe it so.'

Zolko feared that in starting to laugh he might never stop.

'Well, may I say how beautiful things are in the basement, but upstairs too.'

'You may,' she replied, and kissed him. 'The procedure today is relatively straightforward but done under sedation, less because it would hurt, but so the doctor can work without the patient wriggling at what might be uncomfortable. If I'm nervous about anything it's about the result, but at least I'll have you with me then.'

They entered the hospital and then found the department and were shown to the waiting area. Having slept in the car Jerome was awake and interested in what was going on, as well as being a source of attraction to nurses and others who stopped to speak to him. After about 10 minutes a nurse appeared and called Charlotte. Zolko and she kissed before the nurse led her away. Charlotte seemed much calmer than he, not least because he was now at the mercy of Anaïs whose reputation as an asker of penetrating questions had gone before her.

'Sitting here for 90 minutes or so won't be anything but tedious. Shall we try and find a café somewhere nearby? If Jerome wants to make a noise of any sort it will be easier for him and us there than here. We can make sure we are back long before Charlotte has recovered from sedation.'

'Yes, that would wise. Sitting in a hospital waiting room is soul-destroying.'

They settled on the first they came to, the Aroma Coffee Bar, run by the NHS. Jerome was now wide awake and had settled on Zolko's knee quite happily.

'You are clearly most talented, what with being a qualified electrician and totally able to keep at ease an easily bored baby full of energy.'

'He's a delight.'

'Because I too come from a country that sometimes still calls itself catholic, I have met over the years many priests. Forgive me if I say I have not been too impressed with them, but I can imagine that you were a faithful and hardworking priest.'

'So were most of them when they began. They had ideals they sought to live up to and enjoyed the challenges presented by pastoral care. Then, and slowly at first, the institution of the Church began to grind them down. Often at just two days' notice they could be moved and felt that the work they had done counted for nothing. More and more they will have striven to keep an outward face, behind which there was enormous pain and emptiness. They will have seen too the massive processes of secularisation at work as people who once professed a faith realise they can get on without perfectly well. Some took their housekeepers or other women to bed, many will have drunk more than is good for them, and some, alas, fearful of adult sexuality have turned to children, as we know. I saw all this coming and I had simply no idea of what might be a possible way out, until I met Charlotte.'

'Could it have been any young attractive woman?'

'Oh no. I know a few like that in both Warsaw and Hawick and I have always enjoyed their company, but at once with Charlotte I knew, probably because she has had to endure such terrible things in life in Swansea.'

'Because you felt sorry for her, and that the pastor in you sensed a lost sheep?'

'Good heavens, no. I don't feel at all sorry for her because that past no longer exists. If Mrs Muldoon is able to give us something to hope for then the present will have triumphed over the past. And if she cannot it will make no difference. I did not make love to a prostitute last night but to the woman I love. As a psychotherapist I'm sure you will pour scorn on all things coming from religion but I know that when I heard confessions, whether formally in Church or informally, I had one aim and that was to release the knots that so easily bind us to the past. I cannot of course say that I always succeeded and some people still wished to rely on magic week by week but I tried my best and sometimes it worked.'

'Zolko, as a human being I would pour scorn on nothing that brings life to people, even religion, and I'm sure you know Jung thought confession in the catholic church a potentially rich source of therapy. I don't find doctrines even remotely helpful, and I can't stand going to Church. I rebelled when I was nine and haven't returned since and I'm not likely to return, not least because in my work I see many casualties of religion, all religions.'

'I can well imagine, as I am one too.'

'Can you foresee the possibility that you might come to miss it, or regret leaving?'

'I will answer with a questions of my own: do you miss period pains when they have passed.'

She smiled broadly.

'For a man to think that, let alone a former priest, is something of a miracle in itself.'

'Ought we to go?'

Zolko sought to pass Jerome to his mum, but he utterly refused to be handed over.

'I'm perfectly happy with the arrangement,' said Anaïs laughing.

They made their way back in the hospital and to the department.

'Do you have any thoughts about the next stage of life?'

'The Farm electrics are in a terrible state and I am very much hoping Rhona will have been able to obtain what I asked for so I can keep the milking going. It really is near to total failure and that could lead to a fire quite easily. Whether I can use my skills on other farms and communities I will have to see.'

'What would your illustrious godfather say about this change in your life?'

'He would tell me off, and then wish me well. He is a great

man.'

A nurse approached and spoke to Zolko.

'Mrs Muldoon is ready.'

Jerome was clearly aghast at the loss of Zolko and began crying, an opportune moment for a breast to appear. As she had anticipated he was soon asleep. She kept him there and took our her phone and dialled a number.

'Hello. Is that Mr Edward Challen?

Chapter 18

The nurse opened the door and led Zolko in. Mrs Muldoon and Charlotte were seated and Mrs Muldoon invited him to do likewise.

'I'm very pleased to meet you,' she said. Charlotte has been telling me that you are a man of many talents. We are always short of good electricians here at the hospital.'

'Thank you,' said Zolko. 'I'll keep that information in mind, though at the moment I am enjoying working with cows and farmers.'

'Many farmers are good gynaecologists if not quite so hygienic.'

They laughed.

'When I see vets on television,' she continued, 'I am in awe at the range of their skills. No doctor has the same capacity to do all they do. All the same Charlotte you will be pleased to know that I am not recommending you be treated by either a farmer or a vet, though you may well have been better served when you were operated on in Swansea following what happened to you. I think you said she was a young registrar doing weekend cover and I have no doubt that she was seeking to do her best given that the bruising and damage must have been considerable, but no registrar in this hospital would have acted as she did and would have immediately called a consultant. Ironically, in the circumstances, this has worked well for you if you did but know it, because I am certain that in surgery I can undo some of what she did and you will be able once again to have periods (bad luck!), but more especially to become pregnant.'

'Oh, that's wonderful,' said Charlotte, her eyes already full of tears, and in a moment Zolko was out of his chair and holding her and kissing her face.

'I shall be able after surgery to give you some sort of idea as to how easy it might be to get pregnant normally, or whether you might eventually need to consider IVF, but I think you should try as often as you can just to see. After Monday's surgery you will be quite tender for a few days and so vaginal intercourse should be avoided but I feel confident you both have imaginations, so my advice would be to use them.

'So we shall expect you on Monday morning at 7-00 and please no food or drink after midnight, and all being well you will be ready to return home by 9.00 on Tuesday morning when I shall be able to discharge you.'

'Oh Mrs Muldoon however can we thank you?' said Zolko.

'Let's wait until it's all over first. Then you can come and take a look at the state of my electrics at home. My husband has a doctorate in linguistics and can barely change a plug.'

'It's a deal.'

They all shook hands.

After they had left the the room, the nurse said to Mrs Muldoon, 'You made it sound straightforward.'

'In a way it is thanks to two things. The first is that the poor registrar was out of her depth and the other is that it happened recently enough for me to undo it. She's a lovely young woman but what she has been through day after day to feed a drugs habit she has since broken free from is worse than terrible. Most shocking of all, and I will spare you the ghastly detail, is what was done to her by a detective sergeant who some days later raped his own teenage daughter, but now happily, is dead, following a mysterious alleged suicide in prison.'

'O my God!'

'*He* may well have come in the form of Zolko. I hope so. They both deserve good things and I don't hold with compulsory celibacy.'

'Neither do I when they look like he does!'

Anaïs shared their joy as they made their way back to the car and then to the farm.

'What we now need is some good news about Ed, some luck with the marrow bone list,' said Anaïs.

'I am aware that they were both making light of it last night when they told us, but is Stage 2 particularly worrying? Is Stage 3 inevitable?' said Zolko.

'When we spoke with them last night at home, they were both remarkably up-beat. Apparently with treatment that is not delayed the chances are good. But with a bone marrow infusion the chances of a full recovery are considerably higher. All that can be hoped for is that the online register turns up possibilities.'

'I don't know my blood group,' said Charlotte, 'and when I had my operation in Swansea nothing was mentioned about it, so I imagine I'm simply common.'

'Me too,' said Zolko, 'I am A positive and so are most others.'

'Including me,' said Anaïs. 'Now changing the subject. Whilst you were with Mrs Muldoon and Jerome went to sleep, I was able to phone your friend Mr Challen on behalf of my client Charlotte Holly, explaining that I own and run an exclusive literary agency with offices both here and in my native France. I said that you were now my client and I would be representing you in all dealings with him. You have a most interesting phrase in English which cannot be translated into French: "He was gobsmacked".'

'I bet he was,' said Charlotte. 'But what if he checks up your office in France?'

'That would not be a problem. I gave him a particular number to ring which will be answered by someone who will confirm all I have told him.'

'Intelligence?'

'You need not concern yourself with such things. It just means every eventuality is covered. So I described all that you have brought together and said it was very good stuff, the sort that will receive a great deal of attention from the press and television. He tried to play it down, so I said that if it wasn't that important to him I would look to make it available to the highest bidder including the Sunday newspapers. I said I would have no option to do this as it is important for it to be in the public domain, unless of course he wished to make a bid himself.'

'Tell me, Anaïs,' asked Zolko, 'do you have any friends?'

She laughed.

'I have the most wonderful husband in the world, and the most wonderful son, though he is behaving like a traitor with you.'

'So, did he rise to the bait?' asked Charlotte.

'Of course and there was no likelihood that we would not. At first he feigned shock when I mentioned £35,000, but when we settled on £32,000 he knew exactly what it was he doing and how much profit he will make.'

'Oh Anaïs, please always be on my side,' said Charlotte plaintively.

'And mine,' added Zolko.

They were now on the lane up to the farm and Anaïs almost stopped and turned back as they drew near to the farmyard, for there in the middle of the yard was an outside broadcast vehicle for BBC Scotland.'

With a single voice they said:

'Merde,' said Anaïs with considerable force.

'Gówna!' yelled Zolko even louder.

'Shit,' shouted Charlotte, loudest of all.

Anaïs drove round the offending vehicle and turned left round to the back of the dairy.

'Do you feel up to a tv interview?'

'It probably has to happen sometime, so why not now, but only if Charlotte is willing to be with me, hand in hand.'

'Yes. Definitely.'

'In which case go for it. If you want to make a real entrance you should carry Jerome with you!'

They smiled.

'I'm hoping that before long we will have one of our own,' said Zolko.

The walked back around the front of the dairy, where a woman with a microphone, someone with a camera and another man were waiting for them.

'Hello,' said Charlotte, 'and welcome to the best woman-owned and run farm in Scotland.'

This seemed to throw the BBC crew.

'Er, well thank you. Doesn't that make it an even stranger place for a runaway priest to hide?'

'I'm neither a runaway nor hiding from anyone. This is where I live and work with my partner, the woman I love. That's how most people choose to live their lives, so why not me?'

'But haven't you taken a vow of celibacy?'

'I hadn't met Charlotte then. In life things change. People find that work once chosen no longer suits them, couples once vowing permanency find themselves needing to be released from that by a judge.'

'Your Archbishop says there is a process you should have gone through.'

'He's a nice man, don't you think? But he is not my

Archbishop for I have none and I shall not exercise the ministry of a priest again. The process you refer to is designed to grind you down by lasting for ever. Life's too short for that.'

'Will you continue to go to Church?'

'No, but I will continue to take my relationship with God totally seriously, but you don't need a Church or even a religion for that.'

'Are you happy?'

'I love and adore Charlotte and I have every reason to think she feels the same. I think that answers your question. Yes, I can understand the Church gets its ecclesiastical knickers in a twist about what I have done, in case it encourages others, and I very much hope it does, but that's just tough. Now please I am hungry and it's my turn to cook. So thank you for coming and I hope I've not been a disappointment to you, but I'm just another man who's fallen in love.'

They turned and walked towards their door and went into the kitchen.

'My darling,' said Charlotte, 'that was brilliant and I especially welcome hearing that you are cooking this evening.'

'Ah,' replied Zolko, 'I thought you might have heard that. Well, it so happens that when I was in Galashiels I paid a swift visit into Asda and acquired ready meals for this evening, so if I put them into the microwave, I will have fulfilled my obligations.'

'Zolko?'

'Yes my darling.'

How is that you speak English with a far larger vocabulary than I do?'

'Two reasons. The first is that once I learned English at school, I read many books in English. The second reason is that of course you are Welsh and so cannot speak or understand properly!'

'I'm going to hit you.'

'Ah, the first signs of a change of mind.'

The hit became a very long kiss and cuddle on the sofa and the ready meals were somewhat delayed!

Rhona had also used far from lady-like language when the BBC had arrived and she and Andrew wanted to get on with milking. She had said that the person they were looking for was not available and advised them to make an appointment if they wished to meet Mr Zolkiewski. But they were clearly not intending to leave for the time being and the ladies were waiting outside the parlour. She could have called the police and asked them to accompany the BBC crew to the end of the lane, but she hadn't time right now. After milking, if they were still there, it would be a different matter altogether but when she emerged it was gone and she decided not to disturb the neighbours!

On Saturday morning Zolko was up especially early to make sure the electrics were still permitting the milking though he decided to wait until all the cattle were back in their field before beginning his labours of the day in earnest, but he stayed a while watching what was happening, noticing not only Rhona and Andrew as they worked, but that the cows knew what was expected of them. He was greatly impressed by them all, but his priority had to be keeping the show on the road and although he had told Rhona how things were, he wasn't wholly convinced she had grasped the perilous state of the farm electrics.

He set to work with a vengeance after breakfast whilst Charlotte went to the supermarket with Rhona to do the grocery shopping. About an hour into his work he heard the sound of a vehicle stopping in the yard, so he stopped what he was doing and went out of the dairy to meet whoever it was. It was a woman in overalls.

'Hello,' said Kolko, 'can I help you?'

'Yes, I'm the farm's electrician and I've come to check up on a new alarm system I put in for Rhona.'

'Really? Well, Rhona isn't here I'm afraid. What is it you want to check up on?'

'I put in the control box in the kitchen so I'd like to check on it.'

'Good idea. I'll come in with you.'

He led her into the kitchen and gave her space. She opened the box.

'What's happened here? I didn't leave it like this.'

'I'm pretty sure Rhona hasn't touched it, though I know she was rather cross at having to get up in the night because you installed it with positive and negative reversed in the lighting switch.'

She turned and looked at Kolko.

'Did you do this?

'It couldn't be left as you left it.'

'Who are you?'

'I'm the farm's new electrician.'

'I don't think so. My firm is the company used by this farm and there is no other. I shall have to test the whole system now just to make sure that what you have done isn't more likely to lead to a serious failure and considerable consequences.'

'If you feel the need to do so, please go ahead, and then I shall take you in the dairy and show you what your firm has missed completely there, and after that into the milking parlour in which I am doing a major electrical refit because your firm had not bothered to take the time to look properly or test the system, perhaps because whoever it was could not stand the smell. For me, it's the whole system that stinks, not least because your firm has failed to do its job properly. Would you like a coffee and please tell me your name?'

She was completely taken aback by this development in the conversation.

'Anastasia Watson.'

'Hello Anastasia, I'm Zolko.'

'That's unusual.'

'I'm from Poland which is where I qualified as an electrician in case you wondered, and I live next door with my wonderful partner Charlotte. Let's go there and I'll make us both a drink.'

He led her from one kitchen to another and put the kettle on.

'I thought Anne-Marie lived here.'

'She did and one day soon we hope, will live here again. Her husband Ed has an illness especially susceptible to infection and his doctor thought it best he live away from the farm for a while, though she still comes most days with their son Gregor to make sure everything is done properly.'

'I imagine Rhona makes sure that is so. I am told by other farmers that she is a superb stockswoman.'

'And she has a new colleague, Andrew Sinclair, who used to farm with his father near Jedburgh.'

'Andrew? Really?'

'You know him?'

'Let's just say our paths have crossed occasionally.'

'He's not here right now. He's had to go and get fresh supplies for tupping – raddle I think they call it.'

'Yes, its put on the chest of a tup so they know which yows have been served by which tup.'

'Perhaps young men ought to be made to apply it before a Saturday night out.'

Anastasia laughed.

'Tell me, Anastasia, how long have you worked for your present firm?'

'Two years. I was working in Aberdeen but wanted to be nearer my family who live in Duns. I also wanted to have more than Aberdeen can offer in terms of a social life.'

'Totally off the record, what do you think of the firm for whom you are working?'

'They prefer domestic to agricultural work but just as I had to come back here when the alarm failed for the first time, so I think they are not the most reliable, but we are still the electricians to this farm and they will not take kindly to Rhona hiring another firm.'

'I am not sure I have met anyone who is more her own woman and knows her own mind than Rhona. Andrew says she is completely open to argument and will change her mind appropriately when she sees the strength of what is said, but that once she has made up her own mind, then there is no further point debating..

'She's also by far and away the most attractive farmer I know.'

Zolko smiled.

'Now let's talk business – literally. I am wanting to establish a new electrical company here in the Borders working predominantly on farms, stables and similar places. It will require a great deal of effort to become established but our best advertisement will be quality work at a lower price than that asked for by competitors. But it is all far too much to be done by one person, who isn't even a Scot, so I want a partner with whom I can work happily and enjoy their company and can wholly trust in terms of the quality of the work we would be doing. It will be tough at first as I'm sure you realise, but Anastasia I would very much like to go into business with you.'

'I now know who you are. You said a word in an unusual way and you said the same word in the same way on BBC Sotland last night. You are, and it's not my title . . .'

'"The runaway priest" they call me, though actually I left Hawick in a car. Yes, that is me, and I wish they would get it right and call me the "happiest man on earth".'

'My mum said to me that she thought that was how you looked and we all felt pleased for you.'

'Please thank her for me. But Anastasia, you will need time to think this over, but please remember this company will be yours and mine jointly, total equals. There is a lot of work to be done here because both houses need re-wiring but it will be done much quicker by two than one. My wife to be will be much relieved seeing me working with an attractive Scot if she knows that the lady in question is considerably less interested in me than she is in the farmer.'

'How on earth . . .?'

Zolko smiled.

'Who knows? Now I must do some work and so must you. Here is my phone number and call me to say yes when you can.'

Anaïs received a phone call from Wales.

'Ms Clément, this is Edward Challen.'

'Good morning.'

'I've been asking round literary agents including my own publishers and no one has heard of you.'

'Of course.'

'What do you mean by that?'

'That very few, if any, agents in England know anything about the literary scene in France. It's the literary version of Brexit mentality. For example how much do you know about it?'

'Er, well, I've never needed to have contacts because my books don't travel well being mostly about Englishmen.'

'Yes, I know that from checks my colleagues in Paris have made on you. So you think I am swindling you, and claiming the name of Charlotte Holly as my way of doing so, even though it must be obvious to you that being in possession of all the facts in the case, of which I spoke to you last time, I am working with Miss Holly, whom, if I may say so, you were exploiting on this research trip.

'It's wholly up to you, Mr Challen. I am advised that I can obtain considerably more from newspapers alone if I hand over to them the information, which does of course include references to your own unfortunate encounters with McHugh. I have held back so far, because Charlotte thinks we should do nothing for now that would cause further hurt to the daughter of Mr Dickson, your wife Eleanor. Having said, she is realistic enough to know that needs to live and earn, which reminds me that you have not yet paid into her account promised monies. Please do so.

'My agency works on a Saturday so by all means telephone my Paris office who will establish my bona fide. You might also want to check it with Anne-Marie Hunniford of the *Poetry House* in London with whom I work closely although at the moment she is on maternity leave, though she would be more than willing to speak with you. If you insist I will put you in touch. Her uncle Oliver began the publishing house and turned McHugh down. Then, and I mean this morning, please transfer the money to the account you have and then separately pay the money you owe Charlotte into the same account. It's straightforward. By the way, if you want help with the presentation of the material to a publisher, just let me know. Ok?'

She heard a mumble before the line went dead. She was encouraged to feel that she hadn't lost her touch, but just in case dialled a number in Paris and hung up as soon as she heard the automatic voice answer the call. This would set in motion what would be needed if Challen rang, though she very much doubted he would, and less than two hours later she received a notification on her iPad that the money had been paid. In a way it was a great pity because Charlotte really could have obtained a great deal more from the papers and on tv though, thought Anaïs, still could do. Now however she and Charlotte could do with a chat about the £60k job offer from Justine, to whom Charlotte had promised a reply by Monday.

Chapter 19

For almost the first since Anne-Marie first acquired the farm Ed had not done the Sunday morning milking, and it was therefore Adam who arrived early and set to work with the ladies who knew him well. Zolko had left the milking parlour safe and unlikely to fail, but still needing a lot of work. He was hoping that Anastasia might come and join him on Monday as he wanted to go the hospital on Monday afternoon. Anastasia had called him on Saturday evening to say that having informed her boss she was leaving but would work her notice, he had said she could go straightaway as she had totally failed the loyalty test and no one would work with her anymore. So . . . she was glad to be able to accept Zolko's invitation to join with him as joint directors of a new company.

Charlotte was concerned that he had acted without discussion with her whilst conceding that as she knew nothing about establishing a business and that Anastasia knew the country and had contacts.

'I know we have to trust each other, so I have no doubts that you are acting for the best, but I feel a bit jealous about you working so closely with a woman you find attractive.'

Zolko laughed.

'She is, but if you were to ask Rhona if you need to be

concerned about Anastasia working closely with me, I think you would be more than reassured, and when I told her with whom I was hoping to go into business her face was a picture.'

'Why?'

'Because Anastasia is a lesbian, and recently made a pass at Rhona.'

'Her? Rhona told me about her.'

'Well, it's likely that she'll be here on Monday morning, but how did you get onto the subject?'

'It was on the way to the supermarket and I simply asked her whether she had hopes of marriage and starting a family. She said she was still far too young to worry about such things and could not possibly attend to them until she was established firmly on a farm, perhaps even on her own or possibly in partnership with Anne-Marie. I then asked about boyfriends, and she said she had a boyfriend way back in Glasgow who was heavily involved in drugs and who blamed her betraying him to the police. When he left prison he found out where he was and came to settle a score. Anne-Marie and a food lorry driver chased him away when they saw his knife. He ran away and accidentally slipped into the slurry pit and died. No one ever survives in there apparently. There were one or two lads at college she went about with but no one seriously. But no girls either, she said, and that was when she mentioned your friend Anastasia who seemed to have assumed that being single indicated that Rhona is gay which she insists she is not.'

'Somehow or other I shall have to break that news to Anastasia. And as I have made a unilateral decision about my working and business future, I think it is quite important that you feel you can do the same about the job offer from the future Mrs McHugh.'

'No. I really want it to be a joint decision. I know I have spent most of my life not making decisions about my existence and, indeed Zolko, for the very first time I have begun to feel deep shame and sadness about it all, anger above all directed to myself rather than those who used and manipulated me to terribly. And I'm feeling it because I now know what love is, love I have never experienced until we met. You have known a lot of love in your life – that of your beloved mum and dad, your brothers and sisters, and of course your great godfather, and for that matter and perhaps above all you have the known the love of your God. Believe me, I am not feeling sorry for myself because now I have met you and for me the world has changed colour completely, and so whilst of course I wish we had spoken together of your plans for the business I recognise I would have had nothing to contribute, but I will not decide anything about this job offer until we agree about it together.'

'Charlotte I don't deserve you and when we marry I will promise that I will always be with you, care for you and love you . . . and ignore any lesbians with whom I am working.'

'Seriously, do you have problems with those who are gay or trans?'

'There are many gay priests and I have never been troubled with that, and your Queen Victoria refused to accept that lesbians existed so how could I argue with a queen. I know too little about those who are trans to make any judgement. If people are unhappy and can find some peace then who am I to stop them being themselves, but I would be profoundly uneasy about a trans still equipped with male genitalia being admitted to a changing room or public toilet for women.'

'I totally agree. My friend Paul or Paula in Jedburgh would tell you what hell he has been through on the journey to become a woman including having to cope with Anaïs shoving her arm up his dress to discover whether or not he was telling the truth about having undergone surgery.'

'And?'

'She came away satisfied that he was not telling the truth. Whether he was satisfied by the experience he never disclosed.'

Zolko laughed.

'Did she charge him?'

'No, but he can probably eat out on it.'

'But back to the question in hand. I'm supposed to reply by tomorrow but my day will be otherwise taken up. So I need to let her know today.'

'If it were me, I would want to know considerably more than she has said. For example, she may want you in Edinburgh now, but then require you to move to Berlin or Paris for example, or even Warsaw. I am not denying that an income of £60k would be of great help to us, but our new found happiness is worth very much more than that and cannot be bought at any price. And we have a hope that what is to happen tomorrow will change our life in wonderful ways.'

'Yes, it's going to be a big day though it will bring back the reality of periods, which I have not missed.'

'There is a way to stop them again.'

Charlotte smiled.

'For an ex-priest you know more than I would have expected.'

'If you have sisters there are no secrets.'

'Well, there we are, that's decided then. I'll text Justine and let her know.'

'I didn't know we had decided. You haven't said what you want to do.'

'You've said it all for me. Oh, there's one other thing.

'Yes?'

'In this country before we begin discussing the content of marriage vows it is customary for the man first of all to go down on one knee and offer her a diamond ring, asking if she will marry him.'

'But won't that make the knee of my trousers dirty?'

'Oh don't worry about that. I'll take them off for you.'

'What, now? I think you are a wicked woman.'

'I do hope so.'

As they left the dairy after evening milking, Rhona (who had been able to think of nothing else since Zolko had told her) asked Andrew if he had ever come across an electrician called Anastasia Watson.

'Oh yes, I see quite a bit of her one way or another.'

'Was she your electrician?'

'Oh no, she didn't arrive until my dad died. No, I know her through the gay scene in Edinburgh and we've been on gay pride marches together. She stays with her parents in Duns if I remember right. Why do you ask?'

'She and Zolko are going into business together and from tomorrow they will be doing the electrical work here.'

'Oh that's great. She's huge fun and I suspect she works hard too. That's quite a coincidence.'

'The last time I saw her, she made a pass at me.'

'I'd take it as a compliment. The rumour is that she's extremely picky and choosy.'

'Andrew, you are saying all the wrong things.'

He laughed as they reached the door.

Twice a day Ed and Anne-Marie went on-line in the hope that during the time since their last look a new name with the correct blood group had appeared, but this was going to be a long haul. Ed was anxious this evening with his chemo due to begin in the morning and he was also concerned that because he was especially prone to infection he would not be able spend much time with Gregor. He had spent a long earlier in the day talking with his closest friend and former colleague Alex, though as did so he found himself wondering what he was wanting from a former bishop who had left the Church of England after just two years in that position and who now admitted that the only thing he could commit himself to was his wife Emily and their children. Both Ed and Alex were philosophers by training and inclination but admitted to one another that meaning could not be found in Ed's situation which made it extremely difficult to know how to talk about it once the details of symptoms, treatment arrangements and the search for a suitable donor. Ed knew that there was no way he could ask for Alex's prayers, and for his part Alex knew he could not offer any either, but for both there was the wish that it might be possible. It would be nice to be able to believe that there is a God overlooking and caring for everyone below, but they both knew it isn't so, and no divine being would keep Ed alive, though chemo and a bone marrow transplant just might. It was, thought Ed, a simple fact that Children in Need, Sports Relief and Comic Relief had done infinitely more for the suffering children of the world than any of the various deities of the world's religions put together. Ed knew the statistics, that 9,000,000 children under five die each year through illness or starvation. Religious people prayed for them but God wouldn't listen to their prayers, because they mattered not to God. That is an intolerable proposition so you apply Occam's Razor, by removing from the sentence the word or words that make it unacceptable, which in this instance is the double use of the word "God". Without the word, as Ed knew well, the death of all those children was no less terrible, but by abandoning the word "God", we would know that anything was to be done about it, that action has to be ours. Most of the time any propositions containing that word are meaningless. And it was the same for those with Non-Hodgkin's Lymphoma. "God" was meaningless.

Anaïs telephoned Charlotte to find out her decision about the job offer. Charlotte did not know what Anaïs thought of the decision, but she did suggest that she should be the one to give the news to Justine "as your literary agent". Gift horses had not until recently been part of Charlotte's life, but she was not going to count its teeth before accepting Anaïs's offer!

'You have an early start in the morning.'

'I have to be in the Gynae unit by 7-30.'

'And I take it Zolko is taking you in. Challen's money is through so I'll transfer it to your account in the morning.'

'Thank you, Anaïs, you have been wonderful and I really couldn't have done it without you, and not least your very special intervention in the Coop in Jedburgh which I told Zolko about. He laughed and laughed and then said he would be sure to stand one or two steps further from you in future.'

'We are flying to France next weekend to visit my parents and show off our son to them. That will leave the house for Ed and Anne-Marie, who will also be going into the hospital in the morning, so that they can relax and be at ease without us. If you get a new car in time you might be able to come and see them. Anyway, I'm sure we will see you again before we go.'

Charlotte hardly slept but spent most of the night snuggling up close to Zolko but, typically, finally fell asleep less than an hour before the alarm radio woke them. Zolko got up and washed before having a drink and then encouraging Charlotte to get herself going.

Soon it was time for them to leave the house and as they did so they could hear Rhona and Andrew already at work in the parlour.

'We should get going quickly,' said Zolko.

'Why, are we late?'

'No. It's just that if the electrics break down they'll come running to get me!'

'Then drive on my wonderful lover.'

Not a great deal later Ed and Anne-Marie were also preparing themselves but both were at least able to have some breakfast.

'What are you intending to do whilst I'm getting my chemo?'

'I'm not really sure but I might do some shopping, and of course Charlotte is being operated on this morning, poor thing. Rhona tells me Zolko is very good indeed and says the wiring needs a total overhaul including our house. He's also wanting to set up a new electrical business concentrating on farms, and he's got someone willing to go into partnership with him, though Rhona didn't mention who it is.'

'I can't see that going down well with existing firms, can you?'

'No, but we sometimes talk at market about how useless some of them are, and it strikes me that if they do it astutely they could get away with it. And I suspect that more electricians than ever before prefer the warmth of working inside in homes, rather than have to spend long hours up ladders in the cold of a windy winter's day or falling snow.'

Charlotte was shown to a bed in a small ward of just four patients and asked to change into her nightie. Zolko was given his marching orders by the sister in charge and after a kiss and a hug made his way out of the hospital. Habit made him want to pray for Charlotte even though he knew it to be nothing more than superstition, but then how might he feel if it all went wrong and he hadn't prayed? He decided against.

Heading out of the city and away from the considerable amount of traffic coming in, he began to do what many people do in such a circumstance and that was to think the worst. How would he cope if she died? What would there be left for him in life if this happened? He was still in that frame of mind as he drove past the gate into the farmyard where there was car he didn't recognise, and next to it Anastasia and Andrew in animated conversation.

'Is Charlotte settled in?' asked Andrew.

'I'm afraid they threw me out before I could discover that. It was a strange world of women, not a man in sight, so I fled.'

They laughed.

'Now tell me, are you two plotting to paint the farm buildings in rainbow colours?'

'Actually that's not a bad idea,' replied Anastasia with a perfectly straight face.

'What a relief in that case that you are an electrician.'

'I was just saying to Anastasia what a good job you've already done in the dairy as well as keeping us going in the parlour over the weekend.'

'Flattery will get you nowhere, Andrew. As I drove in you were engaged in animated conversation and laughter about something or other and I would be surprised if it was about the dairy. Anyway Anastasia and I need to get changed for the day ahead and you need some breakfast. What else have you got lined up?'

'A hard day, gathering the yows and gimmers for tupping.'

'Well, it's quite a nice day and not too warm. We will see you later.'

A very pretty young black woman came towards Charlotte, pulling closed around her the curtains.

'Hello Charlotte. I'm Dr Wills, your friendly neighbourhood anaesthetist. Whilst Mrs Muldoon deals with the Antipodes, I look after the rest of the world and try to keep you asleep.'

'That's an onerous responsibility.'

'I'll try my best. Now I need to listen to your chest. Mrs Muldoon has acquired your notes from Swansea so I know that when you last had surgery you were a smoker. Is that still the case?'

'No. I stopped then and won't start again.'

'And was some of what you smoked cannabis?'

'Yes. I also also a number of years taking other drugs regarded as illegal.'

'It's in your notes so I don't need to ask what. Are you using any now?'

'I stopped them at the same time as I stopped smoking.'

'Okay, sit up and I'll have a listen.'

She gave time to her stethoscope and then to taking soundings and then sat on the bed.

'I can't imagine what it must have been like living as you did and I'm not being judgemental about it but I'm told that your life has been transformed by a man, when you must have thought all men were were perverts and absolute bastards, so I admire you hugely for surviving and coming through. However, just as you have been treated appallingly down below and it has left its consequences, so your lifestyle has also affected the rest of you and it will take some time for your body to recover. You might find, for example that you are susceptible to chest infections in winter and I must advise you to register with a GP as soon as possible, and make sure you get to see him or her for antibiotics at the first sign.'

'I have done. What about pregnancy?'

'I'm not a gynaecologist and I'm sure Mrs Muldoon will be able to advise you once your procedure is done, though don't forget you will be fertile again, so unless your boyfriend is this so-called runaway catholic priest, you should give thought to contraception for as long as she suggests.

'Right. It's lovely to be able to care for you, Charlotte. For most of our acquaintance you will be asleep but at least it will spare you my inane conversation. I'll see you when you get to theatre and you can meet the team. I'm not just saying this to reassure you but you will be in the best of all possible hands. I'll no doubt see you before I go home to check how you are. Ok?'

'Thank you very much.'

Anne-Marie went onto the ward with Ed, carrying Gregor who was bored by it all and asleep. Ed had been told he would possibly feel sick as the poison hanging above his head on a drip stand like a gibbet was delivered into his system. They kissed before Anne-Marie and Gregor departed to shop and drink coffee or fresh milk.

At much the same moment Zolko and Anastasia entered the kitchen to change and prepare for the day. Totally unselfconsciously Anastasia took off her clothes there and then down to her underwear before putting on her overall, and for just a fleeting moment, Zolko thought there might be a lot said for being a lesbian, but it was only fleeting. He knew his Charlotte was even more stunning without her clothes.

Their first task was to assess what they would need for the day and then to go into Galashiels to obtain it. It also gave them their first chance to share ideas about their business.

'Have you any thoughts about what we should call ourselves?' asked Zolko.

'How about "Runaway Priest and Lesbian Friend – Farm Electricians"?'

'That is brilliant, Anastasia, though we might shorten it to "RP & LF – Farm Electricians.'

'Oh yes, I like that very much indeed. I was only joking, but that is superb.'

'You don't want LF to come first?'

'I appreciate your feminist intentions, but I like it as it is.'

'I've never been accused of having feminist intentions before!'

'It's not an accusation, but a sign of my respect.'

Charlotte walked to the theatre and was met by a host of women resembling the milking parlour when full! Mrs Muldoon came and greeted her and then Dr Wills approached.

'You never mentioned what a very rare blood group you are. We've had to summon all our resources to find some for our potential use.'

'I didn't know. What is it?'

'AB-negative'

'Oh my God. That's what Ed needs. He's got Non-Hodgkins Lymphoma and urgently needs a bone marrow transplant, but potential donors are very rare indeed and all this time I'm the same blood group.'

Mrs Muldoon had come over.

'Do you know his consultant?'

'No, but he's here in the hospital this morning beginning chemo.'

'His name?'

'Ed Hunniford. Until recently he was chief civil servant in Scotland and special advisor to the First Minister.'

'Charlotte, thank you very much indeed. You would also have to have a tissue match but this is important.'

She spoke to one of the SHOs there to watch and learn and asked that as a matter of urgency she was to the Chemo suite and inform whoever was in charge to let Mr Hunniford's consultant know what had happened.

'Dr Wills,' she continued, 'that quite enough excitement for one morning. If Charlotte is ready, perhaps she might appreciate having a sleep'.

Dr Mehta was sitting at the bedside chatting with Ed having discovered, unlikely though it was that they both enjoyed the game of croquet. Ed had discovered it in Cambridge, and his consultant had done the same in Kerala. Anne-Marie and Gregor came in and was pleased to see both men looking very cheerful indeed.

'I was expecting to see Ed looking sick,' she said.

'He might later but we are both feeling cheerful because an amazing thing has happened, and it has happened here in this hospital today,' said Dr Mehta, looking to Ed to continue.

'A match has been found, someone with AB-negative, and although there will still need to be a tissue match, Dr Mehta and the team are optimistic. But do you want to know the real miracle?'

'Isn't what you've said enough?'

'No. The potential donor is not only known to us but is actually living in our house?'

'Charlotte or Zolko?'

'Charlotte, who of course has been having gynae surgery this morning. Apparently that's how it came out. The anaesthetist happened to mention the rarity of Charlotte's blood group to her whilst she was already on the table waiting for the anaesthetic, and Charlotte stopped everything and told them about me. It's astonishing.'

'What happens now Dr Mehta?'

'For this week, there will be no change to the daily chemo. That will give me the opportunity to see your friend Charlotte and discuss with her whether she will let us do a tissue test with a view to a possible stem cell transplant later. If she says she will, then we will change your chemo to something very much stronger which will hopefully kill off all the cancer cells but which leave bone marrow in need of new stem cells and hopefully the donor will provide them. In the light of her surgery this morning, I shan't speak to her today and I gather she will be going home tomorrow morning, but I might persuade her consultant to delay that departure. In fact I'll see if she's finished her list for today and go and see her, plus her anaesthetist, Dr

Wills.'

Chapter 20

Notwithstanding the element of rejoicing that evening in Galashiels and Melrose, there was a major problem of which as yet they were not aware. Dr Mehta had gone to see Mrs Muldoon after Ed and Anne-Marie had gone home and found her in the Surgeons Rest Room next to the Theatre Suites where she had been working all day, and was now dictating her notes into a dictaphone for her secretary to transcribe on the following morning. With her was Dr Wills who had just checked on the last patient of the day in the Recovery Room and those already back on the ward, including Charlotte.

Dr Mehta walked over to the large urn and poured himself a cup of foul and disgusting coffee. He had made sure that in his own department the facilities for staff drinks were a great improvement on this, though cynics maintained that the coffee was deliberately awful to encourage the medics to get back into theatre quickly. He then came and next to Mrs Muldoon on the sofa.

'It's most odd but coincidences do happen, what Jung called synchronicity. Your patient is living in the same house and indeed the same bed as I asked my patient to move out of just last week because of the risk of infection on the farm. What are the chances of them both being AB-Negative? Perhaps I should buy a lottery ticket this week.'

'Perhaps not though,' said Dr Wills. 'Mrs Muldoon has clearly done a great job on Charlotte today, opening up for her the possibility of conceiving but, Dr Mehta, before you celebrate too early there are some things about our patient that you need to know.

'Although she is now clear and has been for at least three months, she smoked and took street drugs regularly. She was a prostitute in Swansea but after an unbelievably savage sexual assault by a police officer, which Mrs Muldoon has been repairing today, she escaped from that life and now works as a researcher for a writer in Wales. I examined her this morning. She is an attractive young woman, but undernourished and has entered into a relationship with a man called Zolko, who is in fact the runaway priest from Hawick whose face face has been on television.'

'She has had rough, even brutal, sexual intercourse many times,' said Mrs Muldoon, 'but you will need a thorough check to see if she has an STI and an up-to-date test for HIV. She maintains she never had anal sex, and I could find no evidence that she might have had, though it makes her rather rare among girls on the street, and she insisted that the men wore condoms for vaginal sex. I didn't ask about oral sex.'

'I did,' said Dr Wills. 'She said she would not agree unless the man wore a condom.'

'Well,' said Dr Mehta, as you can imagine our own screening process is exhaustive, whoever the donor might be and covers everything you have mentioned.'

'I wasn't suggesting . . .' spluttered Dr Wills.

'I know and I think you have done your job well in getting that information. If you have no objections Mrs Muldoon I will ask your patient and the runaway priest to come and see me in the morning.'

'Once I've checked that everything's ok inside, she's all yours. I have just one question and one that arises from the sensitivities of being a female gynaecologist: when you go through everything to do with her former life, is it you or a woman colleague who will see her?'

'I will have my registrar, Lorraine McLeod, with me, but just as you operated today, it has to be me who sees her. She has to have the best.'

Doctor Mehta smiled, rose and walked back to his department. 'Bloody feminist nonsense' he muttered under his breath.

On the following morning Anastasia went straight to work in the milking parlour whilst Kolko set off for the hospital and on arrival was asked to meet Charlotte on the ward and to go with her to Dr Mehta's out-patient clinic where arrangements were made for her to be quickly seen being still post-operative.

'It certainly was tremendous that you were already on the table, probably anxious and awaiting the anaesthetic, and yet you had the wits about you to recognise that you had the same blood group as Dr Hunniford.' Said Dr Mehta. 'However, we are only at the beginning, though being AB-Negative at least means we have a beginning. If we had found someone in China, say, who is AB-Negative, it would be much more difficult, but before we can go further I have to have your signature on a consent form allowing us to proceed with a series of tests and, if we get there, to the bone marrow procedure itself.'

'I am perfectly happy to do so.'

'Have you anything to add?' said the doctor to Zolko.

'Only that this is a very special and courageous woman who will cope with whatever she has to go through.'

'Ok, you need first of all to have a time of convalescence and recovery. I want you to start eating more nourishing food than the ready-meals I gather you've been living on. Unless you're vegetarian and even if you are, if you're going to be of service to Dr Hunniford, I need you to be eating red meat every day because we shall only be able to use your bone marrow if we can be sure your own red corpuscles are up to the mark. Before you leave one of our dieticians will give you some more guidance.

'I gather that Dr Wills spoke to you about those aspects of your former life which have left their mark, not least on your lungs which will make you especially susceptible to chest infections. If you don't smoke again this will improve over time, but you need to avoid contact with anyone with a cold or cough.'

'What about the fact that I live on a farm? Ed has had to move.'

'Do you have any direct contact with the animals?'

'None whatsoever.'

'As you know, farmers build up resistance to many infections and although ideally I would prefer you off the farm that may not be possible, so I ask that you avoid all direct contact with the animals until we have been able to complete the process. Lots of fresh air will help too.

'I can't say at the moment how long all this will take as much depends on Dr Hunniford's condition but we should begin the necessary tests once you've begun to heal inside. I am going to ask Dr McLeod here to tell you about all the terrible things we intend doing to you. Don't tell anyone but she's in fact my rather brilliant niece and if I were to fall off the perch almost certainly she would take my place, though she might also be the person who knocked me off in the first place!'

She pulled a rude face at her uncle and they all laughed.

'So, I must go to my out-patients and I look forward to seeing you again soon. My hope, and I'm sure it's also yours is to do all we can for Dr Hunniford and his family.'

'Thank you Dr Mehta,' said Charlotte standing a little

uncomfortably, and they shook hands, as did Kolko.

Dr McLeod went through the list of all the tests that lay ahead.'

'It's my former life catching up with me, isn't it?' said Charlotte.

'Actually most of us have a former life containing all sorts of things we might later come to feel a measure of regret over. I'm sure Kolko knows from his former life that it is far from uncommon for young men and women to have a prolific sexual life with as many partners as possible, and I mean many, and with whom they have been considerably less responsible than you were. One of the busiest wards here is that dealing with those coming with all sorts of sexual transmitted infections, some of which are very serious. If we find any in you, and we have not done so as yet, we would put you onto antibiotics as soon as we can. The other concern we have is the effect of the street drugs you have taken. I know you stopped some time ago, but it's important we check all your vital organs for long-term effects but especially of course the functioning of bone marrow. We have to start with tissue-typing because although you're the same rare blood group doesn't mean your blood and Dr Hunniford's are a good match. So as Dr Mehta said . . .'

'Uncle,' laughed Kolko.

"Yes, uncle. God. Isn't he embarrassing and it's not false modesty on my part to say I shall never be as brilliant as he is, and he always buy me a nice Christmas present!'

Charlotte giggled.

'As he said, we are just at the beginning and our aim is to save Dr Hunniford's life. Therefore before you go, I want to steal some of your blood.'

'Oh darling what a mess I've made of my life. It's all been brought home to me in the past 24 hours.'

They were on their way back to the farm.

'By what standards are you judging yourself?'

'By people such as those amazing doctors I've met and who have cared for me, by those I have come to know and love via the farm, and not least by those of the man I know I have been made for in this life.'

'Lucky man. Do I know him? But seriously, my love, don't do it, don't judge yourself by what appears to be the case in other people, because for a great deal of the time you'll be wrong. Anaïs, and Ed, when you enable him to recover, in their work as psychotherapists will tell you that just about everyone has a past, and even a present, about which they feel a measure of shame and regret. People behave in all sorts of ways the Pope wouldn't approve of, the main reason being that we only have one life and we cannot misbehave and have fun once we're dead. That's not a charter to cause hurt and pain to others, but it's called being human. To me your past is as if it never happened and I want us both to focus on the present and the future, and that reminds me, did Mrs Muldoon specify a time?'

'Yes, six months.

'What?'

Charlotte burst out laughing.

'To my surprise she didn't at all. The damage was high up apparently and that's where most of her attention was directed. She said I would be tender in my vagina by virtue of what they had to do to get higher but said it was up to me completely depending on the discomfort. She said to stay on the pill for at least two more months however to give the uterus time to heal.'

They were on the long lane to the farm and as they drew nearer they could see a large car parked in the farmyard.

'I don't believe it,' said Zolko, 'it's the fucking Archbishop!'

The man himself was talking to Andrew and from the state of his formerly high-polished shoes had received a guided tour though only the pigs were close by the farm buildings. Andrew looked mightily relieved to see Zolko arrive back but at once went over to ensure Charlotte was ok getting out of the car.

'Good morning,' said Zolko, deliberately omitting the Bishop's formal title. 'Welcome to my home and to the farm. Do come on in and showed his guest into the kitchen and invited him to sit down at the table.

What could not have been better timed was the opening of the door and the appearance of Anastasia.

'Zolko, have we got any OCPDs or should I go and get one?'

'That'll be for the parlour? What sort do you want to use?'

'Medium-voltage, vacuum circuit breaker.'

'Definitely. They could almost have been designed with a milking parlour in mind. But we have not got one here so if you can wait I'll pop into Galashiels after a quick cup of tea with my former boss. You might also just mention it to Rhoda as they're not cheap.'

'Of course. How's Charlotte?'

'She's doing ok and pleased to be home. A bit tender.'

'O God, I can imagine but you two are lucky not being women and regularly getting all sorts of things and shapes and sizes pushed inside you.'

She turned and left, whilst Kolko rose and put the kettle on.

'I've had an email from your bishop in Poland demanding your immediate return. It is your home diocese after all and they were doing a great kindness in lending us to you. So what sort of reply should I make? I had forgotten that you were a qualified electrician and the identity of your nobel-laureate godfather, himself also an electrician. But I find myself in a very difficult position. I have a lot of clergy though I've just lost one, have I not? So many of them seem so unhappy and then I come here and look at you and I see someone totally at ease, clearly in love and already establishing a working partnership with a fellow electrician. By the way I was speaking earlier to your colleague Anastasia and I asked the derivation of the name of your company to be: RP & LF.'

Kolko smiled.

'Perhaps it would be best if you didn't know.'

'Now, that makes me even keener to find out.'

'Runaway Priest and Lesbian Friend,' having no idea what response it might elicit.

The Archbishop burst out laughing and continued doing so for quite a while.

'I love it,' he said. 'What I would love to do would be to offer you the contract for the electrics of the diocese but your LF had already told me you are wanting to specialise on farms and outside work.'

'I will always respond to an emergency from the diocese. It's the least I can do.'

'Thank you, Zolko. I'm aware that you need to be on your way to the electrical wholesalers. Do you think I might be able to come and pay an occasional visit here and see the farm at work? I think I might enjoy that.'

'You could even come into business with Anastasia and me" "AB, RP & LF".'

'You don't know just how tempting that sounds. Before I go there is one final thing. I know from what you have told me in the past that despite ambivalence about the Church, you never stop taking God seriously and that prayer in silence has been your mainstay. Is that right?'

'Yes and believe it or not it was a conversation about that drew Charlotte and I together. Each day I make a good space for that.'

'I've not had the chance to meet Charlotte.'

'She's in bed recovering from surgery yesterday in Edinburgh. She is such a good and lovely woman I decided to hide her away from you, in case you fell for her as I have. She will be sorry to have missed you but she needs a period of sustained rest.'

'Can I tell you I will keep you in my prayers?'

'I am delighted to know that. Thank you.'

Zolko led the Archbishop to his car.

'One thing. These farm visits. Make it soon,' said Zolko. 'You'll always be welcome.'

The Archbishop smiled and said he would be in touch. As he drove away down the long lane, Zolko was already wanting to be with Charlotte and spend time with her before he had to go and obtain the circuit breaker.

Chapter 21

A close friendship had grown up between Francine, Anaïs, Anne-Marie, Charlotte and Rhona and although Anastasia would have given a great deal to be part of the gang, as yet it hadn't happened. Francine had bumped into Anaïs one day when calling on Rhona and was excited to be able to spend a lot of time speaking French as she had done whilst drenching the sheep with Adam. The five women had taken to having a night out together each week, going for a meal either in *The Cobbles* or *The Waggon* in Kelso, the latter famous for its cocktails. The other women marvelled at Charlotte's capacity to eat rare steaks every week until she explained why she had to do so.

'When will this be over?' asked Rhona.

'Not long now.'

'Ed is now on a very powerful chemo till all the affected cells are ready for what only Charlotte can give him to keep him alive,' said Anne-Marie, tears beginning to flow.

'I seem to have passed all the tests to be able to be able to be a donor despite every terrible thing I have done in my life, and when it's over I swear I will never eat a steak again.'

They all laughed.

'Ed quite suits being bald,' said Anaïs, though Anne-Marie is very strict about making him wear his bobble hat and probably in bed too, if I know you.'

'I'm not telling,' she said. 'But have you any details about the wedding yet?'

'More or less,' replied Charlotte with a huge smile.

'Will it be in a Catholic Church?' asked Francine.

'No, in a hotel. We shall be much happier doing that.'

'How is Kolko's new business with Anastasia going? asked Anaïs.

'Really well, thank you. Word has spread quickly that they are farm specialists and a lot of farmers have expressed interest.'

'I'm not surprised,' added Rhona. 'Electricians are getting softer and most prefer domestic indoor work to being in freezing cold and smelly farm buildings.'

'Kolko and Anastasia get on really well, and already they seem to understand each other. He's never worked with a woman before, but he's never been to bed with a woman before he met me either,' said Charlotte, and trust me sisters, he's pretty good at that too.'

They laughed.

'I hope he doesn't bring Anastasia along too,' said Anne-Marie.

'I shouldn't worry as it would be Charlotte she would be more interested in,' added Rhona.

They laughed again.

'I haven't met Anastasia I don't think,' said Francine.

"Oh you must do so,' said Charlotte. 'She is really nice, and thinking of trying to find somewhere to live nearer than Duns. We could then invite her to join us.'

'Charlotte and I are going on a shopping spree in Edinburgh tomorrow morning,' said Anaïs, 'though the bad news is that it is primarily to buy clothes for Jerome. Oh, and for the new baby.'

The excitement and noise level rose considerably as they all congratulated Anaïs, though Anne-Marie silently gave thanks that at last Adam might be allowed some sleep!

As Charlotte emerged from the long lane and drove towards Melrose she failed to notice a car that had been parked nearby and was now following her, nor when she she parked and got into Anaïs's car did he she see it, though Anaïs did.

'We're being followed.'

'Don't be daft Anaïs, who would want to follow us.'

'We both have pasts that might possibly catch up with us, mine far worse even than yours, believe me, so it's more likely that it has to do with me, but then again I was trained to deal with situations like this, so let's put him to the test. At the next junction she turned left and accelerated sharply.

'Well, he's not a pro, that's for certain.'

'Does that mean we can get away from him?'

'I don't want to. I want to know who he is?'

'Don't take any risks, Anaïs. Jerome is is in the back and you are pregnant, remember.'

'And you are here beside me. I will ensure all four of us are safe.'

She had now slowed down to allow the driver to catch up, before turning back to the A68.

'I think we might stop in Lauder. Have you ever been to the Black Bull there?'

'No.'

"I like it and we can get a coffee there.'

'Ok,' said Charlotte, not at all sure what Anaïs in mind. 'Is he still behind?'

'Indeed he is, but he soon won't be, and the Stow and Lauder Health Centre is conveniently close by.'

The sign for Lauder now appeared as Anaïs cut her speed, and then indicated right and pulled up in the car park at the front of the hotel. The other car followed her and stopped behind.

'Stay here', said Anaïs to Charlotte who had every intention of doing so.

Anaïs approached the driver's door with a smile on her face. The driver was unaccompanied and whilst he was winding down the window she opened the door and took hold of his neck far from gently.

'Are you lost?' she said.

'Get your fucking hands off me, bitch.'

'You are in Scotland now, and we do not use such language here. Undo your seat belt and get out.'

She continued to have a tight hold on his neck and getting out she easily manipulated him on to his knees.

'Tell me,' she said.

With some difficulty he spoke.

'You have property of mine with you and I want it back and am taking it back so don't get in my way or there'll be trouble.'

'Oh dear, that's scary. Have you reinforcements following?'

'When I get up I will kill you.'

'Really? I can hardly wait. Now tell me or I will dislocate your shoulder and if I were you I wouldn't doubt that I can do it.'

'You're fucking crazy.'

'I know and that must be most worrying for you. Stop struggling or the shoulder really will go. Tell me.'

'Rosa is my property and she's coming back to do what she does best.'

'Her work as a researcher you mean. She is very good at that.'

'What the fuck are you talking about. She's a tart, a common whore and I own her.'

'Ah, that means you must be Ollie the pimp and genuine shit-bag, but clever enough to make it to here. How?'

Anaïs now genuinely caused Ollie a lot of pain and he screamed out.

'How?'

'The police told me where she had been in their safe house.

Someone told me she'd gone to work for a man called Challen who told me she'd cheated him out of £30,000 and when I told him I'd get her, he told me approximately where she was living and I worked out the rest.'

'So you're a pimp turned bounty hunter now. Well, Ollie, I have some friends, mostly quite big, not too far away, and if I ask them to come they will be here in less than half an hour. They have all worked for French Special Forces and because I am senior to them, will do as they are told and remove you from the UK once and for all, and I have to say that I don't think you'll be missed.'

'You'd kill me?'

'Why not? It would be just like picking up shit on a spade in a farm yard. On the other hand I might decide to give you a sporting chance and throw you into a slurry tank and if you can get out, I'd let you go, though you ought to know that the last guy failed to make it. It took two fireman in full kit with oxygen an hour and a half even to find his body.'

Ollie was looking terrified.

'Or I could let you go and you will return to Swansea, not making contact with Mr Challen or anyone else, but if you ever return I think the slurry will be all yours.'

'I'll go, I'll go, I'll go,' screeched Ollie who was sure his shoulder was dislocated, something Anaïs knew was so for certain, having just done it, something she had been taught by Special Forces. Driving would be painful for Ollie unless he called into an A&E en route. She smiled as she allowed him to get back into his car in a lot of pain.

'There's a health centre across the road, Ollie. Before you drive anywhere I would suggest you pay them a visit as they may be able to help with your dislocated shoulder and let you have some pain killers. If they ask how you did you can tell them that a pregnant French lady did it. Au Revoir.'

She returned to her car and at once they pulled out back onto the A68.

'What did you do to make himscream?'

'I had training before I began working undercover, and they taught me an easy way to dislocate a shoulder. I'll teach you if you like.'

'Er, that's very kind, but I'll try and manage without.'

They both laughed loud enough to wake Jerome. Anaïs spoke to him in French and he smiled back. Then she spoke in French on the hands-free.

'I was just logging in to Intelligence and asking them to watch for Ollie's car to make sure he's heading south. Even after Brexit we retain information exchange so if we ask, we get to know when his car trips a camera.'

'What I don't understand is how you did what you did given that Ollie is bigger than you.'

'It's nothing to do with size but a matter of knowing how to do it. It's the same with shooting a gun. I can always hit a target because I've been taught how to do it.'

'Do you miss it?'

'I've told you before: there was a man standing on my doorstep in the pouring rain, without a coat. At that moment I knew that I had found the most precious and wonderful thing ever likely to come into my life. I don't miss my former life at all, but sometimes, as this morning, it comes in useful. I'm still officially on active duty which allows me to call in assistance.'

'But does that mean that you might be summoned to do something involving danger and so on?'

'In an emergency I might, I suppose, but it would have to be one heck of an emergency for that to be the case. When you are admitted to French Intelligence you continue a member for ever.'

It was beginning to get dark and Rhona and Andrew were on

their way back from replacing some fence posts. They passed through the cattle and it was Andrew who first spotted the casualty. She was in a bad way having a large tear on her nearside belly, probably caused by having been caught on some barbed wire.

'It's too big for you or me,' said Andrew.

'Yes,' said Rhona, who regularly stitched small cuts. 'It's a mess and she'll need her insides looking at too, just in case she's also torn one of her stomachs. I'll get her into the barn if you can call the vet. It'll probably mean starting milking late but could you see if Adam's available?'

Rhona went down with Andrew to get a harness and then walked back to the injured cow and very gently led her down to the barn she and her sisters would all soon be occupying for the winter.

In the yard, Kolko and Anastasia arrived back from work they had been doing at the market in Kelso and went in at once for a cup of tea. Anastasia was now living with Kolko and Charlotte during the week and only returning to parents' on Saturday morning returning early on Monday.

Chatting about nothing, they heard a vehicle pull into the yard and stop.

'It's probably Charlotte back from Edinburgh but when she didn't come in Kolko had a look through the kitchen window.

'No, it's the vet. It can't be a calving because they're all done but it must be something serious as Rhona usually manages everything herself.'

Not long afterwards another car arrived, bur this time it was Adam to help with the milking.

'Gosh, something must be wrong if they have brought Adam in to help.'

Francine had injected the cow with a local anaesthetic before starting to examine what was happening inside her. As with many vets she was working without gloves.

'There's no damage in here, I'm pleased to say, so all we need to do is to sew her back together though it's a very nasty tear.'

'Which is why I didn't want to do it.'

'You know Rhona that you could do it easily and that you should be a vet.'

'Perhaps, but consider what I would be missing out on: carrying heavy fence posts up a hill and getting them deep into the ground.'

Francine laughed.

'I'm sorry, Rhona, but you are wrong. There would be some frustrations of course and you would know a great deal more even that some of your teachers and all your fellow students, and you could still farm in the vacations, but I am perfectly serious. Now is the time to give proper thought to it. I will do half, and you can finish off and then I'll spray the wound with antibiotic and give her an injection too. She will then need milking by the looks of what she's carrying.'

By now Anaïs and Charlotte and Jerome were on their way back to Melrose when Anaïs received a call on the car phone in French. Charlotte could not understand a word but from Anaïs's face she could tell it was a serious matter. She ended the call and turned to look at Charlotte.'

'Do tell me. On a scale of 1 to 10 how stupid would you say your friend Ollie is?'

'Definitely a 10. Why, what has he done?'

'At the moment he is parked near the long lane to the farm, presumably waiting for you to return by yourself after you have collected your own car. So, when we get to Melrose this is what we shall do . . .'

Kolko's phone rang.

'My darling how soon will you be home?'

'Listen please, darling, and do what I ask. Telephone our car insurance company and get Anaïs's name added just for the next two hours. This is urgent and I will explain later.'

'Is everything alright, Kolko?' asked Anastasia.

'I've no idea. I have to make a call to the insurance company. But it's all totally baffling, but I feel that something is not right though I have no idea what it might be.'

Anaïs and Charlotte and Jerome had arrived back in Melrose though not before Anaïs had made two further calls in French about which she offered no explanation to Charlotte. Once in the house she told Ed and Anne-Marie that she had to deal with something and would soon be back but would be leaving Charlotte and Jerome with them. She then asked Anne-Marie if there was a completely secure barn on the farm that could be locked for a couple of hours. She continued by asking her if she could call Rhona to let her know it would be needed shortly.'

'She'll be milking and have her phone turned off or in the kitchen.'

'I'll try Adam then.'

'He will be the same. We don't take mobiles into the milking parlour.'

'I'll call Zolko,' said Charlotte.

The call was answered by Anastasia.

'Charlotte hi. Your fiancé has just gone into the shower. Can I do anything?'

Charlotte passed the message on for Rhona and Anastasia said she would go to her at once. She opened the kitchen door and went into the yard where she met Francine putting her case into back of her and changing out of her work top.

'You must be Francine, the Swiss vet,' said Anastasia. 'I'm Anastasia, half of RP & LF the electricians. I have an urgent message for Rhona. Could you take me to where she is, please?'

She was aware that she was shaking as she spoke. This vet,

Francine, was gorgeous.

Francine led her to the barn where Rhona was preparing to take through the injured cow to the parlour to be milked though she would return to the barn afterwards and spend the night alone. Anastasia passed on the message and she received it without any questions. She passed the halter rope to Francine and went off.

'One of my colleagues told me that Anne-Marie and Rhona are so close that if one asks for anything the other would not hesitate to do it. They trust one another implicitly. Now we must take this poor lady to the parlour and relieve her of some of her baggage.'

They handed her over to Andrew.

'I don't know what's going to happen, Francine, but I would very much welcome the opportunity of offering you some food and drink, unless of course you have another emergency to go to.'

'I'm finished for the day and it's not my night for call so a drink would be most welcome.

Charlotte's car approached the crossroads from where the long lane began leading to the farm. As it moved across the junction suddenly a vehicle shot in front of it blocking the way. The driver got out and came towards the driver's door carrying a jack he clearly intended for a use other than mending a puncture.

'Well Rosa, you little bitch, now that other cow has gone, you are on your fucking own and you're coming with me all the way back to Swansea. I've lost a lot of money because of you and you are going to pay me back the only way you know how, with your legs apart.'

He opened the door.

'Ah good evening monsieur Ollie. We meet again.'

Ollie raised the jack but did so with his wrong arm, the one with the dislocated shoulder, and at once yelled in pain, which gave Anaïs just long enough to put out her leg and gently push him to the ground which made him yell again.

'One kick should do it, don't you think, Ollie. It's so difficult for men with their testicles permanently on the outside, so prepare yourself to hurt a great deal.'

'No, please don't. I'll do what you say.'

'What, like last time?'

'No really.'

Another car was approaching which passed them and stopped at the entrance to the lane. It was Anne-Marie.

'You do know hunting wild animals is now banned, don't you?'

'Oh dear, perhaps you can help me conceal this one in the boot of the car.'

'Gladly.'

They lifted Ollie into the boot and closed the door.

'Do you want to follow me to the farm?'

'I would love to do so and thank you for arriving bang on time.'

'Ed has had a call today and they want to do the transplant next week. Charlotte's busy playing with Jerome and Gregor and they have a chance to talk it over. What about this other car?'

'He won't be needing it again, and it will be taken care of later by one or two of my friends.'

'Please remind me if I'm ever in trouble of any kind, to call for you.'

'What happened today was above all for you and Ed: Charlotte needed a bodyguard because in her body lies the basis of hope for you two. Now let's go.'

Once at the farm, Ollie was moved from the boot into a small barn. Andrew brought him a drink and a sandwich and then locked the door. At first he shouted but then gave up. Kolko left at once to collect Charlotte in her car, and Anaïs and Anne-Marie returned together, the former having given instructions as to what happen in about an hour's time when a van would arrive and take

Ollie away. And the principal beneficiaries of the comings and goings were an electrician and a Swiss vet who had only just met.

Chapter 22

It was only after the train had passed Berwick that either man spoke. Christophe looked at the man with the sling.

'Are you in pain?'

'What do you think after that animal had finished with me.'

Christophe smiled.

'She was only having a bit of fun – this time, but she has asked me to pass on to you the gentlest of warnings that if you are ever seen in the vicinity again you will be unlikely to see Swansea again, or anywhere else for that matter.'

'What about my car?'

'Don't worry about your car. It's been taken care of. When I saw it, I thought you had done well to get to Scotland in it in the first place but there was no way it would have got you back again.'

'So where's my car?'

'I'm not sure where it went to, but it will be a large square of metal by now. If the scrapyard pays us, we'll be sure to send it on.'

Ollie looked aghast.

'Who are you? Who do you work for?'

'Ollie, these are things you don't need to know. What you do need to know is that once we get to Manchester I will make sure you are on the train from Piccadilly to Cardiff Central and I will give you enough money to enable you to buy a drink and a sandwich, plus the money you will need for a bus to get home. Also at Piccadilly Station I will remind you about giving Scotland a miss in future.'

Ollie shut up. Later that day, as he left the train in Cardiff, two police officers met and arrested him and took him to the police station to answer questions about the theft of a car, running a brothel and various physical assault matters with regard to women whose pimp he was. All in all it was not Ollie's best day.

Ed and Charlotte were now just a few days away from the transplant. Ed was already in hospital and aware that after the transplant he would be nursed in a special infection-free environment, a large tent-like structure which would permit contact with neither Anne-Marie or Jerome, for during this time his resistance to possible infection would be extremely low. Six days earlier Charlotte had attended hospital to receive medication that would stimulate the number of stem cells in her blood. Now, lying on a bed in a side-room next to Ed's room a doctor had earlier come and removed blood to test whether or not the blood was ready. A little while later he returned with Dr Mehta.

'Hello Charlotte,' he said, 'good news for Ed. Your blood is up to the mark and we can go ahead. As I have said before what Dr Walton will now do is attach you to this machine for about three hours. It takes blood out of one arm, passes it through a filter, and then lets you have it back in the other arm just so you know we are not stealing it, though we will keep what we need from it. We shall then see if we have enough cells. If by any chance we haven't got what we need we'll have another go tomorrow, but I hope we'll get it done today. You can then go home and become a vegetarian.'

'It's most odd eating all that meat and living on a farm!'

'I hope you haven't mentioned the fact to the animals. Ok, Dr Walton, off you go and I'll leave you both and see you later.'

A nurse or Dr Walton kept a close eye on Charlotte on the machine throughout the morning. She tried reading and listening to her iPod, but kept falling asleep. She could feel nothing.

Kolko and Anastasia also had a medical appointment, attending to the electrics of Mrs Muldoon. It was all very straightforward and considerably warmer inside than usual.

'So when are you moving out?'

'Next Saturday if that suits you and Charlotte.'

'We shall miss you, even if you watch some of the oddest television programmes I've ever seen.'

'Ah but Kolko. You've lived such a sheltered life.'

'I can't deny it, but working with you is an education in itself. You've taught me such a lot about the realities of life I didn't know about before, and you speak of it as being perfectly normal in the lives of so many. I shall never cease to be grateful to you, and though of course I don't mean it in the way I do when I say it to Charlotte, I really do love you, Anastasia. You are simply a smashing person.'

'Well, I love you too.'

'And Francine?'

'She is very beautiful, clever and we are becoming close. She Facetimes me every evening and I long for the moment when my phone rings.'

'Lovers?'

'We're not all like runaway priests who are in bed with a woman on the first night, but No, not yet, and I'm experienced enough to know it might not happen at all. There are some women who know what is happening inside themselves in their attraction to another woman, but are simply too scared to do anything about it. So it may not happen, but moving in with her may make it more likely. I hope so, but it wouldn't be the first time and I have survived before.'

'When did you first know about yourself?'

'When I was eight and I have never felt anything but normal. Mum and dad never questioned it, and they've got grandchildren via my brother.'

Mrs Muldoon, who was having a day off, came into hall carrying drinks and club biscuits.

'Do come down and have a rest. I wasn't listening as such but I have appreciated the care and thoughtfulness your conversation has shown for one another. There are those who say that the modern world is regrettable, but I point to what we can do at the hospital and I would venture to suggest that you two speaking of something impossible a generation ago would certainly convince me that this is a much more adult world than when I was young.'

Anastasia and Kolko looked at her, and then at each other and smiled.

It took over an hour for the stem cells to be tested in the laboratories, and Charlotte had some lunch and chatted with the nurse who had brought it.

'You're very brave,' said the nurse.

'Oh it didn't hurt.'

'I didn't mean that,' replied the nurse. 'I meant it is brave of you to eat a hospital sandwich!'

The pair of them convulsed with laughter.

The were joined at the moment by Dr Mehta.

'It must have been a good joke,' he said.

'It was the one about bravery and the hospital sandwich,' said the nurse.

'The old ones are the best.'

'Yes Dr Mehta, as you often say about yourself.'

He looked at Charlotte.

'Do you see what I have to put up with, Charlotte? My working conditions are appalling.'

'Do you know, Dr Mehta, I rather think you love it with all these lovely nurses around you all the time.'

'Please, I beg you, if ever you meet my wife, don't tell her. But now the excellent news that your stem cell count is good and we shall begin putting them into Ed straightaway. We will also have to give him what are known as immunosuppressants, which will stop his immune system trying to attack the new cells, much as happens with anyone who has an organ transplant. As you know he will be here with us for quite some time to come, say 1 to 3 months before he can return home. But you Charlotte have now done all you can for him, and that is an enormous amount. Thank you. This wicked nurse will now detach you from the machine and unless the sandwich really does kill you, you can go home.'

Anne-Marie received a call from Dr Mehta to say they were able to go ahead with the transplant and that she would be able to see him at the end of the afternoon but only dressed as something from outer space!

'Dr Mehta is really Professor Mehta but doesn't use the title with patients and staff. Ed and I have total confidence in him, though we both know that if it is ever going to bad news, he would not hesitate to give it to us,' she said to Anaïs.

'That is so important to know. Will you come to the wedding at the weekend?'

'I will wait and see how Ed is though obviously he can't go. By the way what happened to that horrible man we threw into the boot of Charlotte's car and was then taken away? I think Charlotte thought you might be having him killed.'

'My friends took him to Manchester by train and arranged for him then to be met at Cardiff Station, and I am reliably informed that he has been charged by the police with various offences though he's now at home "under investigation", what they used to call being on bail.'

'You have some good friends, Anaïs.'

She laughed.

'They sometimes come in useful.'

On Thursday evening, Zolko and Charlotte were at the airport to meet a plane coming in from Poland and Charlotte was able at last to see her fiancé in the context of his Polish family, for his mum and dad were accompanied by his two sisters. She took to them all and didn't understand a word they said, though the two sisters each had a little English. It took quite a while to drive to the hotel in Peebles where their wedding was to take, the venue chosen because it specialised in small weddings. Zolko's family were shown up to their rooms and Zolko had asked that some food be prepared for their late arrival. Just before Zolko and Charlotte left, his father took Zolko aside and Charlotte wondered what they might be talking about. They hugged however as they returned to the others and they then took their leave.

'What were you and your dad talking about. It looked very serious.'

Zolko laughed. 'It was. He told me that he and my godfather had been in touch with the hotel and already paid for everything between them.'

'Are you being serious?'

'Yes. It's astonishing when part of me feared they would come and try to encourage me back into the priesthood.'

The Zolkiewski ensemble were brought by Charlotte to the farm on the following day and were completely taken with the Chinese pigs and Rhona suggested they might like to take them back with them when they returned home! Anaïs prepared a buffet lunch for them all whilst Zolko's father couldn't take his eyes off her, and Anastasia, still awaiting the return of Francine, was drawn to one of Zolko's sisters!

The wedding day dawned cold but clear and was deliberately arranged early so Rhona and Andrew could get back for milking. Zolko had stayed in the hotel with his family overnight. Charlotte had chosen something simple but charming to wear and Anaïs was to be her matron of honour, a title when it was explained to her caused her to laugh and laugh. Andrew was best man and made a lovely speech. There were not many there, but there were two surprise guests in the form of Paul(a) Greene who wore a lovely long green dress and chatted most of the time to Andrew, but much more unlikely a surprise guest was none other than the Archbishop of St Andrews and Edinburgh himself. It turned out he had once spent a year in Poland and was more than competent at speaking with Zolko's family. His presence filled Zolko with such joy that in talking to him, his tears overflowed.

'That lady doing the ceremony was very good,' said the Archbishop. 'Do you think there's any chance she might come to our diocesan conference next year and speak to us about it?'

'Well, Father, you can always ask. But she's also a very attractive lady and you might just lose another of your priests,'

'Zolko, it might even be me!'

For Charlotte, the day was made by the presence of Anne-Marie.

'There was no way I would miss this day. If my beloved Ed survives it will be because of you and you alone. I am so happy for you and Zolko. What a lovely man you have rescued from a fate worse than death. That's two men now: Zolko and Ed, which is not bad. I gather from Anaïs and Rhona that you are going to become responsible for all the farm paperwork and finance, and also be Anaïs's telephone receptionist. That's wonderful.'

'Well it might be once I learn to use the computer properly.'

'Charlotte, I wish for you only good things because you deserve only good things. Everyone who knows you loves you so very much, though I know you are a smash hit with Dr Mehta and the staff at the hospital. We are all hoping that soon you might be pregnant and your taste in runaway priests is very special – and husbands, Mrs Zolkiewski.

'And my wish is only for you and Ed to many more happy years together.'

The hugged and gave a each other a kiss.'

Rhona and Andrew slipped away once lunch was finished.

'Are you going tell me then? said Andrew.

'Tell you what?'

'Your plans for next autumn. The result of your conversation with Francine.'

'Yes, I have finally made up my mind. In the autumn we shall need to buy new tups and then put them to yows and lambs. I imagine there will be TB testing as usual and with luck some oriental illness will kill all the pigs and not touch anything else, and of course there will be milking twice a day. I ask you, Andrew what could be better than what we are doing? I love working with you, and although we're all desperate for Ed to get better and for Anne-Marie to return, even if part-time. I am truly happy and fulfilled. If one day I meet someone special, and you don't try to pinch him from me, then I may have to reassess. Until then, I'm so sorry to have to tell you, Andrew, I'm staying put, and so I hope are you.'

'Well, boss, I rather thought I might.

Printed in Great Britain
by Amazon

76809816R00158